which was just beginning a spin cycle. Angel continued to press forward and put his left hand against the washer, and leaned in close to Rosa. "Jobs around here are hard to find this time of year" he said. He then sniffed. "What is that smell" he said with disdane.

"I was just coming to tell you that you are nearly out of pesticide for the mealybugs." She said as she slipped under his arm and rounded another table with queen sized bed sheets that still needed folding. "You will need more very soon. The bugs seem to be getting out of control."

"You were supposed to have those taken care of days ago!" Angel yelled

"I have been spraying them but it doesn't seem to be working." She said as he followed her around the table. "I've been spraying them every day".

"Is that what that God-awful smell is? You are going to ruin all of the laundry! You ruin anything and it will come out of your pay. You know that." Angel's eyes flared and then something reminded him that he needed to be more persuasive. "I can make it so none of these things are your concern any more. You know that right?" he said with feigned charisma.

"I appreciate the job, Angel. But I need to get back to the plantation and finish before that load is done. Bye!" and Rosa spun around and dashed out the door and into the hallway. Trying to get as far away from Angel as she could, she rounded a corner and her forehead smacked directly into the chest of a tall man. She almost bounced back and she looked up. He was in his early thirties, with dark brown hair and blue eyes. Caught off guard, Rosa immediately said, "Lo siento, lo siento mucho." The towering man instinctively reached out to steady Rosa. His strong hands stopped her momentum immediately as she looked up at him. Her forehead was stinging, she had hit something, but she wasn't sure what. A button? No. He felt it as well because he began to massage the area with a small circular pattern a few centimeters above his sternum. It clearly caused him some pain because and reached into his shirt to pulled out a pendant. It was a beautiful emerald, hanging on a chain around his neck. While normally it would look strange for a man to wear an emerald necklace, the emerald was set in in black tungsten which was very masculine and had a matching snake twist black chain.

His skin was dark, tan, but he was obviously not of Hispanic origin and not from Uxmal. However he didn't look like the standard tourist either. He apologized, "I'm sorry. I didn't see you. I don't speak Spanish very well." Rosa spoke some English which she picked up from tourists over the years and also a little from her mother. Rosa said, "I'm sorry. I should have been paying closer attention," realizing the scent of pesticide was filling the hallway.

"No, it was my fault," said the stranger. "I'm new here, and I think the only way I'm going to meet anyone is by running into them, although I don't mean so literally. Apologies, my name is Edward. I'm here on assignment with INAH to work on the pyramid restoration. Oh wait, how do you say it, ummm, the Instituto Nacional de Antropología e Historia," Edward said with a very poor accent. Rosa was still stunned by her run in with Edward as well as, well…Edward.

"Excuse me," Rosa said as she quickly skirted around him becoming more and more aware of her scent. She shook off the embarrassment, and continued back to the orchard.

The next day Rosa was done with her cleaning a little early at the coco factory when Carlos screamed that he needed her to take a large box to the pyramid site where shops were setup to sell chocolate to those that didn't visit the museum. Carlos received word that two bus-loads of tourists would be at the pyramid early in the afternoon.

Rosa picked up the box and walked 10 minutes south to the archaeological site where Carlos's 14 year-old nephew Miguel, was looking after the shop. Rosa knew he was watching old Bruce Lee movies on the small TV his father had in back of the shop. Rosa carved two wood pieces of similar size and connected them with thin rope to make make-shift nun-chucks as a gift for his birthday.

"Como estás hoy, Miguel?" Rosa said.

"Buenos días, Rosa," replied Miguel. "Me estoy poniendo muy bueno en los nunchucks. Gracias de nuevo por dármelas." This made Rosa smile.

Rosa put down the box of chocolates and heard someone approaching from behind. She whirled around and again found herself in the shadow of Edward.

"Hello again," Edward said with a smile looking deeply into Rosa's very unique amber colored eyes.

"I am so sorry I ran into you yesterday," Rosa said, looking down at the ground. She wasn't shy and it wasn't that she didn't have much self-confidence, there was just something about Edward that took her off balance.

"I'm not," Edward pronounced proudly. "Again, I'm Edward. What is your name?"

"Rosa" she said with her confidence siphoning back. "Are you with a tour group?"

"No. I'm the new researcher here looking at the hurricane damage to the pyramid. I'll probably be here for a few months. I'm staying at the hotel across the way where I bumped into you," Edward pointed in the direction he thought the hotel was, but he actually pointed to the Chocolate Museum.

Rosa and Edward spent a few moments talking, then Rosa excused herself as she had a lot of work to complete. Over the next few days Rosa and Edward did not see each other. Edward kept looking for reasons to speak with Rosa and was quite persistent at it. One day he found her and asked if she would be willing to talk about what she had learned about the pyramid since she lived so close for many years. She indicated that it would be nearly impossible for her to find any time due to the cocoa mealybugs outbreak, which had become worse over the last few days. Edward replied, "So, you are saying that if your bug problem went away, you could spend some time with me?" Rosa responded, "Sure" knowing it wouldn't happen, "But it isn't getting better, and it is worsening so finding time will be unlikely."

A bit later that afternoon, Edward slipped into the choco tree plantation and walked to the center. He saw the mealybug infestation Rosa mentioned. They were everywhere; their small scaly bodies covering nearly every bit of bark on each tree. It was a warm day, cloudless and no hint of a breeze. Edward reached into his pocket and pulled out a small stone, about the size of a quarter. It was a translucent apophyllite crystal with a slightly greenish tint. He held it in his right hand and began concentrating. He then looked directly at the crystal and lightly blew on it. Then he set the stone down and walked out of the orchard.

A few moments later, what can only be described as a nearly invisible orange mist emanated from the stone in all directions. As the mist reached the trees, almost immediately the mealybugs became restless and agitated. They began to release their grip on the trees and fall to the ground. Crawling in every direction, the mealybugs seemed to be disoriented. They were falling off trees like a massive insect hail storm. The ground looked like it was alive, now covered with bugs. Within a couple of minutes everything was quiet. Everything stopped moving and all the mealybugs lay dead on the ground. Edward looked around apparently satisfied, picked up the stone, and slipped out of the plantation.

Later, while laundry was drying, Rosa was exiting the shed with the pesticide and sprayer. Such a beautiful day, she thought to herself. It was warm, but she liked the warmth. She hated being cold. She walked north about 100 paces when she noticed something was different. The normal light brown dirt beneath her feet was a much darker brownish grey. As she approached, she saw the remains of millions of rolled-up bug sized carcasses covering the ground. She looked at a nearby tree which was free of mealybugs, actually every tree was. She saw dozens of bluebirds on the ground picking at the insect bodies and more birds flying in landing on the ground pecking. She dropped the pesticide canister and turned around to go tell Carlos of the good fortune in hopes his mood and advances would calm down when she almost ran straight into Edward again.

"Hello," Edward said. "How is it going?"

"You startled me," Rosa replied, hand on her chest clearly caught off guard.

"Sorry about that. Are you working on your insect problem? Looks like you have done a pretty good job," Edward said, nodding his approval while looking at the trees over Rosa's shoulder.

"Can you believe it? Look. All the mealybugs are dead. There aren't any left on the trees at all. Something killed them all," Rosa exclaimed in a rushed tone as she looked back at the plantation with birds in an all-you-can-eat frenzy.

"That is amazing, your pesticide must be really effective!" Edward said looking down at the canister and then back at Rosa.

"No, it couldn't have been the pesticide. I've been using this stuff for over a week and it hardly made a difference. I haven't even sprayed the Northeast corner of the plantation, yet and they are all dead," Rosa said. She was almost out of breath from talking so fast. "I need to show Carlos," she said side-stepping Edward. She began walking back to the shed to drop off the sprayer and pesticide.

"Hey, now that your bug problem is resolved, do you have time to go out with me?" Edward spoke to the back of Rosa's head. She turned around. Edward continued. " Can I pick you up tonight at 6:00? I want to show you something," Rosa barely knew him, but her mealybug trump card had just been obliterated so she didn't have an excuse.

"I'll meet you at the hotel lobby at 6:00," she said and she ran towards the hotel.

~

AT 6 :00 ROSA HAD ALL THE LAUNDRY and other work finished. She had a few minutes to run home, brush her hair and put on a clean dress, she entered the hotel. The Hacienda Uxmal Plantation & Museum was a highly regarded 4 star hotel, which was pretty amazing for being in the middle of nowhere and Carlos as the manager. The lobby had a checkerboard tile floor of black and travertine tile in a two by two pattern giving the floor a grand and spacious appearance. The ceiling had large walnut beams with a white ceiling. There was a wide formal staircase leading up to the 2nd level with blue smaller tiles with an inlaid flower pattern. The railing was beautifully ornate. Rather than standard balusters or spindles, it had black metal swirls ending in a gold center. The landing had 3 shallow 'light box' frame which each held a woman's traditional Mexican dress.

In the corner was a television with the history channel playing an episode about ancient artifacts that archeologists can't explain. They showed a strange contraption found in a desert in Africa, followed by a small copper polygon with 12 sides. Each side had a circular cut-out of a different size. Each corner had a metal bulb on it. The commentator explained how there was only 116 of these dodecahedrons found in European treasures over the last 100 years. "Decahedron is the Greek word for twelve," he continued and stated that they were found with large treasures and that most archeologists believe that they held special value for the owner. Others speculated they were used as a child's toy, like a large die, perhaps for a game.

Edward was there waiting for her. He was standing in front of three wooden chairs looking at some pictures on the wall which were describing the history of Uxmal and some famous people from the region. As he heard Rosa approach he turned. Edward's eyes dilated as he fully took in the beauty that was in front of him. He smiled. "You look lovely" he said. "How was your day?"

Rosa smiled. "Thank you," She said. "Since the bugs are gone and we will still have an August chocolate harvest, my day was wonderful!

"I'll bet you haven't eaten dinner yet, right?" Edward said. "There aren't a lot of eating places around here, but I'm guessing you don't want to eat at the same place you work. I saw another restaurant across from the pyramid. Ppapp Hol Chac de Uxmal. Is that any good?"

"Alicia's enchiladas with mole sauce are the best I've ever had!" Rosa said smiling.

It took about 10 minutes to walk to the restaurant. Edward asked about Rosa and her time in Uxmal. She didn't feel comfortable sharing her life story, so she skipped over a lot of details. She turned the conversation to Edward's history. Edward talked about being raised by his parents in northern California in a small town called Myers Flat and how much he loved it there. His parents were both park rangers, passionate about the preservation of nature. That combined with his love of history is what led him to his career as a climatologist. His specialty is working to preserve historical sites. He had traveled all over the world working on newly discovered ancient ruins. He would study the environments surrounding ancient sites and the conditions of the ruins before, during, and after an archaeological dig. He would also be called in if a particular site had experienced damage, either natural or human caused, to help identify preservation and restoration strategies.

They arrived at the restaurant and were seated by Gabriela. Rosa would sometimes catch a ride with her to church on Sunday along with her 3 young boys aged 9, 7 and 4. Gabriela's husband, Raul, kept telling Gabriela he would go to church with her, but he never did. The Iglesia Catolica Santa Elena in Calle was about a 15 minute ride east of her home in Uxmal. Rosa asked how the boys were. It was evident that Gabriela had a familial love towards Rosa. Gabriela assumed less than noble intentions of Edward and was quite curt when asking him what he would like to drink.

The Ppapp Hol Chac was small with a single dining room with 12 tables, each covered with a mustard yellow table cloth laying in a diamond pattern over a white table cloth. The room was Pepto-Bismol pink on the walls and ceiling, while the walls were adorned with colorful Mexican sombreros. Gabriela seated Rosa and Edward near the kitchen entrance so she could keep an eye on Edward. A few moments later, Gabriela brought a water for Rosa and a Coke for Edward.

She asked for their order. Rosa asked if Alicia was cooking today. When she confirmed, Rosa said she would love to have her famous enchiladas. When Edward asked for the same, her scowl softened just a bit, but was still suspicious.

"So is that why you are here?" Rosa questioned. "To help preserve the Pyramid of the Magician?"

"That's right. Were you living here in 1988 when hurricane Gilbert came through?" Edward asked.

"Yes, but I was a newborn. My mom told me that she took me and we hid in the boiler room of the hotel during the storm. I have no memory of it," Rosa replied.

"It must have been terrible, that was a major storm," Edward could tell it was a sensitive subject. "I even remember watching the news and hearing about it in California. I was only a young boy but I remember the images on TV. I'm so sorry you had to go through that," Edward said sincerely. "As you know, that hurricane did a ton of damage to your pyramid. That saturation level significantly weakened the Northeast side. You probably know this already, but it wasn't until 1996 that the city of Uxmal was designated a UNESCO World Heritage Site."

UNESCO was an acronym for The United Nations Education, Scientific, and Cultural Organization and was a specialized agency within the United Nations. Through this official designation, resources could be given to save historical sites.

"As you know, they have been working on the preservation for several years now, but they came to a point where they didn't want to proceed any further until a 'specialist' (Edward rolled his eyes while doing air quotes while saying the word specialist) came in to evaluate a certain section of the pyramid, especially with the further weakening due to the moisture this area has been receiving. It is a wall that appears on the verge of collapse, but keep in mind that is a relative term. The pyramid has been standing for over a thousand years."

The Pyramid of the Magician was a massive, 131ft tall, 266ft wide stone structure and was a sight to behold. In its prime, the surrounding area was home to about 25,000 Maya which was about 600-1000 AD. It had several building tiers with a large staircase both on the east and west sides of the building measuring over 50' wide. The pyramid was just one of several buildings in the surrounding area.

"Would you mind telling me (from a local perspective) about the legend surrounding how the pyramid was built?" Edward asked.

"You mean the magic dwarf story?" Rosa said.

"Yes. Tell me what you know," said Edward.

Rosa began, "Well, there is not one version of the story. The pamphlets in the hotel tell a different one than what you can read over there," she said pointing to the small gift shop off to the side of the restaurant. "But it is essentially that an old witch lived somewhere around here and was able to create a dwarf from an Iguana or some kind of egg. There was a prophesy... why is there always a prophesy," Rosa muttered under her breath. "There was a prophesy that the dwarf would control the land, and the reigning King or ruler was threatened by the dwarf and demanded that he be executed. The dwarf asked if he could prove himself, which the ruler allowed, by giving him an impossible task. His task was to build a building, taller than any in all the land and he had to do it in one single night. The dwarf built the temple in one night, became ruler of the land and lived within the pyramid and is known as the magician forever after."

Edward sat intently listening, genuinely interested in the legend then said, "Do you think it is true?"

"What kind of a silly question is that?" Rosa responded.

"I don't know. In my experience, most legends have some elements in truth, but over time the story changes here and there.

Gabriela returned to the table with two plates of enchiladas. "Ten cuidado, Rosa cariño. El plato está caliente," she said letting Rosa know the plate was extremely hot and to be careful. She then placed Edwards down in front of him without a word and went back to the kitchen.

After dinner, Edward walked Rosa back to the hotel not knowing where she lived but didn't want to presume she wanted him to know. He thanked her for a wonderful evening and hoped that he could take her out again. She accepted and they said goodnight.

Over the next few weeks, Edward and Rosa went on several dates. Usually they went to dinner and then on walks, given there wasn't much to do in Uxmal. Additional spring showers brought heavy rain to the area. This slowed everything down in Uxmal. Very few tourists came, Edward and his group could do very little, and even Rosa with the tourism slowdown and the mealybugs taken care of found herself with quite a bit of extra time.

One evening while Edward and Rosa were sitting in the hotel lobby having a discussion about a time when Edward was in Egypt, one of Edward's co-workers came rushing into the hotel lobby soaked from rain. He told Edward he needed to come immediately. Edward followed him with Rosa close behind. Edward saw Rosa following and told her she should stay inside to keep dry, but Rosa insisted on coming. They arrived at the pyramid a few minutes later, completely drenched. The other preservation specialist, by the name of Spencer Adams, a short middle-aged man with extremely thick and bushy hair and a deep receding hairline. Edward didn't think he could see through his glasses with the pelting rain, but it didn't seem to stop Spencer.

Spencer went around to the northeast corner and pointed out the problem to Edward. The heavy rains had saturated the outer limestone walls and the interior of the pyramid. The core of Mesoamerican pyramids were rubble retained by stone walls and adorned with limestone on the outside. It appeared that the water had caused the inner rubble core to have an interior rock slide that pushed the retaining wall off its foundation, and caused severe movement of the outer limestone sections. The lower outer walls looked as if the foundation had been pushed up and over, now leaning outward.

Edward immediately went into task mode. He instructed Spencer to get all of the INAH employees and contractors up and to move some equipment into position to reinforce the wall before further damage was done. Spencer immediately ran off leaving Edward and Rosa. Edward again insisted that Rosa go back. Rosa wanted to help and was resolved to stay.

Moments later, a loud crack and groan from the pyramid was heard, and the leaning wall began to move. It was at this moment that Edward realized more of the structure was unstable and the adjacent wall to the one leaning was moving and that Rosa was directly in the path of the falling wall. There was no time to push her out of the way. Rosa was turned with her back to the falling wall where she would be crushed by gigantic sections of limestone in just moments.

Edward reacted instinctively making a motion with his arms and a green light shot out from the emerald hanging on his neck. The green light changed forme into a plume that appeared to hold a tight column between the ground and the falling wall, directly next to Rosa. Edward was clearly straining when he told Rosa to move. Rosa was holding her ears down on one knee and couldn't hear Edward. Rosa looked at the wall suspended in the air over head and looked at Edward. Edward took his right hand and swung it right to left and at that moment a strong gust of air pushed Rosa about 10 feet away from the wall. Then, the wall fell directly on the spot Rosa was standing just a moment before. Rosa, having been thrown onto her back and the wind knocked out of her, looked at Edward who was now collapsed on his knees. He looked up and crawled over to her. "Are you okay?" he asked. Rosa, still struggling to regain her breath nodded instinctively although she wasn't entirely sure if she was. Edward looked over at the pyramid and watched as the northeast corner collapsed. He helped Rosa up and moved her even further from the pyramid and rain continued to pour down in sheets.

~

SYRPENS SAT UP FROM THE COLD BENCH he was laying upon. Sunrise was still in its final stages and light had begun to flood the room through the glass dome ceiling above him. Meditation was still invigorating, but his frail body had now fallen far behind his mind which was clear, sharp and had perfect recall. The room looked like a small ancient atrium of sorts with no windows and only a single door in the smooth stone walls. Very different from the small room with concrete walls he lived in while growing up in Pakistan. He rubbed his old dark Arab eyes. He had been meditating throughout the night and received a clear signal. Thomas would need to be told immediately.

He walked over to a large wooden chest, his long, dark robe polished the mirror black marble stone on the floor. The old worn walnut chest had over-sized hinges and a latch. He opened the lid. Inside there were several stacked wooden trays, each with a black velvet cloth laid within. There were six trays total and each tray, an assortment of stones, gems and crystals perfectly arranged by color. The top tray had red and clear, the second orange, followed by yellow, green and blue. The bottom tray had purple and black stones. After the top five trays had been removed, he placed the dark purple amethyst crystal wand he had been holding throughout the night into the tray. He set the other five trays back in the box and walked out of the room.

Moments later Syrpens entered Thomas Blood's office but rather than finding him, he saw Alexander Litvienko, a tall Russian man with sharp cheek bones and rigid movements. His pale skin contrasted with the greyish-brown stain that appeared to be rubbed into his many wrinkles, divots, and lines across his worn face. Especially the eyes, jaundice with steely grey orbs that never trust anyone. Alexander was speaking with Asha Sauda, The Blood family nurse, who for a life druid looked remarkably old as well. It was rumored that she had taken care of Thomas Blood's great grandfather as a boy. She had white, thin, short hair, along with large, thick glasses with frames that sat on her cheek rather than her nose and extended above her eyebrows. She was from Africa, Swahili descent, but had lived in England for the majority of her very long life.

"Did you feel it?" Syrpens asks. "Where is Thomas?"

"Feel what?" Asha replies.

"Where is Thomas? He must be told immediately," Syrpens spoke with more force than usual.

"He must be told what?" Alexander asked in his thick Russian accent.

"That it has happened and I know where he is!" said Syrpens.

"I don't know what you're talking about," said Alexander, "but Thomas is traveling, remember?"

"But it could be too late if we wait for him to return," Syrpens said (mostly to himself). "I felt Edward. He used the stone. Thomas had been looking for Edward for years. He would want us to send a team to retrieve it. Who is available?"

"Good God are you serious! Why didn't you say that! The only one available right now is Nephrite. She likes to work alone anyway," said Alexander. "But you are right, he would want someone to go immediately. You give her the coordinates and I'll communicate to Thomas that she is on her way."

"How long has it been since he used it?" Asha inquired in a raspy low voice.

"Years," answered Syrpens with anticipation seeping from the deep pores in his face.

"Do you know exactly where he is?" asked Asha turning all of her focus to Syrpens.

"No. But I have it narrowed down and if we act quickly, he won't get away again," said Syrpens.

"But where is he?" Asha insisted, this time more impatiently.

"The Yucatan Peninsula in Mexico," said Syrpens with a sound of a child describing Christmas morning.

"So, a specific location then," Alexander said with heavy sarcasm.

"There are only so many places he can be when you consider the ley lines, and don't forget, we are nearing Summer Solstice which would be the reason he would poke his head up," Serpens replied dismissing Alexander's sarcasm. "I'll speak to Nephrite immediately." Syrpens left Alexander and Asha alone.

~

HUI YIN ZHANG WAS RETURINING to her home in Dujiangyan City, China after the second most difficult day of her life. The most difficult day was just over 2 years ago, May 12, 2008 when the Great Sichuan earthquake happened. Just moments before her daughter would leave school, one of the 20 biggest world-wide earthquakes of all-time hit. The damage was unimaginable in every direction from their home in Dujiangyan China, at the base of Mount Qingcheng, only 20 kilometers from the epicenter. The news would later report that the 8.0 earthquake ruptured across more than 240km and many places with surface displacement of several meters. It was felt in

Beijing, Shanghai, Bangkok, and even in as far away as Vietnam where buildings swayed. Aftershocks were felt for months, some of them as large as 6.0 on the Richter magnitude scale. Nearly 400,000 people injured and 4.8 million people left homeless including Hui Yin, whose apartment had partially collapsed. She had been waiting outside the Dujiangyan Elementary School when she watched it buckle under its own weight right before her eyes with her daughter Li inside. Li was one of the more than 69,000 that lost their lives during the quake. Later they would learn that many of the schools had been poorly built as a result of corruption and bribery of government officials years before. Hui Yin would never be the same.

Her husband, Ju-Long narrowly escaped his own death. He was working as a sanitation engineer near the Jianfu Palace on Mount Qingcheng very close to the epicenter, however being outside at the time saved his life, despite a large section of roof that broke off and narrowly missed him. They both dearly missed their 6 year old Li.

Most of their personal items from their apartment were recovered, as their home was in one of the least destroyed areas, but the entire building was demolished soon thereafter. Government assistance helped by putting them into temporary housing, and later they were able to get an apartment in one of the newly built buildings on the west side of Dujiangyan near the Minjiang River. They, of course couldn't afford an apartment with a view of the water, but Hui Lin found comfort in taking walks along the riverside as she attempted to heal from the loss of her little girl.

A part of her that she thought could never feel again was brought back to life when she learned that she was pregnant. Chinese law prohibited more than one child, but with the loss of Li, they had hoped to once again add to their family, even though it would never be whole. The medical facilities in Duijiangyan were never exceptional before the quake, but after left much to be desireds. Most people traveled to Chengdu City for medical care beyond a simple cold or flu. Chengdu was about an hour Southeast of Dujiangyan by car, however Hui Yin had taken a series of busses and trains to make the journey for her 16 week ultrasound appointment.

During the train ride early in the morning to the Chengdu Western Hospital, Hui Yin was full of anticipation. Although it was raining, she enjoyed looking out of the window at the countryside and even at the city-scape as she entered Chengdu. It turned out to be over two hours in total including bus transfers, but it felt twice that long. She didn't want to take the journey alone, but Ju-Long couldn't miss a day of work. He worked harder than anyone she knew. He believed he would be promoted in the next couple of years if he continued to work hard and have a pristine work record. With the new baby coming, a promotion would mean a great deal to their financial security. They had been married 7 years saving as much money as they could. Hui Yin had become pregnant shortly after they were married and she made this journey several times alone all those years ago when she was pregnant with Li. Going now brought memories and emotions that were reflected in the rain as it dripped down the train car window.

Hui Yin had taken the entire day off due to the time it would take to go into the city. Hui Yin and Ju-Long lived on the outskirts of Dujiangyan where housing was affordable and an easy bus ride to work each day. Hui Yin worked at one of the souvenir shops near Mount Qingcheng at the Sichuan Giant Panda Sanctuary. In fact, there were several sanctuaries, but they were accessible from a common entrance which had a row of shops for eating and shopping.

Being a popular destination for tourists, Hui Yin stayed very busy at work. What she loved most about her job is that she had access to the sanctuaries long before tourists were allowed to enter at 9:00am. She would often go a couple of hours early (especially on days when her husband left for work before sunrise) and walk the grounds with almost no one else around. There was a very old man who she thought must be a researcher or breeder because she would often see him on her early morning walks. He had high cheek bones, bald on top with long white hair and a beard that split and hung down to his belly. The dark skin around his eyes seemed to indicate his late years but he seemed to move with swiftness and precision around the habitats.

A few months earlier when Hui Yin found out she was pregnant, she literally jumped for joy. That night, Ju-Long took her to their favorite restaurant, JunShou Fu, an amazing seafood restaurant not far from their home. Hui Yin ordered the Seafood Birdsnest, a Cantonese style dish with jumbo shrimp, squid, and scallops that are stir-fried with fresh vegetables, ginger and garlic. Ju-Long got the west lake vinegar fish with a sweet and sour sauce and chopped spring onions. China had enacted the one child policy just a few years before Hui Yin was born. Her whole life she knew she would only be able to have one child. Being pregnant twice was not something she imagined when she was young. The anticipation to hold another baby in her arms was more than she could hope or dream. That was 3 months ago, and it was time for the ultrasound with her doctor. It was against the law in China for doctors to announce the sex of the baby. There had been an enormous increase in abortions after parents would learn that their child was a girl. The boy to girl ratio was already getting to be close to 60% male to 40% female in some areas. So the government placed hefty fines and threats on doctors who revealed the baby's gender during an ultrasound. Regardless, there were plenty of doctors that could be bribed into divulging this information. Not that Hui Yin and her husband had that kind of money, but she did hope that the doctor might give some indication of the gender during the ultrasound or that by seeing the screen, she would be able to determine if a boy or girl was on the way.

From the train station, it was a short bus ride over to the hospital where she had a 10:30 appointment with Dr. Chen. The medical staff called her to the examination room only 15 minutes after her scheduled time. She felt like she could walk on clouds as she entered the room. The ultrasound was scheduled for 30 minutes. After 60 minutes and two additional doctors coming in and looking at the monitor with its black and white static pictures on the screen like watching the television channel with no signal, they wiped the warm jelly from her stomach gave her a few minutes to clean up. She was escorted to a small room where she was told the doctor would be in to talk with her. A few minutes later a concerned Dr. Chen entered the room. He didn't mince words. He told her they had some disturbing news about the baby and he made sure she was sitting down. The heart, lungs and all vital organs looked perfect, however it appeared that the baby had a condition known as Meromelia, which she was told meant that the baby hadn't formed arms. She was assured that the condition was not life threatening, but that the child would be born severely handicapped. For Hui Yin it felt like her life was about to end. All the happiness she had ever felt seemed to evaporate in a single instant. She couldn't feel her legs and had she not been sitting down, she would have certainly collapsed. She didn't hear much of what the doctor had to say after that, although much of it was about the number of babies born with a similar condition, how the causes are unknown but they were certain it was not genetic or hereditary. There were some studies that had begun linking birth defects to water pollution as their seemed to be a rise in such cases over the past several years, but they were early in their studies. After a few minutes, he left and a nurse entered. Hui Yin sat sobbing in her hands for quite some time.

The train ride home was very different than the one she had just a few hours earlier. Her world was crumbling down around her. She felt alone and abandoned even with hundreds of others on the same train. Arriving at the Dujiangyan Bus Station, she felt dizzy realizing she hadn't eaten all day. How could she? She found her connecting bus, paid the fair and sat down in a seat near the front. She just wanted to be home. She just wanted to be in her husband's arms where she could cry and not feel alone and afraid. She arrived home just moments after her husband. He knew immediately something was horribly wrong. She told him the condition of the baby, he held her and they both wept.

Chapter 2

AMELIA WAS STILL REALLY SICK. This was her first pregnancy and she knew the first trimester could be difficult. She still was throwing up at least 3 times a day. She now wished she had never agreed to this. Being a surrogate mother for some rich bastard that wasn't even married. Even while she thought that, she knew she would have still done it. She was financially destitute and the offer was just too good to pass up. The first part of the terms was simple enough. Get artificially inseminated in a private medical clinic, have access to state-of-the-art equipment, and a full-time personal doctor and nurse. Deliver the baby and collect the other half of the $500,000.

The other terms were a bit unusual. She couldn't let anyone know she was pregnant. She couldn't communicate with anyone during the pregnancy. She had to stay in the private facility through delivery. And to think she was just one of over 50 applicants that were screened and she was chosen. Applicants. That was a laugh. No one "applied" for this, the candidates were selected from a pre-screened list of college women between the age of 21 and 24 with top grades. The further screening was even more in-depth. Background checks, drug tests, genealogy tests, genetic tests, physical examinations, and the list went on and on. When she was finally chosen, she didn't know if she won the lottery or was just chosen to be Frankenstein's monster. She chose to think of it as winning the lottery, but it was still difficult to go 9 months without seeing her sister or parents. She hadn't spoken to her best friend for months.

She had told everyone she was going on an international service mission to Africa and would be in a region without service, including phones. She had assumed there were still places like that, but she didn't know. Now she just sat, day in and day out waiting for this baby to grow inside of her, getting caught up on every episode of Downton Abbey and the American TV show, "Friends." She wasn't even sure where she was exactly. She knew she hadn't left the U.K. because she was awake the entire time, although blindfolded. That was a bit creepy. She guessed the drive took about 3 hours and she thought it was north most of the time because she felt the afternoon sun on the left side of her face as she sat in the back seat of the car. But nothing more concrete than that. She wasn't allowed to leave the first floor of the clinic, and all she could see were trees out of each window.

She thought it was odd that they never performed any ultrasounds on the baby. When her sister was pregnant, she seemed to get them all of the time. When she asked why they didn't do ultrasounds, she got a bizarre answer about how it could interfere with the developmental energies of the baby or some nonsense. While she would be the biological mother of this child, she would likely never see it again after the birth. The iron-clad contract whereby she gave away all the rights to the baby had to be finalized before the first installment was paid. She decided to simply try to not get attached to it.

She didn't even know who the father was. She could derive from the situation that he was very wealthy and assumed if he was married they would be doing this more naturally, but otherwise didn't have a clue about whose baby she was carrying. That was a strange feeling. She had always imagined her first pregnancy being with a man she loved and they would care for the baby together. But falling on hard times and the cost of college had made her rethink her altruistic notions. She figured with this money she could finish college with everything paid off and still buy a house. A great jump-start to her life if she could just endure about 6 more months.

Part of her contract was to do whatever the doctor said about her or the baby's care. She didn't know why, but the doctor had her lay in a special room for 2 hours each day. The room was dim with soothing music playing. There was a single bed that looked more like a wide massage table in the center of the room with a soft purple blanket draped over it. Under the table was a series of large crystals organized in a pattern on the floor. There were mostly clear crystals but other colors including purple and pink were the most common. There were also some dark-colored stones set in between the translucent crystals. Down the center had stones that were all long and pointed from the foot of the bed to the top of the bed. On either side sat additional crystals and stones all pointing at the center set of crystals.

The bed was about 2 feet off the floor. Amelia would be required to lay on her back covered only by a sheet, then the doctor or nurse would place crystals on various locations on her body. As she did this each day, she would ask questions. They would answer questions about what they were doing, but never why they were doing it. When she asked about the crystals that they placed on her, they said that these were clear crystal quartz "seer stones." Each seer stone was about 2 inches wide with one side shaven flat so you could see inside the crystal, with the outside having a white hard shell. Without the shaved section it would be difficult to know it was anything special, let alone a crystal. These crystals would be placed down the center of her body. One was on the crown of her head, which meant touching the top of her head while laying down. The next is on the forehead. The third is on the throat. Next on the solar plexus, and then 2 inches above the naval, and then 2 inches below the navel, and the last in the crotch. Additional crystal shards with pointed edges would be placed above the head and below the feet, typically pointing up towards the head. Lastly, there would be a special crystal placed in the right hand. It was called a Vogel crystal. They varied in the number of sides they had, usually between 8 and 24 with a smaller point on one end and a larger point on the other.

This would be held in the right hand pointing to the small end at the left hand wherein would be placed various stones, crystals, and other objects. Amelia found it strange but could feel an energy vibration from these crystals when they were on her, especially the ones on the crown of her head and her forehead. Beyond this slight 'tickle,' she wasn't sure they were doing anything.

Lastly, the room was adorned with other crystals and stones in various locations. The corners of the room had various crystals pointing in particular directions as well as other colored stones encircling the edges of the walls. She could feel a variety of different emotions when different stones and crystals were placed in her left hand. They would have a small towel over her face and ask her to tell them the color of the energy coming out of the stone. Her answers would be "red" or "purple" or "blue" or whatever. They never gave any indication whether she was correct and didn't even know if there were correct answers. But she felt like she could actually see, or more accurately "feel" the color when a stone was placed in her hand.

Two evenings prior, the nurse placed a new stone in her left hand that she hadn't felt before. It was smooth, round, and quite cold. Once it touched her hand, it was like a chill climbed up her arm into her heart and down to her unborn child. It happened so quickly that it startled her, and she dropped the stone that would have shattered had the oriental run on the floor not caught it. She took the towel off her face, stones rolling off her. She looked down on the ground and saw a round stone that looked like a globe of the earth but with continents far less defined. There was blue and yellow swirling throughout the stone with elements of green, gold, and white. Amelia surprised, asked the nurse what that stone was. She responded that it was Ocean Jasper. She inquired what Amelia had felt and she described the sensation. The nurse muttered "Very interesting" while making notes on her digital tablet.

~

ROSA WAS FOLDING TOWELS the following morning. The pounding she felt in her ears was starting to subside. She couldn't stop thinking about what happened to her the previous night when she was nearly crushed by the wall of the pyramid. She was also trying to rationalize in her mind what she knew Edward had done. He had saved her life, but how? She decided she was going to talk to Edward about it right after work.

She was done early with all her duties. The air was muggy from all the rain, much more than usual. The baking sun felt like a sauna as she walked from the hotel over to the Pyramid of the Magician. When she arrived, she saw the mass of people around the collapsed wall of the pyramid. Memories of the previous night again flashed through her mind. Rosa shuttered at the thought.

There was a barrier set up about 30 meters back from the pyramid around the northeast corner. The damage did not seem to extend far into the interior or further around the perimeter of the pyramid, preserving the stairs leading to the top. Large reinforcements were positioned to hold areas of the wall and structure in place with several more being worked on by a large group of men. Edward was in the midst of them pointing and directing. A moment later he saw Rosa just outside the barrier. He spoke to another gentleman making some final gestures, patted him on the back, and walked towards Rosa. Edward had a yellow hard hat and a long white cotton shirt which was dirty and soaked with sweat. Rosa could see the outline of his broad shoulders and muscular chest.

Edward took Rosa by the hand and led her to a shady spot on the east side of the pyramid away from the noise. "While the northeast corner wall is down, it looks like the integrity of the core structure is solid. The rest of the pyramid including the stairs and top are all going to be fine," Edward said knowing the real reason Rosa was there.

"What happened last night?" Rosa asked. "I remember the wall was falling on me, I thought that was the end. Then my ears were pounding and feeling like they would explode and I couldn't even think. I saw you," her voice trailing off. "I saw what you did," Rosa said as if she were explaining it to herself and not Edward. "How did you do it?"

"How did I do what?" Edward said, however, he got an immediate flash of Rosa's amber eyes and realized that wasn't going to work. He changed his tactic and said, "What do you think happened?"

"I don't know but it was like magic," Rosa said with her ears still ringing from the night before. "But since it can't be magic, what was it?"

"Why can't it be magic?" Edward said.

"Because magic isn't real!" Rosa exclaimed.

"How do you know magic isn't real?" he said in a very serious tone now.

"What do you mean?" Rosa said, getting a bit frustrated with the question. "Because it isn't real. There is no real magic. If there was magic, we would see it everywhere. It would be written in books and on the news. There would be evidence."

"There is tons of evidence of magic in history books," Edward said. "Remember the other night when we went to dinner and you introduced me to the woman that you sometimes go to church with, right?"

"Yes," said Rosa thinking of Gabriela.

"What book do you use there?" Edward said. Rosa knew he meant the bible. "Don't you consider the bible to be a historical record?"

"Of course," said Rosa wondering where this was going.

"Well, then you have all the proof you need. How else would you describe Moses calling down plagues on Egypt? Parting the Red Sea? Pillars of fire and smoke leading the children of Israel into the desert? Making water come out of a rock? The list goes on and on, and that is just one of the prophets of the Old Testament. What do you call that?" almost like a professor talking to a student.

"The power of God," said Rosa.

"Well, that may be, but look at it from the perspective of someone else there. Perhaps the Egyptians. What would they have called it?" Edward asked. Rosa thought about this for a moment but Edward answered his question. "Magic. If the magic is sourced from God, or the universe, or whatever, it is still magic. Arthur C. Clarke, a famous author, once said 'Magic's just science we don't understand yet.'"

With what Rosa had experienced the night before, she felt she had to be open to the idea even though it was against everything thought to be true. Edward walked over to a garbage can where an empty soda can was lying on the ground. He picked up the crushed Coke can and walked back to Rosa. He handed the can to her. She said, "What am I supposed to do with this?"

"Just hold it out like this," Edward positioned her hands together out in front of her, palms up with the can laying evenly across them. Edward then closed his eyes and held his right palm out in front of him towards the can. His left hand reached inside his pants pocket and pulled out something he was clutching. Edward, without saying a word sat there concentrating. A few moments later, Rosa was astounded to see the can begin to change. The can was brand new earlier that day and other than being crushed, looked perfectly new. What she observed was unbelievable. She watched as the can began to rust and decay right before her eyes. The can began getting holes as the rust completely engulfed the can until she could no longer see any traces of the Coca-Cola logo.

"What the..." Rosa said, opening her hands right as the entire can dissolved to dust and blows away in the light breeze. Rosa was trying to understand what she had just witnessed. After Edward saved her from the falling pyramid wall by some unseen force, he had now caused a soda can to disintegrate in front of her eyes. A thought occurred to Rosa. "You killed all the bugs in the plantation, didn't you?"

Edward began to explain. "Rosa, I just thought that if you had less work, I'd be able to take you out on a date. That's all."

"How did you do it? How did you make the can disappear? How did you kill the bugs, and, and last night," Rosa started to stutter, "How did you stop the wall from falling on me? How did you move me?" the faster she spoke the thicker her accent became.

"I grew up in Northern California like I told you. At a very early age, my parents showed me how to use magic. They both did magic, albeit different kinds of magic. They helped me discover my magic and taught me how to cultivate it." Edward stood up, reached for Rosa's hands, and helped her up. They started walking north staying in the shade as best they could. "Are you hungry?" Edward said. "I'm starving. Can I take you to an early dinner?"

Edward and Rosa walked to the Coole Chepa Chi's, which was a fresh-air, buffet-style restaurant. The large straw hut offered much-needed shade, although there was no protection from the humidity. The decorative stone flooring and iron statues of several Mariachi band members greeted diners.

The hostess, another older friend of Rosa named Juana, seated them. Juana smiled at Rosa and raised her eyebrows with a quiet approval of Edward. Rosa immediately started in, "So why don't more people know about magic?"

"Kind of a lost art that people don't understand. It isn't easy to do, plus it doesn't work the way people think. It isn't like you can do just anything like it shows in the movies. Listen, I think it is kind of like brain surgery. Everyone has heard about it but very few people in the world can do it. Even if I wanted to do brain surgery, it would take me years of education, training, and practice before I could do it. And then, if I became a brain surgeon, that doesn't mean I can be a heart surgeon, it is a different practice. Well, that is kind of the same with magic."

"So you can't just do anything with your magic?" Rosa asked.

"No, I can't just do any magic. I can do surprisingly few things, to be honest. You can't just do anything with magic. No one can. Magic doesn't work like that. Movies, TV, and books make magic look like people can just conjure up anything and do anything without any regard for science, physics, or nature. It makes you think that magic is about making things like fireballs come out of your hands."

"You can do that?" Rosa imagined Edward with fireballs coming out of his hands.

"No! Of course not," cringed Edward. "Real, true magic is usually more subtle and always adheres to the natural order of the universe. There are different types of magic. We refer to them as 'affinities,' meaning you as a person has a natural inclination towards a particular type of magic."

"So there are different types of magic?" Rosa asked.

Edward explained, "Well, there are six affinities which are like categories of magic. My affinity is environmental magic, or what some like to call atmospheric magic. Controlling things in the atmosphere around us. Wind, clouds, rain, and the like. Even lightning. I can control gasses, atmospheric pressure, and humidity. Those bugs on your cocoa trees, I just simply removed the oxygen from the air, leaving only nitrogen and carbon dioxide and the bugs suffocated and died," he said in a softer tone as he noticed an older tourist couple looking over at them. "I accelerated the environmental conditions around the Coke can to make it rust faster."

"And what about last night?" Rosa asked.

"Well, I used barometric pressure to slow the fall of the stone wall and then a wind gust to move you out of the way. It all happened so fast that I didn't have time to think about it. It was more reactive than anything," Edward looked at the tourists who had gone back to their discussion.

"Is that why my ears hurt today?" said Rosa rubbing her right ear again.

"Yeah, that is likely. Barometric pressure changes are what you feel when you change elevation going up into a mountain or something. That would have been a lot of pressure very near you. I'm so sorry," Edward said sincerely.

"I want to see the lightning magic sometime," Rosa was thinking about Edward in the middle of a storm. "You said there were other types as well?"

"There is cosmic magic, frequency magic, liquid magic (no that is not a super powerful toilet bowl cleaner)," Edward added as an aside. Rosa laughed for the first time in as long as she could remember. Edward continued. "Life magic, and earth magic. Six different affinities," Edward answered.

"So you get to pick your magical powers?" Rosa asked.

"No. Just born with it. Everyone is born with an affinity toward a particular type of energy. But there is a lot more to magic than just an affinity." Rosa was listening even more intently to Edward now. "In addition to what type of energy is drawn to you, there is your ability to control it. This usually takes some outside help. Natural objects can help you control the energy that is all around us. For some, this is a rock, stone, gem, or crystal. For others, it is a staff, a scepter, and yes, the occasional wand. Look at that story from the bible. What did Moses do? He had his brother take his staff and do all those plagues. These objects are uniquely formed to capture, store, enhance, control, or otherwise interact with a particular type of energy. For example, someone that has an affinity towards life magic would more likely be able to draw on that energy from something that was at one time living, like a tree branch. So a branch that is fashioned into a staff, scepter, or wand could help someone harness and control life energy. Like Moses."

"So I could go over there, break off one of those branches from that tree, and control 'life energy'?" Rosa said feeling like she wasn't quite understanding all this.

"As you would guess, it isn't quite that simple. Not all objects are created equal. There are conditions that make some objects more suitable for energy manipulation than others. And with each 'rule,' there are many exceptions, but as a general rule, the older something is the more energy it can store and manipulate. So, the age of the tree the wood was taken from would make a big difference. The type of wood can make a difference. How the wood was cut or gathered, the location of the tree, the conditions that existed when it was cut or carved all might sound insignificant but can make an enormous difference in that object's ability to control magic." Edward looked over as their hostess came over again to the table. She asked what they would like to drink. Edward wanted a Coke and Rosa asked for water. Juana told Edward that it was a buffet and that they could get plates on the counters next to where the food line began.

Edward and Rosa got up from the table, got their plates, and went around from chaffing dish to chaffing dish picking out what they wanted. Edward picked chicken with Spanish rice, black beans, chips, and pulled pork fajitas. Rosa selected chips with guacamole, shrimp, and an assortment of vegetables. She had, of course, eaten here before, but at her income level, those times were quite rare. As they sat back down, the discussion reignited.

"You mentioned something about other types of objects beyond wood?" Rosa asked.

Edward continued to explain. "Yes. Wood is very good for life energy as well as other things. But as you would imagine, wood is not good for liquid energy. For most of the other energy types either gems, crystals, stones, or other things are best. While age plays a part, many of those are as old as time, so other factors play important parts. All gems have flaws, well, nearly all of them, and those flaws cause light, sound, and energy to pass through them differently. Each one is unique and therefore may be more apt to help control energy than another one. Plus the color of the stone, crystal, or gem makes a big difference as well. Some colors are more conducive to controlling liquid, some earth, while others help control atmospheric conditions, etc. For example, my mother had control over liquids and she commonly used a pearl (which naturally came from the ocean) to help her harness and control that energy."

"So what do you use?" Rosa asked just before taking a bite of a large green pepper. "You know, to control your magic."

"I have a variety of things that I use. Rarely does someone strictly use just one object all of the time. You might find that a particular stone helps you do one thing while a specific crystal helps you with another and a certain gem with even another. However, what you might find some use is an object that has multiple types of objects in it. This would be an artifact or a relic. Imagine a staff with a bejeweled handle and a crystal atop. This one object would hold multiple types of energy and therefore multiple magical qualities. This is why old artifacts or relics are highly sought after.

Edward was now digging into his fajitas and Rosa thought it best to let him get a few bites in. "So, is that what I hit my head against the first time we met?" Rosa said. "Something that helps you control your energy?" Edward pulled out the necklace with a green emerald. Rosa examined it closely. She noticed it had some kind of a flaw or marking in the center. Edward put it back in his shirt.

Kevin Prince | 30

"Yes, this is my favorite, a family heirloom, but again, it is just one of several I use," Edward said.

"So a crown from some old Monarch with gold, jewels, etc. could be powerful, right?" said Rosa, starting to understand how this works.

"Yes, plus a scepter with a crystal or diamond atop surrounded by jewels. How do you think they kept all those people in line? These things were used throughout history and do have real power. Who is the king? The one who wears the crown and holds the scepter," Edward wiped some pork from his cheek. "But there is more to it than just finding an object and knowing your affinity. The objects just store, manipulate, direct, and focus energy. We haven't even talked about the energy itself. Energy is everywhere, in every living thing. It is in anything that moves or emits heat or light. Look at the sun, it is nothing more than a huge ball of energy.

There are two main sources of energy. The first type is everything around us that generates or reflects energy. These include natural forces such as volcanos, earthquakes, wind, rain, the sun, a hurricane, waves, an avalanche, any living thing, and the list goes on and on." Edward seemed to explain these concepts from his subconscious without any effort. "Even where we are right now has a tremendous amount of energy. Do you know why your pyramid was built here? It is because there is a ton of underground energy flowing right here. My guess is that it was formed millions of years ago when the meteor that killed all the dinosaurs hit right over there in the Gulf of Mexico. That caused such a massive energy release, I believe that energy is still flowing up right under us."

Edward took another bite and swallowed before continuing. "There are certain geographical locations all around the earth where this energy is very strong. We call these locations vortexes. Vortexes are connected with energy lines that are commonly referred to as ley lines. Often an energy or ley line would be where tectonic plates collide, on a fault line, or you've probably heard of the 'ring of fire' with all the volcanoes, or a large mountain range. You get the idea. So where these ley lines cross are very powerful energy spots. These vortexes are places where magic users can harness a lot of power.

Did you know, your pyramid is on one such ley line?" Edward said rhetorically. "Well, not everyone agrees on every ley line and every vortex, but there are some that are indisputable. Stonehenge for example. A perfect ley line crossing or vortex. The great pyramids of Giza in Egypt are another good example. Everyone knows that is one of the most powerful vortexes. Some people believe these locations can be mapped out mathematically. Others believe they follow geological formations. But one thing is for sure, ancient magic users knew of these ley lines and vortexes. Look at Stonehenge for example. The stones are aligned perfectly at summer solstice for the sun to rise behind what is known as the Heel Stone with the first rays shining into the heart of Stonehenge. So if you combine powerful ley line crossings with a celestial event such as summer solstice, you have a point in space and time that generates tremendous energy." Edward took a sip of his Coke.

"You said there were two sources of energy," Rosa reminded him.

"The other type of energy is from human thought. It isn't raw, natural power, but rather it can be generated by the human mind. The more we think or focus on something, the more energy we give it. And while perhaps a single person can't generate too much energy, many people combined can. This is why religious relics have so much power in them. Thousands or millions of people thinking about some object endows it with power. You know there are churches in Europe that claim to have bits of the wood used in the cross of Jesus Christ. Millions of people believe those are real and because they think and believe that, it fills those relics with power. The crazy thing is that it doesn't even matter if they are the real thing or not. What matters is that people believe that they are, focus on them, have devotion towards them, and then they are filled with power. Same kind of thing with your crown and scepter example from before." Edward stopped talking for a moment and began stabbing some of the pulled pork that fell from the fajita with his fork and put it in his mouth.

"Druids have learned through millennia how to identify and harness this power. It is really that simple," Edward was looking directly into Rosa's amber eyes.

"Druids?" Rosa questioned.

"It is the ancient name of magic users," Edward responded. "It is difficult with names. You say wizards and pointy hats come to mind. You say witches, and you think little kids getting cooked in edible houses and broomsticks. You say magician, and you think Las Vegas. I think that is why most contemporary magic users refer to themselves as druids. For me, the name refers to a person who is in harmony with the natural energy of the universe and uses it to control their environment."

"So you are a druid?" Rosa asked in the most serious tone she had.

"Yes I am," Edward said with a certain finality.

Chapter 3

I HAVE SOME GOOD NEWS for you Thomas," Asha, the old Swahili nurse, spoke in a deep raspy tone that contrasted her petite frame. Thomas held up a finger with the phone still against his ear.

"Call me as soon as you locate him but engage immediately. We can't lose him again." Thomas hung up the phone. "They are zeroing in on Edward," Thomas said with the look of a lion near a herd of gazelle.

"I heard. I'm surprised you didn't go after Edward yourself," the nurse said in a curious tone. Her dark skin looked worn and resembled loose leather after being rubbed with a fine-grit sandpaper.

"I was returning from my trip when they got the signal, and the team decided to move immediately, which was right. But the bigger issue for me is I need to charge some artifacts tonight, or I would portal there right now. So Nephrite will have to suffice," Thomas said, disappointed with his required priorities.

"Well then, things are in good hands. Would you prefer I give you the update later?" said the nurse looking through her thick pink-framed glasses, making her beady eyes look almost regular-sized.

"No. Please proceed," Thomas said, now squarely focusing on her.

"Amelia is doing well," Asha said in a business tone. "Nothing to report there."

"And the child?" Thomas inquired. "Did something happen?"

"Well, yes. In a sense. The baby now has extended responsiveness to crystal divination, and I believe the child is a dé-thugach," The nurse articulated the word with added inflection, knowing Thomas would be pleased.

"Really!? A duel-gifted druid? Are you sure the mother's affinity is not being expressed?" Thomas questioned.

"No. The mother is a freq, although she is unaware of the ancient ways. We tested her before insemination. They are coming from the child," The old nurse answered.

Which affinities were expressed?" Thomas said, this being almost better news to Thomas than identifying where Edward was.

"The child seems to be responding very clearly to Onyx as well as the Ocean Jasper," The nurse said.

"So, in addition to the power of the cosmos, like me," Thomas said with his thoughts leaving the conversation.

"And the child is a Liq," the nurse said, bringing Thomas' focus back.

"The child will also have the power to control liquids. What an interesting combination, being on both ends of the energy spectrum. Well, this is good news and will be very useful. It appears all our preparation is paying off. Imagine what the child may become yet. Despite what so many have said, we can architect foreordination. And you have brought me the first proof of that. Keep me updated. I'm off to charge a rew relics. Solstice is tomorrow," Thomas says and begins to turn away.

"So you will be using your dodecahedron then? I'm surprised with all the moving around you have done that you have any charges left on it," Asha asked.

"Yes, I will portal late tonight, so I will be there for the first sun tomorrow morning. The lack of charges is why I flew on the jet on my most recent tripo. Flying, even if on a private jet, is for peasants and a complete waste of time," Thomas said as he turned again and walked down the black marble hallway.

~

June 20, 2010

ROSA AND EDWARD LEFT THE RESTAURANT. Edward hadn't realized how hungry he was. He had hardly eaten anything all day due to the pyramid emergency. Edward asked Rosa if he could show her something late that evening. She agreed to meet him at the Pyramid steps at sunset.

When sunset arrived, Rosa was walking past the shops, which were all closed. No one was around except for a few workers near the collapsed corner. She walked towards the pyramid. She saw Edward waving at her from the far west end of the pyramid, and she walked in that direction. She noticed she had a nervous excitement in her steps. She had started really liking Edward over the past several weeks since they had been dating. However, these feelings had intensified in the last 24 hours as Edward had saved her life, not to mention everything she learned about energy and magic. She wanted to be with him and thank him for saving her. She felt in shock after the incident and didn't feel she had appropriately expressed her gratitude.

When she reached Edward, he took her by the hand and looked at her. "You look absolutely amazing!" Edward exclaimed in slow, deliberately separate words. Rosa had put on her nicest dress. She rarely wore the red poppy-colored dress because it was significantly shorter than she usually liked. "I'm excited to show you this tonight," Edward said, taking Rosa by the hand and walking around the west side of the pyramid.

"Something good has come out of last night's small collapse," Edward announced. "All tours to the pyramid have been canceled until further notice."

"That isn't good for the local economy. If it doesn't open back up soon, many of my friends will struggle," Rosa said with a concerned look as she thought about all those she knew and loved.

"The pyramid will be open in just a few days. The structure is still solid. It was just that corner edge that collapsed. We got most of the reinforcements put in place today to ensure safety, not to mention something seemed to dry out the limestone, so the saturation issue is largely resolved," Edward winked quickly at Rosa, letting her know he may have had something to do with that part. "A longer-term plan will have to be designed, but for now, it is safe. But I said it is good news because we have the entire pyramid to ourselves tonight." Edward took her hand and stepped up onto the first stair.

"Are you sure it is safe?" Rosa asked.

"Absolutely. That far other end had significant damage, but it doesn't affect the main body of the pyramid," Edward answered confidently. Edward had a large backpack over his left shoulder. He used his right hand to gently pull Rosa from the ground onto the first step.

They began making the 131-foot climb at a challenging 60-degree angle. Edward was in no rush. "Do you remember talking about how this pyramid was created?" Edward continued talking through his rhetorical question. "The reason I'm here at this pyramid tonight is why I came to Uxmal at all. I believe a druid dwarf created this pyramid in one night. A night identical to this night. Do you know what tonight is?"

"No," Rosa said, thinking Sunday was probably incorrect.

"Tomorrow is summer solstice! June 21. You know, the longest day of the year. Well, it is not any longer than any other day, but the time between sunrise and sunset is longer than any other day. This temple was built on summer solstice. That is part of the energy used to build it," Edward sounded extremely excited now. "Not only was it built on summer solstice, but the entire pyramid is designed to be aligned exactly east with the rising sun tomorrow morning. Remember when I told you about the power of crystals, gems, artifacts, and other objects? Well, the magic gets depleted with use. You need to recharge these items, and while there are several ways of doing that, few are as potent as the sun on the solstice, especially at an energy vortex. Not that this is a vortex. I have to avoid those, especially on days like tomorrow, but this is on a ley line and has unique ties to other energy, as I told you."

"Why do you have to avoid other vortexes?" Rosa asked, getting out of breath now and only about one-third the way up the pyramid. They both stopped for a short rest.

Edward continued, "As you can imagine, the rarer and more powerful an object or relic is, the more people want it. Imagine what happens when people show up at the same place at the same time with these rare magic items. That is probably one of the reasons there are so few druids around. So I try to stay clear of the major sites on days like tomorrow. Imagine what Stonehenge will be like tomorrow morning or the pyramids of Egypt. That is why I picked this spot. More or less off the grid. But I still think it will do the trick."

Rosa began walking up the steps again. Edward followed, realizing he should have been following her the whole time with the way Rosa's leg muscles strained as she ascended the stairs. "So your rocks and stuff will be recharged tomorrow? Like a battery?" Rosa asked.

"Uh, what? I mean, yeah, similar, I guess," Edward said, still distracted.

"And to do this, you only have to put them in the sunlight at sunrise?" Rosa said, looking back at him.

"While here at the pyramid, yes," Edward said, feeling his legs getting a little weary now.

"Under what other circumstances can you charge your things?" Rosa couldn't decide what she should call them and wasn't sure if she fully believed what he was telling her. Magical objects? Yet she couldn't dismiss what she had witnessed in the last 24 hours.

"Different types of energy can be used to charge different objects. For example, some crystals need a very subtle, soft energy. So for some crystals, a waxing crescent moon is the best. For others, it would be a full moon. Other objects might need the full power of the sun to charge them. But this type of energy can discharge very quickly with just moderate use. You can have far better results when you correlate a celestial event with the energy charging. That is why a sunrise on a summer solstice is considerably more powerful with results much stronger than just any old sunrise," Edward said this with some difficulty as he was trying to talk and panting significantly now with beads of sweat standing prominently on his forehead. Rosa glowed. No visible perspiration, just a radiant sheen that Edward found irresistible.

"For example, six months from now, on December 21 of this year, will be Winter Solstice, which is a rare enough event by itself with the alignment of the sun on the shortest day of the year, but on that day there will also be a lunar eclipse. Do you know how rare that is?" Edward asked.

"I'm guessing pretty rare," Rosa smirked.

"Yeah. Very. The last one happened almost 400 years ago. That will be a day of magic, to be sure. But some other special times or events can increase the power consumption of particular objects. Certain gems, crystals, or other specific things might generate a tremendous amount of power during rare events such as an eclipse, comet, or solar flare (although, unfortunately, most solar flares can't be predicted). Also, when certain planets and constellations are in specific alignments, they too can impact power absorption." Edward turned and sat down on a step. Rosa did the same. They were more than two-thirds to the top.

Edward reached into his backpack, pulled out bottled water, and handed it to Rosa. He then pulled one out for himself. After draining more than half the bottle, Edward continued, "Sorry. This is probably more detail than you wanted to know."

Rosa jumped in, "No, this is very interesting. I don't understand everything, but I generally get the idea. People have affinities, a propensity to a specific magic type. You said there were six of them. But more is needed to perform magic, so you also need the help of rocks, crystals, or whatever. These objects absorb, store, and focus energy in conjunction with the 'druid,'" Rosa looked over at Edward to make sure she was getting this right. "But the energy in these objects can be drained like a battery when used and must be recharged occasionally. But you can't just plug them into a wall like a phone. You must use energy in nature, a combination of location, time, and other events with different power levels. Oh, and not all energy sources and types work with every kind of object."

Edward sat stunned. "Geez. You just summed it up even better than I could have. That is remarkable."

"I'm a good listener," Rosa said, smiling. In reality, she loved listening to Edward talk. He was so passionate about what he did and everything in his life.

Plus, as he spoke, she could see the gold tooth in the back of his mouth, which she thought was sexy. "But there is still something I don't understand, like why are you telling me all this?"

Edward paused with a self-reflecting stare. "I'm not sure. Part of me thinks you deserve to know based on what you saw. I don't want to lie to you." The two continued walking up the steps to the summit. "But if I'm being honest, there is something more. Spending time with you these past few weeks has been wonderful. I feel very close to you, although I don't know why. Part of me wants you to know my deepest secrets, and now you do! I feel like I can tell you anything, and as you would probably imagine, not many people know this about me."

"So each person can only have one affinity of the six?" Rosa asked.

"Yes. There are some exceptions, and then there is the prophecy." Edward hadn't thought about this in a long time.

"A Prophesy?" Rosa asked with a grin. "There's always a prophecy."

"Laugh all you want, but yes, there is a prophesy, although few fully understand it. It was passed down via oral tradition for generations, so I worry that what we have now isn't even the correct prophesy anyway," Edward continued closing his eyes, "It goes like this: 'When the crimson moon passes through shadow and blood on the darkest day, the druid of destiny will be born of death on the last archer where energies converge to create tension between the heavens and the earth which will begin when the ancestor stone is gifted on the day of becoming.'"

"Oh, so an easy-to-understand prophesy," Rosa said sarcastically. "What does it mean?"

"I have some guesses on parts of it, but no one knows for sure," Edward said, almost entirely out of breath. "But it is believed that the 'druid of destiny' will be a druid that embodies and controls all six affinities."

Just then, Edward and Rosa took the final steps to reach the top of the pyramid. Rosa reached over for Edwards's hand and squeezed it. "Thank you for telling me and saving my life," she said.

Edward stopped and took in the moment. "I love the feeling in a place like this. The breeze. The sights and smells. These places have a life of their own, their breath. The aura is perfect. That is what I want to name a little girl if I ever have one. Aura. It sums up everything good in the world."

"Aura, huh?" responded Rosa. "That is a beautiful name. Very English, but very pretty."

The Sunset atop the Pyramid of the Magician was breathtaking. There was something about how the sunlight hit the stone that created a perfect color contrast between the temple and the surrounding complex, with its orange limestone hue and the lush green forest and grass around it. Both stood taking in the picture-perfect moment while slowly turning to absorb the full 360-degree panoramic beauty. Edward said, "More than anything, this is why I love working with UNESCO, is for moments like these." They walked to the pyramid's center, and Edward pulled a blanket from his backpack. Rosa helped him unfold and lay it down. They sat down as the sun set and twilight fell upon Uxmal with brilliant colors on the horizon and slowly turned darker and darker shades of blue above them.

Edward then empties his backpack one item at a time. He pulls out a bottle of wine and two glasses. Next, he pulls out a plate of cheese and crackers and sets them in the center of the blanket. Lastly, Edward takes out a leather bundle rolled like a small sleeping bag with a leather cord wrapped around it and tied with a bow. Edward carefully untied the leather roll exposing several pockets and compartments, each holding an item.

"Are these all the magic items you have?" Rosa asks.

"All the ones I am going to charge, yes. I have quite a few more in my collection back home," Edward responded. Edward began pulling them out one by one and showing them to Rosa. He would name each one as he went. Carnelian, brown agate, ametrine, crystal quartz, morganite, orange calcite, citrine, orange garnet, orange jade, orange opal, and rhodonite.

"Let me guess, your favorite color is orange," Rosa said with a playful grin.

"No, actually, it is green, but each affinity I mentioned before is associated with a color on the spectrum. As you may have guessed, atmospheric energies are often, but not always, associated with orange-colored objects. It may be easier to remember if you think that the atmosphere brings about sunsets," Edward had been laying them out in front of Rosa as he talked about them.

He picked up each of the stones or crystals and moved them to the edge of the pyramid on the east side, seeming to know precisely where he wanted them. He then pulled out a long brownish crystal slightly thicker than a length of a pencil. It had six straight flat sides with pointed ends, one being slightly larger than the other. He then pulled out another similar long crystal. Still, this one is more colorful, with orange, purple, and different colors throughout. They both looked like miniature crystal versions of the Washington Monument in Washington D.C. "What are those?" Rosa asked, stretching out her hands to hold them. Edward placed them in her hands.

"This one," Edward said, pointing to the brownish one, "is a smoky quartz wand. And this one is a pineapple amethyst wand."

"Wands," Rosa said with a bit of a giggle. "So you are a wizard, after all."

"A druid, thank you very much," Edward said. "I know it sounds silly, but they are called wands." He then placed them next to the others.

"If everyone has an affinity, how do you know what they are?" Rosa asked.

"There are different ways of telling. Some druids specialize in divination magic, whether to figure out your affinity or tell you what powers your stones or crystals have. It isn't easy for most druids to do," Edward said as he sat on his side, picking up a piece of cheese and popping it into his mouth.

"Can you tell what affinity I have?" Rosa asked.

Edward paused for a moment attempting to discern if she was joking. When he decided she wasn't, he said, "Maybe. You wanna try?"

"I'd like to find out. You said everyone has one," Rosa said in all seriousness. Edward went back over and picked up the pineapple amethyst wand. It was distinctly purple on the geometric, pyramid-shaped top. Still, as it went down to the other point, the sides appeared to have white, battery-acid corrosion, although it was part of the crystal. He came back and sat down next to Rosa. Edward asked Rosa to lie flat on her back. He then systematically touched specific points on her body one by one. Rosa felt the wand glide across her body from point to point. Every point Edward stopped at tingled with a vibration that stimulated and energized her. She opened her eyes and locked with Edwards. They both simultaneously embraced and kissed passionately. The following hours were spent staring at the stars together. Edward explained many constellations and planetary alignments, and they talked while holding each other late into the night.

~

June 21, 2010 – Summer Solstice

THEY BOTH MUST HAVE FALLEN ASLEEP because the stars in the sky had wildly shifted positions when Rosa awoke, still on the blanket. Edward was a few feet away on the east side of the pyramid's edge. Rosa could see that he was taking off the necklace with the emerald and setting it as a centerpiece to all the other stones, gems, and crystals he had laid out. Edward's silhouette was unmistakable against the deep blue sky, which seemed lighter by the moment. Rosa realized that it was nearing morning and sunrise would be soon. Edward returned to the blanket lying close to Rosa.

"Good Morning," Edward said, looking into her incredible amber eyes.

"Good Morning," Rosa answered, enjoying his gaze.

"Sorry, we fell asleep up here. I had intended to leave these up here and pick them up again this morning, but I lost track of time and fell asleep. For some reason, I feel very comfortable with you," Edward said as he took his finger across her forehead, moving a lock of hair out of her eyes and behind her ear.

She wasn't sure what came over her, but she turned, rolling on Edward, now sitting up and straddling him. She arched over him, caressing his face while she gave him a deep, passionate kiss. Edward took his hands around her thin waist, up her back, and pulled her close. Edward and Rosa were one as the horizon burst forth with the rising sun upon the pyramid. As Edward had described, the sunrise perfectly aligned with the temple's orientation, but neither seemed to notice.

~

THE SUN HAD FULLY RISEN but was still low in the sky. They took the eastern steps down the pyramid to soak in all the solstice sunlight they could. Edward had placed his necklace back on his neck and the other stones back in the leather roll in the backpack. As Edward and Rosa descended the final pyramid steps, hand in hand, a strange sensation came over them.

Edward felt an overwhelming pull toward the ground. Both knees hit the hard stone simultaneously, followed by his hands. He tried to pull himself up, but it was like having a 300-pound weight pressed down upon him. He looked over at Rosa, crouched down, struggling to move. With considerable effort, Edward pulled his head up just enough to see a figure walking out of the tree line about 100 yards away, heading towards them. The figure wore a black cloak with a hood draped over its face. Tall black boots combined with the flowing cloak gave a shadow-like appearance as it moved closer. The figure then pulled back the hood to reveal thin, feminine facial features, but that is where the femininity ended. Thick, dark copper-colored dreadlocks in a Mohawk crawled down her neck and spine like snakes. Tattoos covered every part of her skin. Purple, blue, red, and orange ink created a creature-like demonic mask across her face. Her cheeks and neck were tattooed with faces of lost souls weeping and wailing as if being pulled into an eternal abyss. Her ears adorned large black gauges. The tops of the ears had four silver clamps. Her nose was pierced with the ring connected to black chains swooping up and connecting to piercings on the edge of her tattooed eyebrows. Her teeth had been filed to sharp points. Edward recognized her immediately. It was Nephrite. She was a dark druid. One of the most disturbing features of Nephrite was that she had sub-dermal implants placed in her head, giving her demonic budges—one above each of her eyebrows and another further above near the hairline on each side. Then three smaller lumps just above the ears going back into her hairline.

These body modifications were not for aesthetic reasons. Nephrite had modified herself to embody the power of particular objects. The ear gauges were made of black jade. The subdermal implants Edward knew were specially shaped red garnets. She wore a spiked choker-style necklace with spikes made of dark silver hematite. Her right hand adorned a ring made from pyrite, holding a large yellow jasper stone in the center. These various stones would endow Nephrite with power and protection in battle.

At that moment, Edward knew what was happening. Nephrite was an earth druid, and she had cast a gravity spell pulling them down to the ground. The force would get stronger as she got closer, so he knew he would have to move fast. With as much effort as possible, Edward reached into his bag and pulled out the smoky quartz wand he had just charged. It was challenging because everything in the bag was about four times its normal weight.

Edward quickly thought through the words that would use his atmospheric affinity, combined with his smoky quartz wand, to reduce the barometric pressure around him and Rosa dramatically. He couldn't undo Nephrite's gravitational pull, but he could offset the effects in a way. However, gravity would be far more potent than reduced air pressure, so he acted fast. His spell gave him just enough pressure release to lift his hand into the air. Almost immediately, dark clouds formed directly above them. Then, using the ever-increasing force of gravity, the hand holding the dark brown wand struck downward as if flipping a whip. At that exact moment, lightning struck from the sky directly toward Nephrite, who jumped to the side, narrowly avoiding the bolt. A massive clap of thunder pierced the air.

With Nephrite thrown off balance, the gravitational pull loosened, and Edward again reached for the sky. With another downward thrust of his arm, another lightning bolt shot down at Nephrite. She was, however, anticipating this and had raised her arm above her head and, by so doing, had pulled a large section of earth up and over her head which the lightning bolt struck. The thunder clap seemed to accompany the uprooted ground with a dramatic boom that Rosa felt go through her.

With the gravitational pull gone, Edward darted over to Rosa, grabbed her by the arm, and said, "Run!" Rosa began to sprint along the side of the pyramid when both she and Edward began to sink. What moments ago was stone and dirt had changed to sand, and as they ran, they were getting increasingly caught in what appeared to be yellow sand. Nephrite had transformed the ground into quicksand, and they began sinking. Edward yelled to Rosa, who was now two human lengths away, to stop struggling, or she will sink faster. His backpack was sitting just out of his reach. With another flick of the dark quartz wand still in his hand, a gust of wind pushed the bag against him. He opened it and pulled out the empty water bottles Rosa, and he used late last night. He removed the lid of the first and pointed the end of the wand against the lip of the bottle. Inside formed what looked like a clear liquid, but plumes of white smoke poured out of the top. Edward put on the lid and threw the bottle toward Nephrite. Edward then filled the second bottle the same way and tightened the cap. Nephrite was less than 15 meters away now.

Fortunately, most of our atmosphere is made up of nitrogen. Edward had used his crystal to quickly condense the nitrogen into liquid form in the two bottles. As nitrogen heats up, it changes into a gas that requires 600 times the space of the liquid, creating a very effective, albeit small, nitrogen bomb. The bottle expanded until the pressure was too much, and the bomb exploded but was out of range of doing any damage to Nephrite. Edward threw the second one, which landed just in front of her. She saw the bottle and immediately cast a spell by pointing at it, and the ground swallowed the bottled, condensed nitrogen to suppress the explosion. This proved to be worse as the pressure build-up was higher and caused an even more enormous explosion, which threw Nephrite back about 5 meters and landed on her back.

Nephrite stood up and began moving her arms and hands in a swirling motion. Some unseen force lifted a section of the collapsed pyramid and was hurled toward Edward and Rosa. Still stuck in the sand up to his waist, Edward reacted instinctively. He used his arms as if pushing the large section of rubble away from him and Rosa. A burst of green energy emanated from the emerald, which hung around his neck, then shortly after that, gale force winds immediately blasted the area, causing him to release the smoky quartz wand which flew out of his hand.

The wind was just enough to push the enormous stone section, which landed centimeters from Edward's head. Unfortunately, the stone section landed squarely on Edward's backpack, crushing the contents and the smoky quartz wand.

The wind pushed Nephrite off her feet into a back flip, but she landed squarely with one knee on the ground. She placed the backs of her hands, fingers together, pointing at Edward. She then pulled her hands apart, causing the ground below Edward and Rosa to open into a fissure. Both Edward and Rosa fell. Rosa slid on a large stone, landing on top of Edward. Rosa screamed, "What is going on?! Who is that?" A section of dirt and sand broke free from the wall, and Edward's legs got caught and could not move. "Get against that side!" Edward screamed at Rosa. She moved beneath an under-hang of earth the crevice had created where Edward had pointed. Both were now under a section of the ground about 5 meters below ground level.

Edward then pulled the emerald gemstone off his neck, the chain breaking. He held it in his hand, then to his mouth, and blew on it up the shaft of the open aperture just in front of him. Moments later, it began to rain. The rain quickly became torrential. Rosa and Edward heard a bellowing scream just outside the fissure opening. Nephrite was in horrible agony, trying to cover her face and head. She screamed something inaudible, and a yellow hold opened on the ground in front of her, beginning the size of a coin and growing in a perfect circle until it was just wide enough, and Nephrite jumped in. The yellow sphere and Nephrite were gone within the snap of a finger.

Water began pouring into the fissure that Rosa and Edward were in. Edward said, "Don't let the acid touch you. Step up on those rocks there."

Rosa jumping up on a nearby stone, said, "Acid?!" as she inhaled and immediately began to cough.

"Well, highly concentrated acid rain," Edward said. "I think she is gone."

"That was a she? Acid rain?" Rosa said in disbelief while continuing to cough. "What is going on?"

"Remember when I told you I had come here so I wouldn't run into other druids? Well, they found me. They have found a way to track when I use the power of the Emerald. They must have detected it when I inadvertently used it to save you two nights ago. I didn't think it was strong enough to track, but it must have been." The words trailed off as Edward said this last part.

"Who? Who are they? Where did she go? Will she come back?" Rosa said all these things in the same breath while choking on a growing cloud hovering around them. She was terrified. The sulfur oxide and nitrogen oxide gave the air a foul smell. It also caused hissing and popping sounds as it crawled along the ground and dripped into the small cavern. A drop fell on Edwards's arm, and he screamed.

"Hold on," Edward said as he made another motion with his hand and blew on the Emerald again. It continued to rain, but within a few moments, the smell dissipated. Edward indicated it was now safe to move out from under the overhang. "Let's leave here before it caves in on us."

Edward helped Rosa climb out of the fissure and back near the steps of the Pyramid of the Magician. As Rosa looked around, a 20-meter diameter area that moments before donned lush grass was now completely dead. Everything else was just as alive and vibrant as it had been before.

"Let me explain," Edward said as he also reached the top of the cavern and realized the view that Rosa was taking in. "The woman that attacked us; her name is Nephrite. She is a powerful dark magic druid. She has an earth affinity. She and many other druids have been trying to get this emerald gemstone for years. It is why I try to stay off the grid. It is why I travel around on the archeological digs, never staying in one place very long."

Edward walked over to where he saw the shoulder strap of his backpack sticking out from under a massive rock section. Rosa said, "I'm sorry about your crystals and stones."

"Me too. Those were rare and had just been charged by the first light of the summer solstice."

Rosa saw something sticking out of the ground a few meters away. She walked over and saw a rather strangely-shaped piece of hollow glass mixed with sand. She was about to touch it when she realized it was scorching. She saw another nearby, also in the sand.

"That is petrified lightning," Edward said. "Some people call it lightning stone. It is technically called Fulgurite. It is formed when extremely powerful lightning hits the ground with a lot of silica or quartz. They are always hollow. These two must have been created with the lightning I tried to hit Nephrite with. They can be powerful magical objects, being forged by lightning.

"Why do they want your gem?" Rosa asked.

"This Emerald is extremely powerful. If you look at it closely, it has a marking in the center of it."

Rosa looked, and she saw small but distinct markings that read "יהוה."

"That mark is written in Hebrew and says 'Judah.' I don't know how deep you get into your Old Testament history, but this gem was once part of a breastplate that the high priest in the temple of Solomon wore." Edward was somewhat out of breath as he explained this.

"You mean the actual Solomon's temple?" Rosa asked.

"Yes. It is a mighty jewel, and therefore, many druids want to get their hands on it. One in particular," Edward was looking around. His hands shook with adrenaline still coursing through his veins.

"You mean that monster that attacked us," Rosa said.

"No, I mean the man she works for, my cousin Thomas Blood."

~

HUI YIN HAD SEVERAL DIFFICULT DAYS since learning her child would be born handicapped. She couldn't even go to work which put a significant financial strain on them. When she did go, she was all but a zombie, going through the motions to make it through the day. Her only solace was her early morning walks around the Giant Panda Sanctuaries before work. Still, they didn't come close to quenching her inner anguish and sorrow. Her husband was supportive but hadn't realized the gravity of their situation. How could they financially survive with her out of work caring for a baby with all special needs, let alone the additional medical costs?

While walking past one of the sanctuaries, she saw that same aged man with a long beard among several pandas. Knowing that humans were to stay away from the bears confirmed he must be a researcher or otherwise works for the sanctuary. As she passed by, the old man said, "Ni hao," which is the traditional Chinese greeting. Still, this morning, the literal translation of "You good?" brought the emotions under the surface, spilling into the sanctuary. She sobbed, and the older man walked through a door in the sanctuary, then through another door to where she had been walking, and came over to her.

"I am sorry to have upset you. I didn't mean to. Is there anything I can do for you?" he asked with complete sincerity and concern.

"No. It is me. I'm sorry. I'm just having a difficult few days," Hui Yin said.

"Is the pregnancy difficult?" he asked.

Hui Yin wasn't even showing yet, and felt somewhat offended. She then realized that it would be silly to get upset about it under the circumstances. "No. Well Yes. But not in the way you think," She told him.

With a curious look, he took his hand and held it, palm forward at Hui Yin's stomach, and closed his eyes for a moment. Hui Yin didn't know quite what to do. After an awkward moment, and she was about to turn and leave, he opened his eyes and said, "I see. I am so sorry about your child. But you should know, your child is very, very special."

"Excuse me?" Hui Yin said, not knowing if she should be frightened, offended, or comforted.

"I am sorry. I didn't introduce myself. My name is Min."

"I'm Hui Yin," she said almost automatically, still wondering how to react.

"I sometimes care for the pandas and other wildlife in and around the sanctuary. Some say I have a special gift for sensing illness or when something isn't quite right. I apologize. I didn't mean to offend, but I could sense that there was something out of harmony regarding your child and pregnancy, and based on how you were acting, it seemed that you were aware of it. It is a delicate subject, and I did not wish to offend. I am just very sorry for your struggle," Min said.

Understanding he wasn't trying to offend, Hui Yin asked, "So you help the pandas when they are ill?"

"Yes," Min answered. "Like this Panda here. This is Xiong Yi. She is the mother of these other three pandas. Xiong Yi hurt herself by falling from a tree yesterday. She is having difficulty walking now, as you can see." Hui Yin began to notice that the panda that was larger than the others was walking on three legs while the other was dragging behind.

"Can you do anything for her? She looks like she is in a lot of pain," Hui Yin asked.

"Yes, that is what I am doing. Would you like to help?" Min asked.

Hui Yin didn't know how she could be of any assistance. Still, she said, "Sure," and followed Min back through the door, which led to a small hallway, then to another door that was more of an access port into the sanctuary. To their right was a large trench that separated the bears from the humans. Pointing to the trough, the old man spoke, "This isn't to protect the humans from the bears, but rather to protect the bears from humans. The giant panda is one of the most docile animals in the world. I am sure you have seen visitors feed the bears by extending long poles of bamboo over the trench and allowing them to eat it." Min and Hui Yin were inside the sanctuary and walked over to Xiong Yi as she sat on her good leg, licking the wounded one.

"Could you stroke her neck as I help her?" Min asked as he moved in front of the bear. Hui Yin moved around the back of the bear and timidly began rubbing the bear's neck. "She likes that," Min said. "Is this your first child, then?" Min asked.

Hui Yin wondered how many sensitive subjects he could hit in a first discussion. "No. This is my second pregnancy. My first daughter died in the great earthquake two years ago."

Min paused his work. "I am very sorry to hear that. Many lives were lost. Many more hurt. It was a devastating event. I am sorry you had to go through that." The sincerity of his words could be felt as if he had also had a significant loss due to the earthquake.

"What did you mean when you said my baby is special?" Hui Yin asked as Min felt the leg with Xiong Yi gently swatted at him when he got to a sensitive area.

"Your child is extraordinary. I can feel a great power within your child. He will do many great things," Min said.

"He? You believe it will be a boy?" Hui Yin asked in wonderment.

"Oh yes. You will have a boy. And he is very special. Full of power and balance, your son is. Was your first child a boy?" Min asked.

"No. Li was my daughter. I miss her very much."

"There is no greater loss than the loss of a child," Min said as he pulled a stone the size of his thumb from his robe. He held it to the panda's hurt leg.

"What is that?" Hui Yin asked, pointing to the stone in his hand.

"This is just petrified wood. It helps with the healing," Min responded.

"Oh, you are one of those types of healers. Stones, mystic arts, incense. I thought you were a real animal doctor. I thought you would be bandaging or casting the panda's leg," Hui Yin said, realizing as she said it, it could be taken offensively, but he had said worse.

"Yes," He said. "I am one of those types of healers." He held the petrified wood to the leg of the panda and closed his eyes. She could see that he was concentrating and didn't want to disturb him. Now that she knew he was a crackpot old man, she wanted to continue her walk. The bear began to squeak and huff more intently. She decided to continue to rub her neck.

A moment later, the panda flipped over onto all four legs and ran off to the back of the sanctuary with full use of her legs without any sign of weakness or injury. "How did you do that?" a shocked Hui Yin blurted out.

"Sometimes the oldest techniques are the best," He answered.

"What does your husband do for a living?" he asked.

"His name is Ju-Long Zhang. He works as a sanitation engineer at Mount Qingcheng."

"I am up there often at the temple," He said. "Thank you so much for your help today. You can't imagine what a difference you made in her healing."

"My pleasure," she responded, following him to the door where he let her out. She finished her walk, pondering what Min had said to her.

~

"They will be back for me," Edward said in a worrisome tone. "It isn't safe for you while I'm here. I need to leave."

"You can't leave!" A horrified Rosa exclaimed.

"I'm the one they want; well, really, this Emerald is what they want, and they will do anything to get it. If I'm not here, they will have no reason to return," Edward explained.

"Then let me come with you," Rosa begged.

"No. Then you will be in constant danger. I'll call for you to come once it is safe. Just give me a little time. It happened because I accidentally used the gemstone to save you from that pyramid collapse. I'll have to find a way to separate myself from the Emerald, so I don't mistakenly use it again. Once I know it is safe, I'll come for you," Edward said as he quickly put his things inside his knapsack. They were in Edward's small hotel room in the Hacienda Uxmal Plantation & Museum. Rosa sat on the edge of the bed made with the sheets she had folded the day before. It seemed like another world a long time ago. Her entire world had been turned upside down in a matter of hours.

"Where will you go?" Rosa asked.

"I'm not sure. I know someone who may be able to help. I'll go to him. He lives near where I grew up," Edward said in a distant but rushed voice. His thoughts were going a million miles an hour.

"What about me? What about us?" Rosa said, still frightened.

Edward snapping back to reality, finished putting the last of his clothes in his bag. "Rosa, I care about you deeply. It is for that reason I have to leave now. Things are not over between us. I will come back for you. But to keep you safe, I need to leave right now. They could have someone else on the way."

Edward rolled the two fulgurite (lightning stone) wands in a dirty shirt and put them in his bag. Edward pulled Rosa close and held her tight. Rosa felt the warmth and genuine care. "Be safe. I'll send a message soon." He gave her a deep warm kiss that held a history he hoped they would one day share. Rosa was soon left holding the space before her as the hotel room door closed. She fell back onto the pillow and instantly smelled Edward billowing up from the pillowcase again. She sat up, removed the case from the pillow, and took another deep breath as she held it to her face and breathed him in.

~

Alexander opened Thomas's bedroom door and shouted, "Nephrite is back. It isn't good news."

"What happened?" he said in a furious tone.

"You need to hear it from her."

Thomas wrapped a robe around him that hung on the tall bedpost and stormed out the door and down the hall, following Alexander, the tall Russian. They went down the grand staircase in the foyer. He could hear screaming and moaning. He turned right into the parlor. Asha was hovering over a gurney where Nephrite was lying in agony when he walked in. Steam seemed to be coming off her body, then Thomas noticed the terrible smell of burning flesh. Asha looked at Thomas and said, "She has third-degree chemical burns over much of her body."

Nephrite screamed again. Thomas approached her and said, "How did he do this? Where did the acid come from?" Nephrite's skin over areas of her body was eroded where you could see down to the muscle and, on her left hand, her bone. The top of her head looked like it took the worst of it. All of her skin looked red and blistered, with some looking melted. Several of her sub-dermal implants had fallen out. The gauge from her left ear was missing, and the ear loop was dissolved at the bottom and hanging loose.

She could only muster the strength to say one word before she lost consciousness, "Rain." Thomas thought for a moment. "Get her into a bath right now. Get the acid off her skin. The water should neutralize it." They wheeled her away. He looked at Asha and said, "Make sure she lives; she has the answers I need."

Chapter 4

August 15, 2010

Hui Yin continued to struggle over the coming months. Usually, mid-August is her favorite time of the year due to the celebration surrounding the Torch Festival, when many different ethnicities, especially those in central and southern China, celebrate. The festival was thousands of years old and celebrated humanity's triumph over things out of their control. Things like destruction, plagues, disease, and evil were subscribed to ancient gods.

People wore lavish, colorful costumes and carried torches to drive off evil spirits. It was a celebration of tigers, fire, and the color black. They would throw Rosin, a powder that, when it came in contact with the torch, flames burst with light of various colors.

When Rosin was thrown in the direction of an elder, it would grant them a long life. Thrown in the direction of an eligible person would indicate to them you are interested in dating.

This was originally how Hui Yin met her husband. He had thrown some Rosin in her direction, which burst into a bright blue flame. But this year, even the torch festival couldn't resolve things out of her control. She had done the minimum, lighting a torch and walking around their home to ward off evil spirits, but that was all. Ju-Long knowing it was her favorite, asked if she would like to join the special celebration held in the front court of the Jianfu Palace. He would have to work late into the night cleaning up from the festival, so he thought it would be good for Hui Yin to get out and have fun.

Ju-Long had told her of the preparations that, much like other torch festival celebrations, the Jianfu Palace courtyard had a large cauldron on an elevated stand in the center of the square. The metal cauldron had four strong metal legs just over a meter off the ground. The cauldron, which was a meter and a half wide, was overloaded with wood, and when dusk fell, the pot would be lit, and a magnificent glow would fill the clean night air. But despite Ju-Long's attempt to get her to go, she refused; and so he kissed her and left for the bus. She knew he wouldn't be back until morning due to the workload.

As the first shadows of the evening were seen, she knew everyone would converge and light a cauldron set on a tall pedestal, where there would be singing and dancing while it burned throughout the night. Her mood couldn't have been more contrary to the festival.

After the celebration and the cauldron fire had been extinguished, Ju-Long surveyed the damage. Food wrappers, used torches, resin residue, and pieces of clothing littered the multi-colored ground. He realized this would take him longer than he initially thought.

He walked past the large, ash-filled cauldron, which was still smoldering. There were several people on his same team sweeping with brooms and tall dustpans cleaning the area, including a very old man he didn't recognize below the cauldron working. As he looked closer, he realized the man wasn't cleaning but collecting something on a miniature stand directly under the big black kettle.

Ju-Long approached the old man and asked, "Can I help you with something? The festival ended almost an hour ago. Everyone was supposed to leave by now. The last bus has already left."

"I don't live far from here, thank you," The old man responded.

"What are you doing? And what do you mean you live close to here? No one lives close to here," Ju-Long asked.

"Just finishing up. I'll be out of your way momentarily. My name is Min, by the way."

Ju-Long, trying not to get frustrated with the old man, said, "I am Ju-Long, and we are trying to clean up from the festival before Mount Qingcheng, the palaces and temples open tomorrow morning."

"Ju-Long? Is your wife Hui Yin?" he asked.

"Yes. How do you know my wife?" Ju-Long inquired, somewhat baffled.

"I met her one morning at the Panda Sanctuaries a while back. She helped me heal a mother panda."

Ju-Long now remembered his wife talking to him about a strange researcher that asked for her help one morning. She said he was very kind and made her feel better after a strenuous morning. She also told him he had said their unborn baby was a boy. This caught her off guard. The following day she returned and asked one of the other workers at the sanctuaries where she could find him, but they said that no one with that description worked there.

"Yes, my wife told me about you. You told her our child is special," Ju-Long said.

"Your boy is extraordinary. His aura that day startled me," Min said. "It is for your son that I am here. I have been waiting for tonight."

Ju-Long was getting very confused and now understood why his wife was also baffled by her encounter with him. "Wait, wait, wait," He said very rapidly. "First, how do you know we are having a boy?

Second, what do you mean he is special, and third, what do you mean you are here for him?"

"I am sorry," Min started. "I was planning to go to your wife's work tomorrow with a gift for your son." Min opened his hand and showed Ju-Long an intricately carved black stone. The sides were cut as wings, with the middle a flower with oversized pedals. "I made this for your son," Min said. He then took it, pulled a silver chain from the inside of his robe, and fed it through one of the two carved openings that curved near the tops of the wings. "Would you give this to your wife and ask her to wear it?"

Ju-Long didn't know what to think. He waited for Min to answer his other questions when he placed the beautifully carved stone into his hand. "Well, thank you," Ju-long said, "but I still don't understand."

Min said, "Let me explain. The energy I felt from your unborn child is very rare and unique."

"So you are a Daoist? You believe in energy healing and all that?" Ju-long said.

"Not exactly. I follow a more ancient path. And the energy in the universe goes well beyond healing. It is the power by which everything around us is animated and alive. This is Jet Stone gesturing to the carving. Stones such as these have unique capabilities. Tonight I activated and charged this stone to help your wife and son.

"What do you mean you 'activated and charged' the stone?" Ju-Long asked, needing clarification.

"Objects such as these can store energy that trained hands can use later once they have been activated. Activating an object means initializing it to store, transmit, or focus energy. It isn't difficult to do. The trick is to know where and when to do it." Min was talking while circling the carved stone Ju-Long was holding. "The universe around us is full of energy, but not all energy is equal. There are places on the earth that have more energy than others. And sometimes circumstances can increase that power. If you place the right kind of object in the right place at the right time, it will fill the thing with concentrated energy to be used for any number of purposes.

"And this is the right place and time for that Jet Stone, you called it?" Ju-Long asked.

"Tonight was the perfect time and place for this type of stone. The festival. This place, Mount Qingcheng, the home of Daoism, one of the sacred mountains, is one of the most powerful energy vortexes in the world. Tonight, everyone celebrates protection from unseen forces, drives disasters away, and wishes for a successful harvest. They celebrate driving evil spirits and misfortune away with fire and use color and light to bring a promising future, love, and healing into their lives. These traditions were passed down for centuries. The culmination of the people's energy on this spot tonight was a powerful and perfect energy signature for a Jet Stone to be activated and fully charged," Min explained.

"And you carved this and, what did you call it, activated it and charged it for my wife?" Ju-Long said suspiciously. "Partially. It is also for you and your unborn child," Min said, looking at the stone, very proud of his work.

"It doesn't feel like it is full of energy to me. What is it supposed to feel like?" Ju-Long asked.

"Not everyone is sensitive to the energy that flows around us. Many go their entire lives completely unaware. However, your child is potent in understanding and using mystic energy. In that way, he is extraordinary," Min focusing from the stone up to Ju-Long's eyes. "A Jet Stone is a natural, organic, fossilized wood long considered one of the most powerful healing stones; everything from physical healing to mental and emotional healing. Jet stones release anger, fear, grief, and feelings of depression, bringing them to the surface and forcing you to deal with them, so you can begin healing. Jet stones are also beneficial for anyone pregnant. Pregnancy always comes with fears. However, your wife's fears have been realized. But your child is very special. Tonight with all the colors and frequencies of light, is exactly what your special son needs."

"Oh, when you said my unborn child was 'special,' I thought you meant his condition that he (if it is a boy) has."

"If referring to his deformity, you needn't worry about that. Yes, I sensed that too, but that is only what makes him unique, not what makes him special," Min said as he wrapped Ju-Long's fingers over the stone.

"What do I do with it?" Ju-Long said, very confused.

"Give it to your wife. Have her wear it. Find comfort, peace, and healing with it," Min said.

"I'm not sure I believe any of this, but thank you. But let me ask you one other question. Why are you doing this at all? Do you give gifts like this to all random strangers you meet?" Ju-Long asked.

"Your wife told me of the horrific circumstances you both have gone through with losing your daughter. I cannot tell you how sorry I am for that happening to you. There are not enough days or stone carvings to undo that travesty, but when your wife told me of your circumstances, I wanted to help you. This stone will help! Have her wear it. It will make all the difference in the world. I promise," Min said with sincerity.

At that moment, two other sanitation workers called out to Ju-Long, clearly upset that he wasn't pulling his weight while they cleaned up. No one wanted to stay later than they had to. Ju-Long said thank you again and began cleaning up the square.

~

IT HAD BEEN OVER A MONTH since Edward had left, and Rosa hadn't heard anything from him. She began to think the whole thing was a dream until she walked over to the magician's pyramid and saw the damage and destruction from the storms and the battle with that demon person that had tried to kill her and Edward.

It was still hot, but the fall tourist season was upon them, which they were making the best of, despite the restoration project to fix the grounds and corner of the pyramid complex. This kept Rosa busy, and she hadn't felt well for weeks. She thought it might be the effects of all the excitement when Edward was around, but something was different. She was also more fatigued and couldn't do as much work for the Choco bean harvest as she would have wanted to.

There was a moment of absolute panic when she realized she had missed her period. She sat in the middle of the floor in her bungalow and couldn't get up or even move. Her breathing became fast-paced and labored. She couldn't control her emotions and felt very alone. She wished that Edward was there to hold her.

When she got up, she went to the hotel, where they had a small convenience store off the lobby where customers could buy snacks and personal hygiene items they may have forgotten. In the back corner, under a large assortment of antacids, she found a single purple box with the words' pregnancy test' written on it. The date on the bottom had expired a month prior, but she hoped it would still work because she had no idea how to get another one. She took it to the counter, where she saw a short, heavy-set older woman she knew well. Rosa (and everyone else) called her Lita, a nickname for everyone's grandmother. When Rosa placed the box on the counter, there was a certain feeling of shame and guilt. Lita looked at Rosa and said, "They didn't have these fancy tests when I was your age. It sure would have saved me a lot of worry and stress if I had been able to tell Hector I was pregnant. But when I started to show is when we got married. Let me know if you need help with anything at all." She gave Rosa an understanding smile.

Twenty minutes later, it was confirmed. Rosa was pregnant. She knew Edward was the father but now felt more alone than ever, not knowing where he was or when he would be back, as all she could do was wait.

It was mid-September when a package arrived for her at the hotel. The package was quickly wrapped in thick brown paper and placed within a packing tube with lots of clear packaging tape. No return name was written, but there was a return address on the top was written in thick black ink, which read:

12848 CA-254, #12 Myers Flat, CA 95554

Rosa raced to the back storage room to find a box cutter to cut an opening in the side. It took her a moment to see it, and if it had taken any longer, she would have torn into the package with her teeth as she was so excited. She opened the side of the package and removed some bubble wrap holding a smaller box. She pulled out the slender box with the rest of the plastic filler. A folded piece of paper fell, which had been held on the side by the bubble wrap. She opened the folded paper and read.

My Dear Rosa,

I miss you so much. I feel terrible that it has already been this long, but it still isn't safe for me or you if we are together. I am working on something that should make it so we can be together, and I'll contact you then. It shouldn't be much longer. In the meantime, I wanted to send you this. It is stronger now but still delicate, so be careful with it. Think of it as a memento of our time together so far and an emblem of the time when we will be together again. Know how much you mean to me and how I look forward to being with you again soon.

Love

Edward

Rosa took the tube, opened one end, and turned it upside down, allowing the contents to fall into her hand. Out came the fulgurite' lightning wand' formed during the battle with the demon lady. She held it in her hand as emotions swept over her. How could this be all he sends? Why didn't he tell me how to contact him? No phone number? Is he alright? It sounds like he is still in danger. How long until I can see him again? These thoughts were like individual notes playing inside Rosa's head while the rest of the orchestra bellowing that HE DOESN'T KNOW I'M PREGNANT! He will be a father. I will be a mother. He needs to know this. He might make different decisions if he knew that. He would certainly want to see me sooner, right?

For the next several days, Rosa was on an emotional roller-coaster. One minute so excited, she heard something, and her dreams of being with Edward again were still moving forward. While at other times, she couldn't help but feel carelessness and neglect coming from Edward, who should be taking her needs and feelings more into account right now. But how could she expect him to know any better when so much of this was based on her being pregnant and Edward not even knowing?

Several times she would pull out the note she had rolled up and put inside the end of the fulgurite wand. At first, she couldn't stuff it in because something was lodged in the shaft. Rosa remembered that it was initially hollow and realized that this was what Edward must have meant by strengthening the wand. She had to fold the paper three times to roll it up and place it on one end of the rod. Rolled inside the wand was also the original packaging section with the return address written. She knew she could have rewritten it, but there was something about knowing Edward had written it himself. So she decided to keep it.

She was starting her 2nd trimester now, and the weather had begun to cool off. She hadn't heard from Edward again and decided to take things into her own hands. She would travel to California, where the return address was, and find Edward. Her grand plan began with needing to get a passport so she could travel out of the country. She had saved a little money over time. She stored it in a brightly-colored yellow and blue clay pot on her shelf. The cash was hidden under some decorative shells that filled the pot. She didn't have much money, so she would have to be extremely frugal. By talking with a few people in Uxmal, she realized she would need to go to a Mexican consulate. The closest was in Merida, a town just over an hour's drive from Uxmal.

She used the hotel's phone to schedule an appointment for the following Monday. She had asked Angel when the next time he would have to go to Merida for supplies for the hotel. He agreed to allow her to come along so she could go to her appointment. She made sure she had all of the documentation they needed. During her meeting, she learned that getting the passport mailed to her would take six weeks. She could have paid additional money to expedite it, but she needed all her money for the trip to California.

While waiting for the passport, she planned her trip carefully. She would have to get a ride to Mexico City, where she could take a bus to the U.S.-Mexico border. From there, she would take another bus up to Northern California. Making the trip with all the stops and transfers would take about a week. Over the years, she had made friends with some tour bus drivers who brought the tourists into Uxmal. One was a woman who was very Westernized and spoke excellent English named Juliana. Rosa often gave her an extra box of chocolates to return to the tour office (Juliana had confided to Rosa that only empty boxes made it back). Carlos had told her to do it so the tour company would always bring more people. Still, Juliana had always associated the extra chocolate with favors from Rosa.

Juliana's tour bus came from Mexico City. It would do tours up and down the western side of the Yucatan peninsula, with its furthest stop being the Pyramid of the Magician in Uxmal. Her bus only came once a week, always on Saturday at the same time. When Juliana arrived, Rosa greeted her with three boxes of chocolates and asked if she could take her tour bus back to Mexico City in a few weeks. This was, of course, against company policy. Still, Juliana knew she couldn't refuse after years of getting her favorite chocolate from Rosa.

It was mid-November when Rosa's passport arrived in the mail. She was halfway through her pregnancy, and travel would only become more difficult the longer it took. She wanted to leave that week, but Angel would only allow her to take time off the second week of December due to the tourism increase. He was upset with her plans to be gone and her continual avoidance of his advances.

Again Rosa waited and saved every penny she could for her trip. When the day finally arrived, she packed her clothes, put the fulgurite wand in a small grey duffel bag, and left. Juliana had arranged for her to have both seats in her row to rest comfortably during the ride. It would take three days to return to Mexico City with overnight stays in Ciudad del Carmen and Veracruz. Juliana had offered Rosa to stay with her in her hotel rooms for the trip. Her kindness was beyond what Rosa expected and wasn't about extra chocolate.

The queen bed in Ciudad del Carmen was softer than she was used to in her bungalow in Uxmal. Still, the sheets were soft and smelled of the same cleaner she used to do the laundry at the hotel, which oddly made her feel more comfortable. She was almost six months pregnant. She couldn't believe it had been half a year since Edward had left with only a single package sent to her. She held the fulgurite wand firmly, thinking of him.

Her bed was situated next to the bathroom, which she utilized frequently. Driving the following day, Rosa realized she had never sat in the same position for so long. Besides being six months pregnant, she looked very pregnant. Being such a petite girl, she looked like she was ready to begin contractions any moment, and being required to sit that long on the bus made her feel like she might. She was very grateful for the somewhat frequent stops at various tourist locations for her to stretch her legs and go to the bathroom.

The next night in Veracruz, Rosa got very little sleep due to the loud tourists in the next room. As a result, she slept most of the way to Mexico City, where the tour bus would drop off the tourists, pick up another group, and start it all again. When they pulled up to the bus terminal, Rosa exited the bus. It was a bit before 10:00 a.m. Above her head were power lines going across the intersection in every direction. They were so low she couldn't believe the bus hadn't hit them. There was a small market on the corner of one of the buildings where she went and got some chips and bottled water. Juliana had now assisted the other tourists from the bus, and she went up to her to thank her for her assistance. Juliana had a smile. "What are you smiling about?" Rosa asked.

"Well, I pulled some strings, and I got you on another tour bus with a good friend of mine, Yesenia. She will be leaving this afternoon and heading north. It should get you most of the way," Juliana said, very proud of herself.

Rosa threw her arms around her crushing the chips. "Thank you so much," she said.

"The tour bus goes as high as the Naica's Cave of the Crystals and then would head back South, but if you get out there, it is only another day's bus ride to the U.S. border." Rosa was so excited. This was incredibly helpful, saving Rosa hundreds of dollars in bus fairs, not to mention the tour bus seats were much more comfortable than a regular bus.

Juliana told her to head over to a Café that was a couple of blocks away. Her friend Yesenia would come and get her around noon. They didn't want her to wait in the cruise office lounge because they didn't want their boss to know what they were doing. Apparently, there was going to be a government official with them on the tour, so they needed to lay low. Rosa thanked Juliana one last time and headed off to the Café.

Just before noon, a large Hispanic woman with short dark hair and glasses walked into the café, spotted Rosa immediately, and walked over to her. "I am Juliana's friend, Yesenia," she said.

"Nice to meet you," Rosa said, smiling at her.

"Well, the bus leaves in a few minutes. Being just before Christmas, the tour is pretty full, but there is enough space for you. Come on," Yesenia said as she waved her arms, the same way she probably led tours, and walked back out the café door. A few minutes later, Rosa was on another bus. Yesenia spoke perfect Spanish and English, and she repeated everything she said over the intercom in both languages, as there were Americans and natives on the bus. An old couple from Ohio sat right in front of Rosa. The woman with short curly white hair turned around and began talking with Rosa. Not wanting to get Yesenia or Juliana in trouble, she pretended she didn't understand English, and the older woman gave up and went back to reading her tour guidebook.

An hour later, the bus reached the Teotihuacan Pyramids just north of Mexico City. Rosa looked out the window as the bus pulled into the extended, oversized parking area next to several other buses.

She couldn't believe the number of pyramids in this complex, especially the enormous pyramid, which rose 216 feet above ground level, more than twice the height of her Temple of the Magician back home. Not traveling far from Uxmal in her life, she couldn't believe there were pyramids this tall, and it made hers look almost miniature.

"We would like to give a special thanks to Julio Marques, our Secretary of Tourism here in Mexico, for making it possible to get a special tour here at Teotihuacan," Yesenia said. As Rosa was getting off the bus, Yesenia told her she didn't have an extra ticket for entry, so Rosa spent a couple of hours looking around the gift shop and restaurants near the entrance.

By 3:00, they were back on the road heading West on the 15D freeway towards Guadalajara. They pulled into the Westin Guadalajara at 9:45, and Rosa couldn't wait to get off the bus. Yesenia was kind enough to let her sleep in her bedroom like Juliana. However, Rosa didn't get as good of sleep due to Yesenia's snoring which could have disturbed the guests in the next room as the tourists did to Rosa in Veracruz. But she was still very grateful for her kindness.

~

"CAN WE JUST BACK UP FOR ONE MINUTE?" Alexander Litvienko said with a thick Russian accent. "You can't just book Stonehenge for a private gathering. What did you do? Just call up Stonehenge and say, "Hello. I want to book the Neolithic stones for a private party on winter solstice". Even you don't have that much money, Thomas."

"Influence is what it takes, although money is often required to garner enough influence," Thomas Blood said to the group. "No one can book Stonehenge for a private event, so I did the opposite. I created a public party. I got special permission from my friend, the Parliamentary Under-Secretary of State for Arts, Heritage, and Tourism, to hold a special celebration at Stonehenge on winter solstice next week."

"I'm sure your generous donations to UNESCO and the VisitEngland initiative helped make this possible," said Asha.

"Yes. So I'm throwing a little party for the general public that afternoon for anyone who wants to attend. As you all know, winter solstice focuses on the sun's setting on the shortest day of the year. But it is the blood moon lunar eclipse in the morning we need the site for. But naturally, if we are going to donate all the food, audio, video equipment, and everything else for the party that night, we need some time to set up without interruption by tourists that morning. The government has granted us this exclusive time at Stonehenge to prepare for the evening event. They said as long as the party is open to the public, we can have some time to set up. This is our cover so we will have uninterrupted access to Stonehenge during the lunar eclipse," Thomas explained.

"Sorry for being new guy," Alexander said, struggling with his English, "but I don't understand what you are trying to do. Are you activating an artifact or charging a relic or something?"

"You know, recently archeologists found animal bones at Stonehenge that they have determined were nine months old when they were sacrificed. They believe that the animals born in the spring would be killed at the winter solstice in a sacrificial ceremony. Or they had a grand celebration. Or both! Imagine sacrifice and celebration on winter solstice with a blood moon lunar eclipse. My ancestor, Thomas Blood, was at Stonehenge 372 years ago with this sapphire," Thomas held up his hand with the sapphire ring on it. Alexander, we all know the prophecy," Thomas began quoting.

'When the red moon passes through shadow and blood on the darkest day, the druid of destiny will be born of death on the final archer where energies cross to create tension between the heavens and the earth which will begin when the ancestor stone is gifted on the day of becoming.'

Thomas continued. "I believe the prophecy is speaking of December 21, 2010, just a few days from now. The last day of Sagittarius, "the archer." When the red moon passes through shadow and blood on the darkest day. That must mean a blood moon eclipse on the winter solstice, the darkest day where energies cross. A ley line crossing which Stonehenge is one of the most ancient. I believe this is where and when the druid of destiny will be born. When my child will be born. You all have your assignments. Follow them to the letter. There is no room for error. You are dismissed."

The room emptied of all the closest, most trusted associates of Thomas Blood. Thomas had carefully selected three brilliant and healthy women to be artificially inseminated with his seed which happened 38 weeks ago. Amelia's pregnancy was successful and progressed nicely. Tradition held that the druid of destiny would grow to have all six affinities. The baby had already shown signals to be a dé-thugach, a duel-gifted druid. Thomas' plan was coming together perfectly. "Who said you can't architect destiny" Thomas often thought.

~

THE NEXT DAY, Rosa andt the rest of the tour group arrived at Puerto Vallarta, a seaside port on the Pacific Ocean. While Uxmal was only a two-hour drive to the Gulf of Mexico, Rosa had never seen the coast, beach, or ocean before. She found it breathtaking. They spent lunch seaside, but she found this tour to be significantly different than the last. It appeared that that group was religious, and many stops were churches and cathedrals. They spent time at the Nuestra Señora de Guadalupe church, translating to the Basilica of Our Lady of Guadalupe. They were back on the bus heading north, staying close to the ocean, which Rosa enjoyed looking at through the bus window.

In Mazatlán, they stopped at a few places, including the Basílica de la Inmaculada Concepción. Since the entry was free, Rosa could visit these churches and cathedrals, which were wonderfully ornate compared to the small church she had attended since she was a young girl. The giant statues of Christ, stained glass windows, and paintings were overwhelming.

But even with her interest in these things, Rosa was getting sick of all the stops after three days when they arrived at the Naica's Cave of the Crystals. This, for some, was to be a highlight of the trip.

"In a few minutes, we will reach the Naica Crystal Cave. The cave was discovered in April 2000 by brothers Juan and Pedro Sánchez while drilling in the Naica mine, Mexico's largest zinc, lead, and silver mine. Naica lies on a fault above an underground magma chamber approximately two to three miles below the cave. The magma heated the ground water, which was saturated with sulfide ions. Cool, oxygenated surface water contacted the mineral-saturated heated water. Still, the two did not mix because of the difference in their densities. The oxygen slowly diffused into the heated water and oxidized the sulfides into sulfates precipitating as anhydrite," Yesenia said effortlessly in English and Spanish but was reading from a sheet. This was an unusual stop for her tour company. "When the overall temperature of the cave started to drop below 56 $^\circ$C (133 $^\circ$F), the hydrothermal and sedimentary anhydrite crystals dissolved, and gypsum crystals formed. The hydrated sulfate gypsum crystallized at a prolonged rate over the course of at least 500,000 years, forming the enormous crystals found today."

Yesenia again said, "Let's give a round of applause to Julio Marques, our Secretary of Tourism, for making it possible to tour the Cave of Crystals today." Everyone on the bus clapped. "Normally, we can only tour the much smaller and less impressive 'Ice Palace' cave. This could be one of the last tours of the Cave of Crystals for anyone, as the cave has been flooding recently. The scientists believe it will soon be entirely underwater and unavailable for tours or exploration."

"The entrance to the cave is at an astounding depth of 980 feet and can only be accessed through the mine. The temperature in the cave is 122 degrees Fahrenheit with 100 percent humidity. After all those churches we have been touring, this will be our tour of hell," she said with the laughter of many of the bus, including the tourism secretary. "Due to the extreme conditions," she continued," you will each only be able to spend about 3 minutes in the cave, so we will do it in small groups. Many of you have opted out of visiting the cavern due to health concerns, claustrophobia, or other reasons."

"I mentioned the smaller Ice Palace Cave, discovered in 2009. It is half of the depth of the crystal cave and is a bit more hospitable. In the Ice Palace cave, you will notice that while the crystalline structures are much smaller than the crystal cave, there are other unique formations, including what they call cauliflower formations which look like fine threadlike crystals. So for those visiting the caves, today you will see some of the largest and smallest crystals in the world. Know that you are among only several hundred people that have ever seen the Crystal Cave other than those that work in the mine. You will each be required to wear a helmet and follow all safety instructions, which will be explained to you before descending. "

"You have all already opted into visiting both caves, just the Ice Palace cave, or opting out of the visit today. Those of you who will not join us in the cave this afternoon will walk two blocks to the Naica mining museum while the rest of the group visits the caves. When we stop the bus, those of you who will be going all the way down to the Cave of Crystals and then onto the Ice Palace cave, I'd like you to line up near the front of the bus. Those going in but only visiting the Ice Palace cave, please line up near the back of the bus. The rest of you will be taken to the museum. Each group will be led by a representative from the mine. If you have changed your preference regarding visiting the mine or which caves you want to visit, please see me as you get off the bus," Yesenia finished.

The timing was perfect because they entered the city of Naica just as she finished talking. It was a small town tailored to the miners and their families. They were on the edge of town with the shops and museum on the far end of the mining property. They filed off the bus and headed to their various groups, some to the front of the bus where a short man in an orange jumpsuit was waiting. Others went to the rear of the bus where another man dressed the same as the first was waiting, only this man wasn't wearing a helmet but was holding it under his arm but in every other way, looked identical to the first. The rest were walking across the parking area where a third person, a woman in regular clothes, was calling people towards her, indicating she was taking them to the museum.

As Rosa exited the bus, assuming she needed to head to the Museum, the couple from Ohio spoke with Yesenia. Rosa waited for them to finish and head off the bus. Yesenia said, "Rosa, do you want to see the crystal cave? That woman," pointing to a white-haired woman from Ohio, "says she doesn't feel comfortable going down there now, so there is an extra ticket if you want to go. I'm not kidding, this is a once-in-a-lifetime opportunity."

"Do you think it will be okay even though I'm pregnant?" she asked.

"I'll make sure, and if so, you need to come, okay?" Yesenia said in a confirming tone.

"Okay," Rosa said, not having time to decide how willing she was to do this.

Rosa went to the line at the front of the bus next to the older man from Ohio waving to his wife, who was joining the museum group.

Only nine people, not including the guide from the mining company, were in the group to see the Crystal Caves. They entered a building with a mine shaft elevator in the middle of the room. It was circular, with a double metal grate on the bottom and a railing around the perimeter. Everyone was given a helmet and safety instructions. Then they filed onto the metal grate, and the guide signaled the operator, and the elevator began to go down.

As they descended, the guide explained that they were lucky to be on the new "high speed" elevator as the old one (still in use in another part of the mine) was considerably slower and could take an hour to go to the bottom. With this, it would only take 15 minutes, which seemed like forever to everyone except the guide. The elevator had lights affixed to it, and they also passed several levels where they could have gotten off. This alleviated claustrophobia when the shaft opened to a large room or area. Rosa felt like she was in a giant ant farm, as you see on TV, with glass on both sides where the ants dug caves and pathways. As they descended, they felt the temperature get higher and higher, and the humidity get thicker and thicker. The guide passed around bottles of ice-cold water from a cooler he had at his feet that Rosa didn't notice until he opened it.

When they reached the bottom, the elevator stopped with a jerk. He opened up the railing, and everyone was excited to get off. They only had to walk 150 feet, but it was over 100 degrees with high humidity. Rosa felt a breeze which the guide explained was an elaborate cooling system using fans and surface air. He also said the cooling system would not be in the Crystal Cave. As they approached the opening, the guide explained that for safety reasons, only two people and himself would go into the cave at a time. The rest would wait here. Each group of two would only be inside for about 3 minutes.

The first group to enter was the cabinet member and his teenage son. Almost precisely 3 minutes later, they came out, covered in sweat with big grins on their faces. They walked past the rest of the group, talking about what they had seen. The next group went in and out three minutes later in the same condition as the first group. Yesenia, who was planning to go in with Rosa, now decided she needed to help a man from their tour group experiencing some anxiety coming down the shaft and heading into the cave. She took him by the hand, and they went in together and, 3 minutes later, came back out. The man seemed glad he had done it, and Yesenia looked like she needed a drink of ice water. The next group was the man from Ohio and another man who had also been abandoned by his wife for the museum.

Finally, it was Rosa's turn. The guide took her in alone as she was the last of the group. She walked down the cave entrance that turned sharply. As she entered the Crystal Cave, she felt like she had put her face over a boiling pot of water. The heat and humidity were stifling. She could immediately see why you could only be here a few minutes without specialized gear. She looked around and saw they had put up some essential lighting to illuminate the cave. The crystal structures were enormous. Some appeared to be 4' or wider and 30-40' long in every direction, like being inside a gigantic geode as it formed. She had never seen anything so beautiful and never felt so frightened all at the same time. The ground she was walking on was a crystalline structure. The walls were crystals. The ceiling was crystals with selenite columns, looking like a crystal giant was trying to reinforce the roof of his home haphazardly. It wasn't easy to breathe. The guide was pointing to one of the largest formations when something began to happen. The Gypsum crystal began to shimmer and illuminate from within. At first, Rosa thought it was part of a light show, but when she looked at the guide, he was more startled. They looked around in amazement as a soft golden orange glow beginning at Rosa's feet cascaded from crystal to crystal like the ocean waves at sunset washing over the cave. When it hit a new crystal, it would travel down the shaft to the end and then flow to another. After a few moments, the entire cave was filled with pulsating orange light. The guide began speaking very rapidly in Spanish. Rosa understood it to be a prayer to Saint Benedict for protection against evil spirits. The orange glow did make the cave appear like paintings of Dante's Inferno. At the same time, there was a peacefulness that Rosa felt as she saw it.

The guide, clearly spooked, took Rosa's hand and pulled her back through the cave entrance and into the hallway. The rest of the group, including Yesenia, tried to understand what the guide was saying. Rosa didn't know what to think. While trying to explain what he saw, the guide led the group quickly back to the elevator. He pushed a button, and they began heading back toward the surface. The more the guide talked, the more he realized how crazy he sounded. He kept gesturing to Rosa for confirmation of what happened. During the ascent, most of the group concluded that some chamber flooding began to happen below and affected the makeshift lighting system in the cave. The guide decided to act professionally and agreed that might be what happened but looked wholly unconvinced.

About 7 minutes into their ascent, he stopped at one of the immense underground openings and let everyone off. They were now about 500' below the surface. This is where they found the cave they now call the Ice Palace just one year ago. They walked down a narrow pathway, down a flight of metal stairs, and took a right at a corridor intersection that opened into a small room with a smaller cave entrance on the other side, maybe 4' tall and 2' wide.

"This chamber is much smaller than the last, but we can all fit inside. Please do not touch anything, as the crystal structures are very delicate, unlike the crystal cave. Watch your backside and helmet to ensure you don't hit anything." He walked over to the cave entrance, ducked down, and entered. Rosa was closest to him, so she went in next. The entrance was small but quickly opened into a room you could stand in but completely covered in crystals. These crystals were indeed much smaller than the Cave of Crystals, but by any standard measure, these were enormous. Many more than a foot long and 1-2" thick.

The rest of the group carefully came through the opening. Many "oooohs" and "aaaahs" were heard as the group took in what they were seeing. As the group continued, Rosa needed to move to the cave's far end, where the crystal structures changed. There was a wall where fragile threadlike formations hung from the ceiling. They were so thin and delicate. Rosa thought if she breathed too hard, they would break. Below them, they looked like popcorn balls. Seeing that these enthralled Rosa, the guide said, "This is called Cauliflower Calcite." He reached into his pocket. "This piece was broken off the first time I came into the cave, and I have kept it for good luck." As he extended his hand towards Rosa, it oscillated between orange and white like the other cave. With a curious look on the guide's face, he moved the calcite higher towards Rosa's chin, and the phenomenon stopped. He lowered it again towards her belly, and it began changing colors again. He took in a breath about to call out to the others to show them the phenomenon, when Rosa took her finger to his lips in a gesture to stay quiet. She then whispered in Spanish, "Can we keep this between us? I don't want to be made into a spectacle." He nodded. But then, with his other hand still holding the cauliflower calcite, he opened Rosa's hand, placed it in her palm, and closed her fingers around it. He said, "I don't know what it means, but this needs to be for your child. Please accept it. I have never seen anything like what we have witnessed today." Rosa didn't feel like she should take his good luck charm but knew it would bring more attention to them if she didn't. So she nodded and whispered, "Thank you."

After ten more minutes, the group filed out and headed back to the elevator and up to the surface. They walked to the museum, where the other two groups were waiting. Yesenia announced that the bus would be leaving in 15 minutes and for everyone to get a snack for the road if they wished and to go to the bathroom as they would be on the road for several hours.

Rosa went to Yesenia and said, "Well, this is where I leave you, I believe. Thank you so much for taking me this far."

"No problem at all," Yesenia said. "I hope you can find your boyfriend."

"I hope so as well," Rosa said. "I'll pull my bag off the bus and head to the bus station. Thanks again for all your help."

"Anytime," she said, and they embraced.

Twenty minutes later, Rosa watched as the bus drove out of the small town of Naica. Rosa looked down at the cauliflower calcite. She put it next to her belly but didn't see anything happen. She then wrapped the calcite in several napkins from the restaurant and placed it in a corner of her bag.

The bus station was next to the museum as several men were bussed into the mine daily. She looked at the bus schedule and saw that in thirty minutes, a bus would be heading north to the city of Chihuahua. As she studied the map, she thought it would be an excellent place to stay for the night as it was just over two hours away, and from there, she was sure there would be many buses that could take her up to the U.S.

The bus came, she paid the fair and was now sitting on a very uncomfortable seat, and the bus was not air-conditioned. She silently thanked Juliana and Yesenia for making the last week's journey so much more comfortable than it would have been otherwise.

When she arrived in Chihuahua, she found a small 3-star hotel called the Ibis Chihuahua and paid the fee for one night. It was close to the bus station and included a complimentary breakfast buffet. She settled into her room and turned on the television. The news anchor was near the start of a segment.

"...this is an infrequent event as the last time there was a lunar eclipse on a winter solstice was 372 years ago in 1638. The eclipse will be visible to everyone in North America and Central America, weather permitting. Areas of Northern Europe, South America, and Eastern Asia will also see the full or partial moon eclipse." The news anchor, a man in a tan suit with a blue tie with thick brown hair combed up and over like there was a giant curler he had forgotten to take out of his hair, continued speaking. "As this is a lunar eclipse and not a solar eclipse, you can look at it directly without any eye protection. Again, tomorrow night, the eclipse will begin at 11:33 p.m. Still, the full shadow of the earth will not fully cover the moon until 12:41 a.m., and the full eclipse will remain until 1:53 a.m. During this time, the moon will appear blood red! Then near 3:00 a.m., the shadow will fully pass off the moon in this once-in-a-lifetime event." The screen cut to a different newswoman who said, "Thanks, Gabriel, sounds like it is a once-in-many-lifetimes event.

Let's take the newsroom to Mateo to tell us what the forecast will be like for the eclipse."

With that, Rosa turned down the television. She didn't realize until right now just how tired she was. She was sure a daylong bus ride and the events of the cave were enough to exhaust anyone but add her pregnancy. She realized why profound tiredness washed over her, and she couldn't keep her eyes open any longer. Without turning off the light in the room or the TV, she fell asleep.

The following day was busy. She woke up early, knowing there was a 12-hour ride ahead of her with two bus changes. She had decided that the best route would be to go through the US Customs and Border Protection in Lukeville which closed at 8:00 p.m. Thankfully, there was a 5:00 a.m. bus leaving. Without delays, she would make it just before they close. She took out her cauliflower calcite and held it in her hand for good luck.

This was the most challenging day for her as it was not only the longest, but the bus was extremely uncomfortable. However, she made the best of it. She enjoyed looking at the scenery as this was the furthest she had ever been from home. Things went very smoothly the entire day. The buses were on time, and the transfer happened as described on the bus route map at the train station. It was a short walk from the bus station to the U.S. border patrol office. She walked on the sidewalk while cars were lined up, waiting between orange dividers as they passed through border patrol. Many more people went through here by vehicle than by foot. She put the calcite she got from the man at the mine in her bag.

She entered the building and waited in line. It was 7:45 p.m., but she felt confident she could make it through in the next few minutes based on how quickly the line was moving. There were eight stations, 2 of them with agents working this late. Their desks were behind a yellow divider with Plexiglas above to protect them. Each desk had a computer and phone. When it was Rosa's turn, she walked toward the agent, a squat, curly red-haired woman with long thin glasses. She had an agency uniform and a gun holstered on her left side. As Rosa approached, the woman took a long look at Rosa. Rosa handed her the passport. She opened it to the first page, slid it through the machine, and a photo of Rosa appeared on the screen.

"What is the purpose of your visit?" asked the agent.

"To find my boyfriend. He is an American," Rosa responded.

"It appears that you are pregnant," the agent stated as a rhetorical question, but Rosa answered. "Yes. That is why I need to find him and tell him we are having a baby."

"How far along are you?" the agent asked.

"I think I'm starting my 3rd trimester," Rosa replied

The agent looked unconvinced as Rosa did appear further along than that. "Why didn't you just fly to see him?" she asked, looking over her glasses. Rosa was beginning to feel uneasy.

"Well, I was told you shouldn't fly when you are this pregnant. Also, flying is more expensive. And I'm not 100% sure where he is, so I thought driving would be better," Rosa explained.

The woman flipped the pages of her passport. "Is this your first time in the U.S.?" she asked.

"This is my first time anywhere," Rosa said.

The agent picked up the phone and held up a finger. Rosa couldn't hear what was said, but a moment later, two men came out from an office and stood behind the red-headed agent. The older one on the right spoke.

"Miss Rosa, is it? Yes, as agents of the United States Government, we have protocols to prevent the entry of people in your condition, by which I mean to say pregnant and close to delivery. If you have the name, phone number, and address of your boyfriend or any family members whom we could call and validate the purpose of your entry, that would be helpful."

"I don't have his phone number, but he sent me a package, and the return address is here." She pulled the fulgurite wand out of the bag and the paper with the return address from the center. She handed it to them. "His name is Edward Blood."

"I'm sorry, without a way to call him, I'm afraid we can't allow you through. I hope you can appreciate this, but many women in your condition want to come to the United States and have their babies to gain U.S. citizenship. The policy is that women as far along as you are only permitted into the U.S. if we can validate your purpose and ensure you will return to Mexico before the baby is born. You may need to wait, have your child, and then travel to the U.S."

"But Edward is an American citizen, and he doesn't even know I am pregnant. He needs to know we are having a baby," Rosa exclaimed so loudly that the couple and the agent behind the other desk looked over.

"So your American boyfriend doesn't know you are pregnant, and you want entry into the U.S. to find him. You don't have a phone number or way to contact him, and you haven't spoken to him since you found out you were pregnant. I'm sorry, ma'am; this is precisely why this policy is in place. This agent here will see you out, and we will welcome you into our country for a visit after your baby is born," The other man who hadn't spoken walked around the barriers and gestured for Rosa to leave the building.

"No. You don't understand," Rosa explained. "I have spent the last week on busses getting here. I got my passport. I should be allowed in!"

"I'm sorry, Ma'am. The office is now closed as well. Good luck." The officer then escorted her out the door and locked it. He then stood inside the door with his back to it.

~

TWO TEAMS LEFT to drive down to Stonehenge and arrived just after 5:00 p.m. the evening before the event when the English Heritage site closed to the public. It would take all night to prepare for the event. One team was setting up "party headquarters" with drinks, food, and music. The other team set up a portable surgical center in the middle of the Neolithic Stone Circle. The team aligned the tent opening to the southwest direction the eclipse moonset would happen, which would also be aligned with the winter solstice sun. It was just after 4:00 a.m., and they were fully set up.

Asha woke Amelia up at 4:00 a.m. and told her to get ready. They were going on a trip today and needed to leave in 30 minutes. She told her to bring a coat. For being 38 weeks pregnant, she felt pretty good. Every morning since passing 36 weeks, she wondered when she would go into labor. It could happen anytime, but there had been no contractions, and she felt well. Asha handed Amelia a new gemstone and told her to keep it with her throughout the day. It was a polished stone with waves of differing shades of green and a touch of sea blue with what looked like fossilized images around the surface, making circular shapes. Amelia asked what it was as she hadn't seen this one before. Asha answered, "Malachite."

They both walked out of the wing Amelia had been confined to for the past nearly nine months. She was excited to see something different, although everyone was rushed and anxious for some reason. Being so early, it was still dark, but the grounds were softly illuminated through the typical English haze of the full moon that was slightly visible as it sat high in the western sky.

They walked outside and down a pathway. Amelia looked back and saw that she was staying in a giant castle. There were three levels above ground, including one within the mansard roof with large dormers extending outwards through a worn black slate roof where recent snow had nearly melted off. The facade was a brownish-red stone, including the battlements with merlons and embrasures alternating across the top of the center portion of the structure. Amelia had looked out of many large arched windows with a pointed capstone and white grills on the main level. She saw now that there were long rectangular matching windows with the same white grills on the upper levels.

Asha and Amelia, both in thick fur coats, walked further down the snow-covered path into a grove of trees, where there was a helicopter with the blades beginning to whirl and spin slowly. A pilot and co-pilot were in the cockpit of the Sikorsky S-70, preparing for flight. As Asha and Amelia got up and in the helicopter, they saw that 4 of the 14 available seats (other than the pilots) were already occupied. One seat had a man in his early 60s with a Russian jaw and deep groves in his white-washed face. He had a black leather ushanka hat covering his head and ears with light brown fur around the edges.

A woman wearing all white, including white leather pants and a white parka, sat next to him. She was probably in her late 30s or early 40s with butch short hair without a part but with long bangs that hid most of her eyes.

Across the aisle was a short bald man with a sizeable reddish nose and oversized ears for such a small body. He had a cleft chin and thin lips sticking out from a two-day unshaven face. He wore a black button-up colored shirt with a vest and jacket. The jacket was too small with an orange and brown chevron pattern. Hanging from his vest pocket was an old pocket watch on a gold chain.

Sitting behind him was a scary-looking creature. Amelia was curious to know if it was a man or a woman. It had tattoos over every part of its body that could be seen. Gauges hanging from the ears, piercings across both eyebrows spaced only a few millimeters apart. A nose ring and teeth filed into sharp points. There were bumps across her head, giving the look of demonic horns with a long red braided Mohawk hanging down its back. With long black pointed fingernails, eye makeup, and what appeared to be breasts under a black leather coat, she thought of it as a girl but wasn't entirely sure.

Amelia was not introduced to any of them and was glad she wasn't. Only the Russian man paid her any attention. He stared at her inquisitively as she boarded and sat on the third row behind the tattooed woman. She saw that much of her skin was deformed, bubbled, and scarred.

Asha sat beside Amelia and told her they would leave in a few minutes. They were waiting for a few more people.

"Where are we going" Amelia wanted to know.

"You will see. It won't be a long flight," Asha responded just as four other men climbed onboard. The first was a broad, strong man Amelia had seen from time to time in the complex. He wore a black suit, white colored shirt, and no tie, with a submachine gun under his jacket. Next was a very old Arab man with a white beard and bushy white hair. He wore a long, comfortable-looking black robe with a purple hue in the moonlight. He was followed by Thomas Blood. Amelia recognized him from television. He was wearing a light grey suit with a lavender shirt and a green and blue patterned tie. His long hair pulled up into a man-bun, thick beard, and half-circle scar around his left eye made him unmistakable. It was at this moment that Amelia knew whose child she was carrying. She was struck with fear knowing that Thomas Blood was one of the wealthiest people alive and one of the shrewdest.

Thomas was followed by what appeared to be a twin of the first dark suit, but he was carrying a large, somewhat heavy wooden chest. He carefully placed it across from the Japanese man. He sat facing Thomas, having an identical Heckler & Koch MP5A3 submachine gun under his coat jacket. Thomas gave the pilots a signal, and they were in the air within moments. The helicopter flew South. Asha leaned over to Amelia and said, "We should be there in about 40 minutes."

Amelia turned to Asha's ear and said, "So this baby is Thomas Blood's?"

Asha smiled as the hazy outline of the moon dropped further toward the horizon on their right side.

The helicopter landed on the far end of a parking area. As Amelia got off, she saw where they were and said, "This is Stonehenge! I haven't been here since I was a little girl. What are we doing here?"

Without an answer, the entire group moved across the parking area, the road, and the snow-covered paved path leading to the stones. The tent preparing for the evening food and music event was pitched outside the Neolithic structure. A sound system booth was adjacent to the food tent, with wires running all around Stonehenge with speakers facing towards and away from the center. A smaller tent was pitched directly within the circle itself.

During the flight, Amelia began to feel pains in her abdomen. They slowly intensified, with a significant contraction happening while she was walking. She had to stop, hunched over. Asha put her arm through Amelia's and asked if everything was alright. Amelia told her about the pain. Asha said, let's get to that tent, and you can lie down. It was now 5:15 a.m.

As they approached the tents, Thomas Blood began barking orders to everyone. Various members of the group broke off following their instructions. "Mercurius, I need a clear view of that western sky," Thomas said, and the short bald man with the pocket watch headed to the west side of Stonehenge. "Bryne and Asha, take care of Amelia," Thomas said next, and the woman in all white came over and took Amelia by the other arm as they helped her towards the central tent. Thomas then instructed the two guards, one of which was carrying the wooden chest again, to follow the Arab man, who he called Syrpens, who was heading to the same tent as Amelia. Lastly, he instructed Alexander (the Russian) and Nephrite (the demon woman) to get some music going and bring some drinks into the tent.

Amelia made it to the tent right as another contraction hit. Each one was far more painful than the last. Asha and Bryne had to support her fully. They carried her into the tent and sat her in a blue and grey electrical obstetric birthing chair. It was partially reclined with leg rests protruding from each side. This was when Amelia realized what was happening.

"no. no. no. no. No NO!" This is not happening today. I will not give birth to a baby in the middle of a field. At, at Stonehenge," Amelia screamed.

"Amelia, look at me," Asha said, drawing her attention. "You are going into labor right now. You are having the baby today. The more you fight it, the more it is going to hurt. Relax, and let's get this done."

"You did this to me!" Amelia said, now looking at the malachite stone. She threw it across the tent, hitting a sizeable portable heater.

"Amelia. I want to do this easy, but we will have to do it the hard way if you are difficult," Asha said in a firm tone. Bryne looked at Asha, who signaled her to get the malachite stone. Bryne fished for it under the heater, brought it back to the chair, and held it out for Amelia to take.

Amelia looked at the stone. She looked at Bryne, then Asha, and slapped the stone from Bryne's hand as she said, "NO!" Syrpens, who had moved behind Amelia, threw a gag in her mouth while Asha and Bryne took one of her arms and strapped them on the armrests. Ameilia kicked wildly with her legs. The two women quickly braced the legs into the leg rests. Syrpens finished tying a knot in the gag and said, "Well, I had hoped she would have been more accommodating for a little longer."

It was now 5:30 a.m., and Thomas walked into the tent. Amelia's wild eyes shot at him, hoping she would tell everyone to release her. He looked down, picked up the malachite stone, and walked to Amelia. Syrpens handed Thomas a necklace chain with a cage hanging from it. Thomas opened the cage, placed the malachite inside, and hung it around Amelia's neck. He then said, "Let's get this over, shall we? But not too early. We need to be precise about this."

Amelia began to scream as loud as she could through the gag. "See, I told you music would be a good idea," Thomas said, and a moment later, Celtic music began to play loudly over the speakers. Asha started to connect the monitoring equipment to Amelia. At the same time, Bryne went outside the tent and adjusted some settings on the three large power generators.

At 6:32, Thomas looked up in the sky and said, "Look! It is starting," as the beginnings of a shadow were crossing the moon. "Asha. How is she progressing?"

"Her contracts are getting stronger and more frequent, but she is behind schedule," Asha said.

Thomas went over to Amelia, who was still fighting her shackles with sweat-soaked hair. "Do you want the gag off?" he said. She nodded. "Will you keep quiet?" she nodded again. He motioned for Syrpens to remove the gag. As soon as he did, she began yelling, "I'm going to sue you. You are going to JAIL. You can't do this to me!" Syrpen's looked at Thomas clearly asking if he should replace the gag. Thomas shook his head. "No one can hear her anyway," he said.

"Look," he said to her. "We have a very tight window for you to deliver this baby. The more you can help us hit that window, the better it will be for you. It is a little after 6:30 now. The baby must be delivered between 7:40 and when the moon goes over the horizon at 8:34. That is less than an hour, and you are behind schedule. So you can help, or there is more we can do."

Amelia responded by spitting in his face, which had a tinge of blood in it. Thomas pulled a handkerchief from his suit pocket and wiped it off. He stood up fully and nodded to Syrpens, who immediately opened his wooden chest and began pulling out various crystals and stones. He arranged them around Amelia in a distinct order and even turned and pointed in specific directions. Using clear bandages, he started taping stones to multiple locations on Amelia's body. Amelia was overcome with pain when he had completed, and a powerful contraction began to put tremendous pressure on her pelvis. "This is what it feels like to be induced," Thomas said. Her scream blended with the Celtic sounds blaring over the speakers.

~

"IF YOU DON'T NATURALLY GO INTO LABOR in the next three days, you need to be induced," said Dr. Chen via a phone call with Hui Yin. "We have you scheduled to come in Tuesday, December 21. If your water breaks before then, immediately come in. If not, be here by 1:00 p.m. on Tuesday. We will induce you, and you will deliver your baby within a few hours. Sound good?" Dr. Chen said in a tone that didn't leave room for negotiation.

The following three days were miserable. She felt fatigued, she couldn't sleep, she needed to run to the bathroom every 30 minutes, she couldn't walk very far without running out of breath, and the stretch marks were getting pretty bad, not to mention the varicose veins. She was ready to have this baby. She grabbed the Jet Stone necklace from her neck, kissed it, and said, "Come soon." Monday evening came without incident, so she packed what she needed in a brown leather suitcase. Ju-Long packed some things as well. They were going to Chengdu Western Hospital tomorrow and would come home together with their baby.

The following day, they slept in, a rare thing for the Zhang family. Ju-Long had the next few days off work, so he made them both congee for breakfast, but Hui Lin couldn't stomach any rice porridge today. The morning went by very slowly, then at 11:40, they walked to the bus station and got on the bus with the Chengdu. Hui Lin was familiar with this bus ride now, having taken it many times during her pregnancy. During this last trimester, she had gone every three weeks with a call with the doctor in-between visits. The bus pulled into the station in Chengdu at 1:08. They were already late for their appointment, but Hui Lin didn't care. They walked the two blocks to the hospital and entered the maternity waiting room through the doors. She got in line at the check-in desk. A few minutes later, it was her turn. She approached the desk with a large analog clock on the wall with the small hand on the one and the large hand pointing straight down, and just then, Hui Lin felt something pop and warm liquid cascade down her legs. "My water just broke," she said to the young woman at the front desk.

"How long ago?" the woman said in a bored robotic tone.

"Just right now," she said.

The woman stood up and peered over the desk. "Oh my goodness," she said and picked up the phone. Two other women wearing masks and gloves came around the corner with a wheelchair. One put a clean towel on the chair and had Hui Lin sit. Ju-Long sat there stunned and almost began following his wife when the young check-in girl said, "Hold on. I can work with you on her check-in, and then you can return. But please hold on a minute." Ju-Long had yet to move when another older gentleman came around the same corner with a mop and bucket. He set a "plastic sign that folds out on the floor that at the top said "Caution Wet Floor" on the top in English and then the same in Chinese below a red figure of a person slipping and falling. The older man mopped up the floor and wheeled the bucket back around the corner. The young woman said, "What is your wife's name?"

A few minutes later, Hui Lin started feeling contractions. Dr. Chen came in and examined her. She was dilating nicely. Dr. Chen said that because this was her second pregnancy, it would likely go significantly faster than her first. The doctor wasn't kidding because she had dilated to an eight over the next 2 hours. Her contractions were severe and only 90 seconds apart. Dr. Chen returned and commented on how quickly her labor was progressing."At this rate, you will be done before dinner," he joked. "You know, it is a full moon today. That may be why you went into labor and are moving through it quickly. Isn't today the eclipse?" the doctor asked no one in particular. "I think only those on the East coast of China can see the full eclipse. I think it may be happening now but below the horizon. I think we here will only see a partial eclipse. At least, that is what the news said. You know, you have an east-facing window; you might see it come up."

Hui Lin didn't care about moons, eclipses, or anything else except getting this baby out of her. Ju-Long sat helpless, reaching over and holding Hui Lin's hand. The nurses encouraged her to change positions and work through the contractions as best she could. At 3:40, the doctor confirmed she had dilated to 10 cm and was ready to push actively. Each time a contraction came, she pushed as hard as she could. Even after 30 minutes, she was exhausted and didn't want to try any longer. The nurses kept encouraging her, then the doctor said, "I can see the baby's head." This seemed to give Hui Lin enough strength to continue a little longer. Six contractions later, Dr. Chen pulled the baby from Hui Lin, and it immediately began crying. The look on the doctor's face was sheer confusion and wonder.

Ju-Long walked around a nurse to where the doctor was, and he immediately had the same look. "What is it!" demanded Hui Lin. "Is the baby okay?"

Ju-Long looked up, smiled, and said, "Yes. The baby is," and he paused, looking down at the baby again. "Perfect." The doctor lifted the baby and placed it on Hui Lin's belly—a perfect baby boy with two perfect arms.

One nurse worked with the doctor to cut the umbilical cord and clean and sew up Hui Lin from some tearing. The other nurse took the baby, cleaned it, and weighed and measured it. She wrote on her chart the time of birth at 4:16 p.m. December 21, 2010. She wrapped the baby and laid it again in mother's arms, and the baby quieted down. Ju-Long and Hui Lin held their baby, looking at each other in wonder when the baby's arm escaped from the blanket and rested on the Jet Stone necklace still being worn by his mother. His little fingers curled around the angel's wing. That is when they realized what had happened.

A few minutes later, Dr. Chen and a team of doctors returned with printouts of the ultrasounds. Three had been performed in the previous months due to the child's condition. The doctor passed around the printouts, and then one by one, they each inspected the baby. This went on for some time when Ju-Long seeing how tired his wife was, asked if the doctors could leave them for a little while so his wife could rest. Frustrated and confused, they all left, still discussing what had happened. Some were saying the ultrasound machine was broken. Others were saying that the ultrasounds were from another mother. Others were calling it a miracle. Ju-Long returned to the bed where Hui Lin and the baby were resting. They looked out the window a little after 6:00 p.m. when a partially eclipsed moon rose from the horizon. They watched the end of the winter solstice eclipse for the next several minutes.

~

AT 7:00 A.M., AMELIA WAS STILL NOT DIALATED to a 10. "The window is closing," Asha said to Thomas.

"No, the window isn't opening fast enough," he said. He reached into his suit jacket and pulled out a red adularia gemstone, more commonly known as a Moonstone. Looking at Asha, he said, "You are the life druid. You do it."

Asha took the stone from Thomas and sat down to face Amelia. Just above her head was the moon in partial eclipse. Mercurius had been using atmospheric magic to clear the winter haze and allow more moonlight into the tent. The eclipsed moon was quite evident as it descended toward the horizon. Asha held up the stone between her straight palms enabling it to take in the light from the eclipsed moon. She then lowered it and concentrated through the stone towards Amelia. She let out another incredible scream. Asha then moved the stone closer to Amelia's pelvis. The closer she got, the louder Amelia screamed.

Alexander came in and saw the state of Amelia. He looked at Asha and then to Thomas. "Is this necessary?" he asked.

"Alexander, you know very well what is at stake here. If she doesn't deliver this baby before 8:34, we don't get another chance at this until 2094," Thomas said this without even looking at Alexander.

"This is wrong," Alexander said, and he walked out.

"Keep going," Thomas directed Asha. "More!"

Asha moved the stone closer to Amelia, and another scream rang out.

At 8:00, Amelia had no strength left. She had indeed dilated to a ten, but with no energy to push, the labor slowed. "I'm afraid we have only one choice left," Asha said.

Thomas looked up at her. "I wanted this to be a natural birth. Okay, do it." A frenzy for work began between Asha and Syrpens. Asha pulled a tray over and gave Amelia a shot, and she passed out almost immediately. She poured a disinfecting solution over Amelia's entire abdomen. She then took a scalpel from a tray and made an incision in a wide U shape just below the waistline in the abdominal wall. It was 8:15, and Thomas told Asha to stop. "I can't stop. She will bleed out if we don't hurry.

"Wait!" Thomas demanded. "The apex of the Eclipse is in 1 minute".

"Thomas, we can't wait," Asha exclaims as she looks at the blood pressure and heart monitor dropping quickly. "Any more, and you could endanger the child's life."

"Hold. Hold," Thomas said as he looked at his Rolex, which was recently synchronized with the atomic clock. "Hold," he paused. "Just a few more seconds," he paused again. "Now Go!"

Asha worked quickly, making an incision horizontally across the lower part of the uterus. She opened the uterus and was shocked. "Syrpens, Thomas, I need your help!" She exclaimed. They both rushed to her side. She pulled out a baby girl, the light of the blood moon eclipse darkening her already bloody body. She handed the baby to Syrpens, who had gloves on. "Thomas, get some gloves on," she demanded. Thomas quickly pulled on some sterile latex gloves. She reached into the uterus and pulled out another baby. This time a boy and put it in Thomas' hands.

Thomas was shocked and sat stunned.

"This explains a lot," Asha says. She moves quickly to sew and staple Amelia while her vitals plummet. At the same time, Syrpens, with one hand, works to pinch and cut the umbilical cords of the two children.

"I need more time," Asha frantically calls out to Thomas, hoping he would cast a time-dilation spell. Thomas did not move. She quickly pulls off her gloves, runs to Syrpens wooden chest, and pulls out a red agate. She runs back to Amelia, goes to her forehead, places the stone on her third eye chakra, and begins chanting. Amelia's abdomen comes together and heals like no incision was ever made. Her breathing becomes steadier, and her heart rate returns to normal.

Thomas, blood, hands his baby boy over to Asha. He takes his left hand and covers his right hand, which has the sapphire ring, as he focuses his thought. Even while unconscious, Amelia began to struggle. Her oxygen levels went to zero, and within a few moments, she began to turn blue. Thomas continued concentrating. Amelia's heart rate redlined within a minute, and she was no longer struggling. Her limp body, still restrained, lay in a heap on the chair. Thomas looked around. Asha was stoic. Syrpens had a satisfied grin. Mercurius and Alexander standing in the doorway, looked shocked. Bryne turned away.

They saw the blood moon lunar eclipse drop below the southwestern horizon through the tent door.

~

ROSA COULDN'T BELIEVE WHAT JUST HAPPENED. Never in a million years did she think she wouldn't be allowed into the U.S. She had a valid passport. She didn't know what to do. All of her plans rested on this. It was now after 8:00 p.m., and she didn't know where to go or what to do. The couple that had been in the booth next to her was now outside the building as well. The husband approached Rosa, handed her a folded paper, and said, "This might help you."

Rosa opened the paper. It said "Peluqueria Beltran entre 4 y 5 #334 Calle E". It was the address to a barber shop close by. Rosa was perplexed. She walked away from the border patrol building heading southwest down the road. She had seen a hotel not far back with its green Hotel Excelsior sign flashing "Vacante." After a few minutes, she passed a street that said 5. She looked at the paper again, saying that the Barber was between streets 4 and 5 on E street. It was only a few blocks away. So she took a right on 5 Street, passed B, C, and D streets, and took a left on E Street. She was now between 4 and 5 on E Street. She looked for #334. She saw an alleyway with a sign above it with numbers 330-340 with an arrow pointing down the dark passage between red brick buildings. With a deep breath and a sense of foreboding, she walked down the alley until she saw an old door that had more grey wood than forest green paint left on it. She knocked. A man, skinny with a scruffy beard, answered. "Hola" in a rough voice that matched that of a man Rosa knew from church who had smoked three packs of cigarettes daily for his whole life. She handed him the piece of paper that she was given and said, "me dijeron que me podrias ayudar."

He then asked what she needed help with. She began to explain the last hour's events with the border patrol when the man pulled her in and looked down the alleyway, left and right. He then shut the door. Rosa was in a barber shop with two high chairs for patrons. They had old, faded red fabric on them. The lighting was dim, and a curtain pulled over the window. He then gestured to Rosa to continue. She explained how she has a valid passport, but they won't let her cross. She explained that she needed to get to the U.S. very desperately. The man said, "hay un costo" as he rubbed his fingers together.

"How much?" Rosa asked, now realizing what this whole thing was about. This man smuggles people across the border for a fee.

"20,000 pesos," he answered.

Rosa felt even more defeated. That was more money than she had. But she also realized then that she didn't have enough money to return to Uxmal. She pulled out 10,000 pesos and offered it to the man. He waved his hands, showing that wasn't nearly enough. As she reached into her bag, the man saw her cauliflower calcite and pointed to it. She pulled it out. He asked to look at it, and she handed it to him. After a moment, he said, "10,000 y esto". Rosa didn't want to part with the stone but felt she had no choice and nodded and handed him the 10,000 pesos. But when he went to grab the calcite, she pulled it back and said, "When I am safely in America." He looked at her and decided that was fair.

He took her through a small doorway into the back and down a set of stairs into a darker room where seven other people were sitting on the floor. He told the group that she would join them and they would leave in 2 hours, and he walked back up the stairs. Rosa, all of a sudden, felt like a fugitive. What was she doing? What had she done? How did she get into this predicament? Why couldn't Edward have just called or given her some more information? A woman about Rosa's age came over and sat beside her.

"Do you speak English?" She asked in very broken English, "I am trying to practice."

"Yes," Rosa answered. "What exactly will happen in 2 hours?"

"Hector, that is the name of the man that brought you down, will help us cross into the U.S.," she said excitedly. "I have been waiting for years to do this," she said surprisingly, with more excitement than fear. She was an impoverished-looking woman with rough hands and a worn face for her age. But she had bright eyes and a kind smile. They spoke for a while. She learned the woman's name was Lula from the gulf coast city of Bahia Kino, where she worked in a restaurant. She pulled out some rolled-up tortillas and handed two to Rosa. She had just begun to realize how hungry she was, said thank you, and devoured them.

In addition to Lula, a young couple in their 20s looked married. There were also two men who looked like brothers but very close in age, with the same hair and eyes. One was only slightly taller than the other. Rosa learned that Lula was the younger sister of these two men. There were two other men, one in his 40s and the other in his 30s. Both men were asleep with their heads on their bags.

About two hours later, Hector returned down the stairs and told them it was time to go. They all got up, grabbed their bags, and followed the man back upstairs and out a back door. They approached a small two-door truck. He looked at Rosa and her belly and gestured for her to get in the front seat and another woman who looked like she was in her 30s. The other six people had to get into the truck bed, lay down, and they were covered by a tarp which they were told to hold onto. They were folded into the back of the truck so everyone was on their sides, laying on the truck's bed like a jigsaw puzzle with legs interlocking with others' heads or legs. Hector walked around the truck, got in the driver's seat, looked back at the cargo through his rear-view mirror, and started the vehicle. They pulled back onto the main street heading towards to border patrol office. It was almost 11:00 p.m. He took a right off Highway 8 two blocks before the U.S. border, going east onto a dirt road.

They drove along the border fence for 3 miles which took about 10 minutes. Rosa started feeling pressure in her stomach like nothing she had felt before. She had been told about Braxton Hicks contractions and wondered if that was it. It was an uncomfortable tightening of the abdomen. She had enough going on tonight. She hoped they would pass soon. They drove until they came to a tiny grouping of buildings with most structures and shelters in shambles.

There was no movement other than a cat Rosa saw dash across the headlights as they turned left onto the first street, and he parked. Hector got out, pulled the tarp off the back of the truck, and motioned for everyone to get out. He led them through old sheds and makeshift housing to a 10'x10' wooden structure with green corrugated thick plastic for a roof. Rosa felt the contractions again, this time stronger.

She knew she needed to not show any weakness, or they may leave her in Mexico.

They went inside, where there were old cans and debris everywhere. Hector walked to the back left corner and kicked some garbage to reveal a small wooden hatch that opened. He went down first, and after a moment, a light from a flashlight turned on. The group began to climb down the stairs.

This was quite difficult for Rosa with the ever-increasing pressure of the contractions. Still, she tried to pretend everything was fine. However, her new friend Lula was now looking at her concerned because Rosa kept holding her belly and breathed heavily.

They descended 15 feet. At the bottom was an even smaller dirt room with a hole on the north side about 3' tall and 3' wide. Flashlights were handed to the group from a small box next to the tunnel opening. Rosa got a flashlight, but almost no light was emitted upon pushing the button.

The batteries were almost dead. She looked, but no additional flashlights were available.

They crawled through the tunnel individually, waiting about 30 seconds for each person. When it was Rosa's turn, she got down on all fours and pushed her bag in front of her as she made her way through the dark tunnel. She felt a sharp pain after only a few seconds and cried out.

Hector called into the tunnel, "Don't be scared. Just keep going." She pushed her bag and kept crawling. A few moments later, she felt a rumble, and dirt fell from the ceiling onto her hair and back. She paused and thought the better plan might be to hurry. She continued for five more minutes when another contraction lasted about a minute. She tried to move but simply couldn't. She looked back and saw flashlights getting close to her, and as she looked forward, the flashlights were getting smaller and smaller.

She was finally able to press on. She would have stayed in Uxmal if she had known she would have to crawl through a claustrophobic tunnel with this kind of pain to enter the U.S. illegally. After about 10 minutes of crawling and another contraction, she came to another room, much like the one she left with a wooden ladder going up.

She climbed up the ladder and out to find she was outdoors in a thicket of juniper trees. Leaves and branches had been placed over the trap door to keep it hidden but were now pushed out of the way.

Slowly the group escaped the underground tunnel, including Hector. The thicket of trees was most dense between the border wall and an adobe building where they stood. The trees engulfed the back of the small structure, but its front was wholly exposed with desert landscape, including giant cacti. They were now in the United States of America at the Organ Pipe Cactus National Monument in Arizona.

The group followed Hector out of the thicket and around the adobe building. The full moon's light was not quite as bright as it had been a few moments before crawling into the tunnel. Rosa looked up and saw that the eclipse was happening. The shadow of the earth had just started to cover the moon. However, the moon's brightness still made them feel incredibly exposed, and they wondered if the red-haired border agent would come driving up and arrest them at any moment.

Hector went to the front of the building and opened the door, which had a torn screen on it. A sign next to the door said "Gachado Line Camp," then another sign read "Closed until further notice." Hector collected the flashlights as they entered and then closed the door. It was filthy, with two cots against opposing walls and a small table in the middle with four chairs, only two of which looked sturdy enough to use. There was a wooden box with large hinges, but it was empty.

Hector's Spanish was good, but his rough voice made it difficult to understand. He told them that the building was used by ranchers decades and decades ago to house their workers on the furthest parts of their lands. More recently, it had been part of a tour for the national park but had been closed for a few years due to tour cutbacks. He then told them they just needed to wait a little while for another truck to come and pick them up and take them to Tucson.

Hector walked up to Rosa with his hand out. "Not until the truck comes," Rosa said.

"Listen. I need to go back through the tunnel. Give the stone to the truck driver, who will give it to me. "Hector said. He then asked one of Lula's brothers to follow him back to the tunnel to cover it with dirt and leaves after he went down. The brother came back a few minutes later. The eight people waited quietly in the small adobe building. Lula, seeing that Rosa was beginning to struggle, helped her up to one of the two beds and asked if she were alright.

"I don't think so," said Rosa. "I shouldn't be going into labor, but I feel strong contractions."

These are probably just early contractions and will go away soon. Perhaps because you are stressed or had to crawl through that tunnel," Lula said.

"I hope so," Rosa Said, but hope was not enough. The contractions got worse and worse and were happening every few minutes. It had been an hour, and everyone in the room was nervous about Rosa. She began to cry out when a contraction came, and the others would try to "shush" her. The last thing they needed was to draw attention to themselves. They didn't know how far anything or anyone else would be, and they knew that the border crossing station was only about 10 minutes away.

Lula kept trying to help Rosa, but she could do nothing. There was no food. No water. There wasn't any bedding or anything. She felt helpless. Rosa was now starting to think she could lose the baby. She was only six months pregnant. She shouldn't go into labor for another three months. Perhaps if she could make it to a hospital, they could help her. Even if she did enter illegally, she isn't trying to stay. She has a passport. But she had no idea how long until the truck would be there, and then she didn't know how far of a drive to a hospital. "What if he won't drive me to a hospital?" she thought. "The last thing he will want to do is drop me off with seven other illegals in the back of a truck." She started to get worried about what might happen. "And what if he doesn't come soon!" Rosa's water broke at that moment.

An hour passed. The contractions were getting very close together, maybe a minute apart. She was on all fours again, which seemed the best position as the contractions came on. The room was a buzz. Everyone was pacing and worrying. Lula, her brothers, and the young man's wife seemed very concerned about Rosa and doing their best to help her, although there wasn't much they could do.

The woman's husband and the other two men were gathered in a corner, arguing and talking and occasionally hushing the others and Rosa. However, they were often the loudest ones. They were concerned someone would hear them. They were supposed to be quietly waiting for the truck when it sounded like a bar fight was happening in the room and likely could be heard for a quarter mile in every direction.

Thankfully, the young married woman had limited nursing training in her hometown of Hermosillo, Mexico. She had begun working to become a nurse when her husband's friend had convinced him to come to the U.S. on a construction project that he was told would be very lucrative for him. However, he had to be there by a specific date, preventing him from getting a work visa. The nurse in training, Rosa learned her name was Isabella. She was kind and would hold Rosa's back and allow her to lean against her. She was just doing what came naturally rather than anything from her training.

It was now almost 1:00 a.m. The eclipse had become a full blood moon about 20 minutes prior when a truck's engine was heard. Lula's brothers peeked out the door and saw an approaching truck. Paralysis struck everyone as they didn't know if this was a border patrol vehicle or the man who was supposed to pick them up. The two older men ran out the door and into the juniper trees to hide in case it was border patrol. The truck's headlights grew further apart as the truck pulled up only feet from the front door. It was an old 1976 Chevy Blazer Chalet with a camper over the truck bed. It was white with dark red thick detailing down the side. The camper had a matching red top with orange and yellow pinstripes both above and below the window going from the front and wrapping around the RV to the other side. Everyone breathed a sigh of relief except Rosa, holding her breath through a contraction.

A Hispanic man that looked even older than Hector got out. He wore a white cowboy hat with a wide brim and a black band with perforations at the top. He had dark eyes and a similar scruff to Hector but with much larger ears. He exited the truck and walked over to the adobe structure as the two men walked around from the back where the juniper trees were.

The two men stopped him and filled him in on the situation happening inside. Rosa then screamed, "I CAN FEEL THE BABY COMING!" Lula opened Rosa's bag and pulled everything out, looking for anything to help. The calcite rolled out on the floor. Lula grabbed two shirts, not even knowing what she would do with them.

They all went inside, and the truck driver froze, not knowing what to do. After a moment, he snapped back, ran to the back of his truck, opened up the camper, and pulled out two lavender sheets. He ran back inside and laid one on the cot. Rosa had gotten up but returned to all fours on the cot, attempting to stay off the dirty floor. Blood was running down her legs. She couldn't help but push when the intense contractions came. Isabella took the other sheet and covered the bottom of Rosa, which was now bare. Lula saw the baby's head protruding from Rosa, and she put her arms out and caught the baby before it hit the floor.

Rosa, sobbing and in pain, turned over and saw the tiny baby girl being held by Lula. While mother and daughter were still connected via the umbilical cord, Lula placed the baby in her arms. The baby was so tiny and yet cried out. Lula noticed that Rosa continued to bleed heavily even after the placenta had passed. Rosa seemed to sense something was wrong. She took the shirt the baby was wrapped in and cleaned off her eyes, face, and chest. Rosa felt weak and dizzy. She reached down with her finger and caught some blood from her leg. With her finger, she wrote A U R A on her chest just as her arm went limp. The strange light from the blood moon streaming through the southern window on baby and mother as Rosa passed.

Everyone stood in stunned silence.

The older two men said, "We need to get out of here NOW!"

"What do we do with her?" said Isabella.

"We will have to leave her. We can't take her with us," said the younger of the two men.

"We can't leave her here!" said Lula.

"You are already an illegal alien in America. Do you want to be accused of murder as well?" asked the older man again.

Isabella turned to the truck driver. "Can we take her?" she pleaded with her eyes.

The man in the white didn't say anything for a long moment. He then turned to the group and said, "We cannot take her."

"But what about the baby!" Isabella and Lula said in near unison.

"Look at that baby. It isn't going to make it. It is too small and too unhealthy," said the married man.

Isabella turned to her husband and said, "You will not leave that baby here, or by GOD, you will not see another day do you hear me!" All the men got the message very clearly.

The man in the white hat returned to his trailer and pulled a clothespin from a wire where a towel was hanging. He returned, folded and clipped the baby's umbilical cord, and put the cloths pin on it. He then pulled out a knife and lighter. He flipped the spark wheel, and the flame appeared. He held the flame under the knife's blade for several long seconds going back and forth across it. He then cut the umbilical cord next to where the cloths pin was.

Lula and Isabella were both sobbing. Lula picked up the baby and wrapped her using the other lavender sheet. Isabella took the items that had fallen out of Rosa's bag. She threw them back in, including several articles that were drenched in blood. Among them was the Cauliflower Calcite that was now more red than white and covered in Rosa's blood.

"Are we going just to leave her here?" Lula said between sobs.

"If we don't hurry, her baby may not make it," Isabella said, holding her. "We need to get this baby to a hospital. Everyone into the truck!"

Everyone, including the driver, scrambled as quickly as they could. They were on the road driving in less than a minute. Lula and Isabella were in the front seat with the Hispanic driver in the cowboy hat. Lula still held the baby while Isabella asked the man, "Where is the nearest hospital?"

It would be a pretty long ride to the Sells Indian Hospital, a tiny town between where they were in the Organ Pipe Cactus National Monument and Tucson, where they were going. The baby sat quietly, but both women could see she was having difficulty breathing. "You go as fast as you can, do you hear me!" Isabella exclaimed as the man pushed even harder on the accelerator.

Forty-five minutes later, they entered Sells, and the man knew where to turn onto Indian Route 19 and right into the small hospital. The flat, one-story white building had only a few lights, including those shining through the Emergency Room double doors under a covering that could be driven through. They were careful not to pull into the parking area, fearing security cameras might catch him. Not knowing what they would do with a baby with no mother this close to the border, Isabella didn't want to leave Rosa's passport for fear they would deport the child under the pretense it may have been born in Mexico. So she pulled out the blood-stained calcite and put it under the sheet leaving the rest of Rosa's items in the truck, including the fulgurite wand, which was sitting in her bag. She then ran as fast as she could through the doors.

"I found this baby!" she said. "Please, it doesn't look like it is doing well," which was true. Over the final 20 minutes of the drive, the child had become almost entirely motionless with a grey hue. A nurse and a doctor (the only ones in the waiting area) flew around from a check-in area and looked at the baby. The nurse darted to get a bed while the doctor opened the sheet. He said, "It's so small. How is she even alive?"

The nurse was back in a flash, but the doctor ignored the bed and ran through another set of swinging double doors with baby in arms. The nurse said, "I'll be right back. Stay here. I'll be right back. Stay right there!" and followed the doctor.

Once the doors had swung shut, Isabella ran as fast as she could, got into the truck, and they all sped away just as the earth's shadow pulled away from the clear full moon.

~

THOMAS BLOOD WALKED DOWN the three sets of staircases from his bedroom to the dungeon on the lowest level of the castle. Once he reached the bottom, he walked down a long stone corridor. It was dark, with only tiny bits of light coming from the staircase he had just descended. A large black metal door was at the end of the hallway. He pulled out an iron key matching the color and texture of the door from his suit pocket, inserted it into the keyhole, and turned the key with a loud CLANK! He then pulled the door open. Inside was a large room divided by thick iron bars going from floor to ceiling just 4 feet into the room. The rest of the room was a makeshift bedroom with a plain bed, table, chairs, and a toilet in the corner. The only light came from a bulb above the door covered in a metal grate. On the opposite wall was a window that had identical bars to the ones in the room. It looked out onto a cement wall with a shaft that led up to ground level. Hanging on the wall next to the metal door was a picture of a young Mexican woman with beautiful amber eyes in a brass frame.

On the far end of the room, on the floor, there was a man covered in two old blankets with his face in a small opening in the wall. On the visitors' side of the bars sat a single chair which Thomas pulled over to the doorway, being sure not to go too far into the room. He sat down and said, "Hello, cousin."

Edward Blood turned to see a blurry Thomas Blood sitting in the doorway. His eyes shot to the picture of Rosa next to Thomas.

"Happy belated Winter Solstice," Thomas said. Edward seemed disoriented. "Where is it? Where is the emerald?" Edward turned his head back towards the wall.

"You disappoint me, cousin. I know you just got here, but let's give this some time and see if you become more communicative," Thomas said as he set the chair back in the room and closed and locked the door.

Chapter 5

Eight Years Later – September 2018

"In this second half of the documentary on the life of Thomas Blood, we are going to look at his rise to fortune." said the commentator as a photo of Thomas Blood in a dark navy suit, checkered blue and orange shirt, and crisscrossed tie change to a panned out view of the Thomas Blood estate and mansion fill the screen. "Earlier this year, Forbes declared Thomas Blood the 2018 wealthiest man in the world, but for the first time, also granted him the title of the wealthiest man that has ever lived. Some claim the famed Mansa Musa from the 14th century may still hold that title" The screen changed again to a painting of a black Arab man holding a golden staff and wearing a turban. "However, Thomas Blood has famously built some of the most profitable companies in the world. "His family inheritance from generations of oil money, including his great grandfather's ownership in British-Mexican Petroleum, certainly helped him launch his empire. In 2004 he started 'Chip Wireless,' which now one in every two phones worldwide is a chip wireless phone. In 2010 he bought StarFlight Enterprises, a rocket company that has grown faster than any other company in the last decade and deploys more satellites and additional payload into orbit each year than all other companies or countries worldwide. His revolutionary approach to rocket reentry and reuse reduced the cost of deploying payloads into space, effectively destroying all competition and government groups resulting in StarFlight being used by most governments and enterprises.

In 2012 he revolutionized the cloud computing movement, making moving to the cloud easy and affordable for everyone. Now, 30% of all computing power worldwide comes from CloudSpark, whom Thomas Blood is the majority owner and chairman. In 2016 all of the Thomas Blood enterprise companies were rolled up under an umbrella organization named 'Next.'" The screen changes to the logo of the Next Corporation. "When asked why he called it 'NEXT,' Thomas answered, 'I'm always looking for what's next, and I thought the companies name should also reflect its vision.'"

"So what is next for NEXT? Thomas Blood appears to be at the forefront of space mining, the next 'Gold Rush' according to the New York Times. According to a recent article, the prediction about who will be the first trillionaire is paired with who can successfully mine the moon, meteors, comets, and other plants. On November 25, 2015, United States President Obama signed the Spurring Private Aerospace Competitiveness and Entrepreneurship (S.P.A.C.E.) Act into law. The law, a first of its kind, gives U.S. citizens the right to "engage in the commercial exploration and exploitation of 'space resources' including water and minerals. The goal of the U.S. Government is to boost the commercialization of space, an important first step towards defining property claims on resources outside our world. Now legislation through the United Nations is being evaluated to adopt the S.P.A.C.E Act globally to ensure worldwide legalization of property claims of these resources. To the chagrin of investors and private equity groups worldwide, Thomas Blood has kept StarFlight Enterprises and the rest of the companies under the NEXT umbrella as private companies leaving outside investors chomping at the bit to invest. And while rumors continue to swirl that Thomas may take NEXT public in an Initial Public Offering or IPO, details still need to be formally released. The rise in the companies' value under NEXT has taken Thomas Blood from being the 97th wealthiest individual to #1 in just three years." A line graph animates as it takes a headshot of Thomas on a line surpassing all the top wealthiest people in the world, ending with Thomas' head far above everyone else.

"But not everything has been easy for Thomas Blood, the technology and space mogul.

Manufacturing costs in several key demographics have gone up, such as the Chip Wireless facilities just outside Chengdu, China, where not only have there been labor challenges, Chip Wireless has been hit with several lawsuits regarding manufacturing waste being dumped into local rivers, which some believe has caused congenital disabilities, birth defects and other ecological problems in China. "The screen cuts to a birds-eye-view of a manufacturing plant and then zooms in to where waste is pouring into a river.

Thomas has been known to move manufacturing from one country to another when allegations start. Some commend his actions as showing quick responses to address issues. In contrast, others say he uses this technique as leverage to ensure local and national governments keep litigation to a minimum. Otherwise, geographies may lose the industry they rely upon to support families, villages, and even some cities.

"Likewise, key cloud computing datacenters in locations such as India, Africa, Europe, and many others consume tremendous natural resources, especially water from drought-stricken regions leaving the area and people in abject poverty." The screen shows a picture of a lush green landscape encircling a lake with birds and other wildlife; the year 2000 is displayed prominently in the bottom right corner. The screen morphed into a dry lakebed, and yellow straw sticking up from dry, cracked mud folded at the edges with the area completely devoid of any living creature; 2018 is now shown in the same corner.

"The company has provided watch groups with all the legal documents from the various governments granting the rights to perform what some consider shady or unethical business practices. Others have come forward saying these agreements are done under duress or other measures of force. Many areas of the world have blamed Thomas Blood and his conglomerate for financial and social devastation in many geographies. Poor labor practices, especially those of child labor, is the most recent set of accusations against Thomas Blood and his empire."

"However, children are one of the things Thomas has enjoyed these last eight years since the birth of his Twins at the end of 2010 with an unknown surrogate mother. Denebula, his daughter, and Kai, his son, are fraternal twins largely out of the public eye, as is Thomas Blood. His marriage to Jessica Bettencount, the cosmetic industry heiress, in 2015 was held on a private island in the Turks & Caicos under a media blackout. Their first and, to this day, only child together was born on September 23, 2017, but no photos of the child have ever been made public. Many thought the date fitting for a child of Thomas and Jessica Blood as September 23, 2017, is widely believed to correspond to an alignment in the stars as described in the Bible's book of Revelation. A fitting date for the child of the couple owning the largest space company in the world."

The documentary continued on the monitor in the corner of the room on the other side of the thick steel bars. The thin, frail man lay on the floor at the far end, turning his head into the opening on the wall. His clothes in tatters. Eight years. For eight years, he had been imprisoned by his cousin Thomas Blood. For eight years, he had been tortured. That short bald weasel of a man Mercurius, an atmospheric druid like himself. He had cast a spell causing the oxygen level in the room to drop to somewhere between 16-18%, Edward guessed. A spell is cast on an object, and the effects radiate a certain distance in all directions. Edward had found that if he stuck his face inside this vent of sorts in the wall, the spell didn't extend that far, and he could breathe normally. But anywhere else in the room and the lack of oxygen took effect within seconds. It wouldn't kill him, of course. It limited cognitive function and physical stamina, but the psychological effects were the most difficult. Not being able to take a full breath or get enough oxygen into your lungs makes you feel asphyxiating without actually passing out or passing away. Like waterboarding, only slightly more subtle but lasting continually for weeks, months, and, in Edward's case, years.

He honestly couldn't give them what they wanted. They wanted the Emerald gemstone he wore as a necklace for much of his life. But after the attack by Nephrite at the Pyramid of the Magician, he needed to get as far away from Rosa as he could to protect her. He knew she wouldn't understand, but if he told her anything, they would torture her to get information. So to protect her, he left Uxmal and returned to the U.S. He wanted to lay low for a while, which he did. He didn't want to go to his home for fear they would be looking for him there, so he stayed with a friend, Daniel Silva, up in the Redwood Forest in Northern California for several months.

Daniel was a true hippie living entirely off the grid. His place was quite tricky to find, being a tree-house high in the Redwoods, and he had used various spells to make it almost entirely invisible. Edward had given him a clear crystal quartz of remarkable quality to help him, but even having been there many times, it was difficult to locate.

One afternoon, Edward had walked down a long path to a large stone that overlooked a beautiful gully. Atop that stone, Edward would often meditate and rehearse the incantations he felt he should have memorized and be able to recall quickly and effortlessly. Returning to Daniel's tree house, he noticed two figures a long way off leaving the forest. When he asked Daniel about it, he brushed it off as unimportant. When pressed, Daniel said two old friends had come to visit. They were among the teaching circuit for druid children.

They had asked him if he would be willing to teach for just one year as the previous life magic druid was no longer available.

"Did you tell them I was here?" Edward asked with a great deal of anxiety.

"No. Well, not exactly. They noticed that someone else was living there. They asked if it was a girl. You know it is nearly impossible for me to say no to girls. But I told them it wasn't a lady, just a buddy that needed a place to crash for a while," Daniel replied very casually, like nothing could ever possibly go wrong.

"This is bad, Daniel. Really Bad. I need to go!" Edward said as he began picking up some of his clothes and throwing them in a bag.

"Dude, seriously, you don't have anything to worry about. Relax," Daniel said, attempting to reassure Edward. However, this did not slow Edward down. Within 5 minutes, he had everything, hugged his friend, and was back on the path. He knew he needed to get some more things. He would have to risk going to his home quickly before heading out. He also wanted to get a message to Rosa, who had been waiting far too long to hear from him. But he also didn't want to give too much information, which could put her or himself in greater danger.

At a brisk pace, Edward walked just over two hours south to his home just outside Myers Flat, a small home almost entirely surrounded by National Parks and California State Parks. A damp morning left most of the open ground muddy, slowing him down. He didn't want to travel by magic as sometimes it can be traced, and he didn't want to take any chances. As he approached his home, which was initially his parent's home, it looked like the coast was clear. The house was a small cabin with aged cedar shingle siding. Two chimneys protruded from the asphalt roof, which sagged over the porch, perhaps due to insufficient supports. Three wood steps, the first of which had broken, led up to the patio and a wood bench. Several oversized windows with green trim and a matching heavy wood door appeared.

Edward spent over 10 minutes waiting for any sign of people before approaching the cabin, wiping his feet on the mat, pulling out a key, and proceeding through the front door. Inside the three-bedroom cabin was a family room with a fireplace, stone hearth, and wood mantle over which hung an old family photo in a thick wood frame. The picture was of Edward, his two younger sisters, and his parents in a European country, but Edward couldn't remember where. They stood before a bridge over a small creek with beautiful trees in bloom behind them.

The simple kitchen connected to the family room. There was a small white stove and oven, a double sink, and a fridge. To one side was a dining table which Edward remembered eating many meals. A hallway led to the master bedroom, which had another fireplace. There were also two smaller bedrooms, one of which was Edward's childhood room. The other was his sisters, where there were still stacked bunk beds.

Edward went over to the stone hearth in front of the fireplace in the living room. He heaved the large block of stone up and rested it against the wall. Below the stone was a hidden storage chest framed out with unstained oak. Within was a box as well as two bags. The box was about a foot long and half as wide and deep with a lid on hinges. One bag was black lace with a round flat bottom and a golden rope that had cinched the top closed. The other bag was dark leather with a black string wrapped around the top to keep it closed. The leather bag is the one that Edward grabbed when he heard a sound outside. By stretching up and looking out the front window, he saw two figures walking towards the house. They had just rounded the corner at the far end of the driveway, about 200 feet away.

Edward quickly replaced the large stone, grabbed the leather bag, and moved on all fours to the kitchen with a back door. He quietly opened the door, locked it from the inside, and shut it. He then moved around the side of the home to a wood pile next to the porch. Edward hid behind the chopped cedar logs as the two figures approached. He reached into the leather bag, pulled out a white aventurine stone, and closed the bag. He put it in the larger bag over his shoulder and quietly zipped it up.

One of the approaching men was short and bald with a wrinkled black button-up shirt and vest with a chain hanging from the vest pocket. The other was tall, pale, and overdressed with an overcoat for the time of year. He had a large mole on the back of his right cheek. As they approached, the tall one looked down and said, "Look. Fresh footsteps going in and none coming out." With this, both naturally distanced themselves from one another. One carefully moved towards the front door while the other moved to peer through the master bedroom window. The short bald man tripped on the first step causing quite a bit of noise, and the tall man came over with a look of "What kind of an amateur are you?" They both stopped and waited to hear something. Edward didn't move. The short one made it up to the front door and, in checking the door, found it unlocked.

"It is unlocked," he loudly whispered to the tall man.

The tall one used hand gestures to say that he would go around back, and they would both enter the cabin simultaneously. He held up three fingers with one hand and no fingers on the other, trying to tell the bald man to count to 30. The bald man didn't understand. The tall man gave up and began heading around back. Thankfully, he was running around the cabin the opposite way Edward was. Edward quietly moved away from the place into the forest and then, staying within the tree line, moving towards the front of the house. At the exact moment, both men burst into the cabin, one from the front and the other from the back. Edward couldn't hear what they were saying or doing inside but positioned himself behind a large tree trunk about 80 feet from the cabin and waited for them to come out. After just a minute or so, both men walked around the back and side of the cabin the same way Edward left. They were examining the fresh footprints on the ground. Both were holding something in their right hand.

"We won't be able to follow him in there," the tall one said, pointing into the thick redwoods. "There is nothing for miles and miles in any direction except back towards town. He may have heard you and snuck out the back." If we hurry, we may be able to catch him." They moved quickly through the open area in front of the cabin when Edward concentrated through the white stone in his hand.

A few moments later, a giant golf ball-sized ice chunk from the sky whirled past the bald man's ear. Then another struck the tall man's leg dropping him to the ground. Then scores of similar extra-large hail stones pummeled a 10x10' area around the two men. One hit the bald man on the cheek, and he dropped to the ground without even raising his hands to brace his fall. Another golf-ball-sized hail hit the tall man in the same leg again, but this time on the knee as he raised his right hand and said some words, and the hail began melting on an invisible force an arm's length above his head. As the large hail passed through the heat shield, they disappeared, replaced by melted water pouring down on the ground. He moved to the left to block further strikes of his partner.

Edward knew this would only slow them down. He was only a few minutes from town, so he ran out of the forest at top speed and onto the 254 (better known as the Avenue of the Giants road), curved to the Southeast along the river. When he got to the large tree that cars can drive through called the Shrine Drive Thru Tree, he knew what he had to do. He saw the United States Post Office up on the right. He sprinted to the old strip mall with cheap wood paneling painted a dark brown. The post office was between a vacant space and a restaurant selling sandwiches and sodas. The window into the post office had the words "U.S. Post Office Myers Flat, CA 95554". Out front was a blue mailbox sandwiched between two newspaper dispensers. One had graffiti on it and hadn't been used for many years. The other had a local paper. He pushed the door to the post office open while pulling something out of his bag and said to the middle-aged woman behind the counter wearing a blue uniform, "What sized mailers do you have that can hold this?" as he held up the fulgurite wand. The woman looked curiously at Edward, shook her head, turned around, and pulled from a stash of shipping containers and mailing tubes about 18" long and 4" wide. "That will be perfect," Edward said. "I'll be right back."

Edward went back outside and to the end of the building, where there was some dirt and sand beneath some foliage. He reached into his shirt and pulled out the Emerald. He carefully dropped it down the center of the fulgurite wand, including the chain. Then he packed some dirt down the middle and the other side, holding the gemstone in place. He then focused on the wand, and the sides got quite warm such that Edward said "ouch" and had to hold it by the very end with his other hand while he sucked the finger of his left hand that was slightly burned. He shook the wand, and nothing moved.

He went back inside the post office. The woman handed him the tube and some brown wrapping which he used to roll the wand in and then pack around it within the box. She asked him the address he wanted to send it. He told her the address of the Hacienda Uxmal Plantation & Museum hotel in Uxmal, Mexico. However, he didn't remember the postal code. "That will be the first time I've ever mailed something there," she said as she looked up the postal code on her computer. The rest of the information was put on the outside of the mailer, including the return address of 12848 CA-254, #12 Myers Flat, CA 95554, which was the post office's address. He then asked the woman for a piece of paper, and he quickly scribbled a note and placed it in the tube with the fulgurite wand. He closed and taped it up. First class delivery, Edward said. The woman looked up and said, "How much would you like to insure this for?" Edward tried to imagine the response if he put an accurate figure to that question. "Whatever will get it there safe and sound," He said. She added $100 insurance which didn't cost anything additional. Edward gave her some cash, and she placed the tube with a small pile of packages just behind her in a large white bin.

Edward went outside, walked across the parking lot, and back into the forest. He found a dense area behind a giant redwood and took out his four-sided tetrahedron, which had the circles on all four sides filled with light orange. He blew on it, imagining the destination he wanted, and from it seemed to have a coral mist that formed an orange circle in harmony with a light breeze blowing in front of him. He stepped through the portal, and then it closed behind him.

The following two months, Edward spent on the island of Lovoni—a Fijian island northeast of Suva. Edward wanted to ensure no trace spells had been placed on him or anything he owned. He needed to be sure his cousin didn't know where he was.

As the winter solstice approached, Edward felt it would be safe to travel back to Uxmal and see Rosa. He wanted to be with her for the eclipse, as they had spoken about it just before he had to leave. It had been nearly six months, and he missed her greatly. He also didn't know if she would forgive him for being away this long. It was for her safety, but she didn't know that, nor did she know how ruthless Thomas Blood could be.

He packed his bag again, walked out of the small beach hut he had been in, and took out his tetrahedron. All sides were again charged. He had a four-sided polygon for an atmospheric druid like himself, with each side being a triangle. Edward remembered the day he got his after completing his educational circuit as a child. Every druid that completed the circuit would get one. Your affinity would determine your polygon. Your polygon would determine how you could travel by portal, each having different benefits and requirements. Edwards being 4-sided poly, had a severe limit of 4 charges, meaning he could only travel to 4 destinations without recharging it. The other polygons had more sides and could be used more times before recharging. However, his tetrahedron would allow him to travel anywhere in the world where all other polygons had other limitations. A tetrahedron was also the easiest and quickest to charge. He held the silver triangle in his hand. He thought about the hotel he first met Rosa at, blew on the polygon, and an orange portal again appeared as if part of a breeze. He walked through it.

Edward appeared in the lobby of the Hacienda Uxmal Plantation & Museum as the orange portal disappeared like a whiff of clouds. It was 6:00 am on December 20. It was a short walk to Rosa's home, but she wasn't there. He thought she had an early start at the hotel, so he returned there. He looked around and entered the laundry room, but she couldn't be found. He walked to the plantation, but she wasn't there either. He decided the hotel lobby would be the best place to wait for her, so he stepped back, sat on the couch, and waited. The television in the corner was playing a rerun of a news program from the night before, where they were talking about the upcoming lunar eclipse.

At 7:00, Angel, who runs the hotel, approached the front desk and saw Edward. "You have a lot of nerve coming back here," he said to Edward in his thick Spanish accent.

"Excuse me?" Edward said, confused.

"What you have done to Rosa, leaving her like that in her condition." Angel said while shaking his head at Edward.

"Where is Rosa?" Edward asked, now more concerned.

"She left to find you. She left about a week ago. She couldn't wait any longer. She didn't know how to get ahold of you to tell you, so she finally just left to try and find you," Angel replied.

"Wait. What? Where exactly did she go, and what do you mean she needed to tell me?" Edward held up his hands, wanting Angel to slow down and explain.

"She said she needed to find you to tell you she was pregnant. She waited and waited for you to return, but when you didn't, she got a passport and left to find you in America," Angel said in a deeply angry tone.

Edward froze. Rosa is pregnant? This would have changed everything had he known that. He felt ashamed for failing Rosa but, simultaneously, even more connected to her somehow. He sat back down on the couch, taking this all in. After a moment, he looked at Angel and asked, "Where was she going? How did she think she would find me?"

"She was going to follow the return address on the package you sent," he said. "She hitched a ride on one of the tour buses that go to Mexico City and from there was going to go up to that address."

"Which tour company was it?" Edward asked quickly. Angel hesitated for a moment but then typed on his computer, found the address, and wrote it down for Edward. He reached under the counter and pulled a picture of Rosa in a brass frame. "Here," Angel said. "Take this. You may need to show it to people to help you find her." He handed Edward the photo and the address in Mexico City. He spent a few minutes apologizing to Angel, telling him he had no idea and he would find and make it right with Rosa. He walked out of the hotel door and across the street, where he pulled out his poly.

Only three of the four circles were filled with light orange energy. He thought about the place in Mexico City and blew on the tetrahedron, and a portal appeared, and he walked through it.

It opened on a busy street corner, where people screamed and jumped back as he walked through. Usually, he would have more discretion than this, but he was too worried about Rosa to care about what strangers thought. He had been here before. That is why he could imagine Mexico City. There was a great restaurant just around the corner. But now he needed to get to the travel company. He hailed a cab and got in. It took over an hour in traffic to get to the travel company. After he paid the driver in U.S. dollars, he was dropped off on a corner with many power lines running overhead. He looked around and saw the cruise company's office next to a corner market. He ran inside and up to a man at a counter already speaking to a woman and said, "Excuse me, this is an emergency," Edward said forcefully and then didn't wait for a reply. "I need to speak with Juliana." Another woman at a desk with a customer both turned with curiosity.

"She isn't here. She is on a tour," the man said with better English than Edward had expected.

"Where is she? When will she be back?" Edward pushed again.

"I'm sorry, miss," the man said to the woman he had been talking with. "He looked down at some papers going line by line with his finger. He stopped and then went to the right and then stopped. "She will be back in two days," he said.

"Is there any way I can speak to her now?" Edward said.

"I'm sorry. The drivers are not allowed to talk on a phone while driving the bus. We may be able to get a message to her tonight when they stop at the hotel. What is this in regards to?" the man asked.

"I need to ask her about someone on the bus with her from Uxmal," Edward said, realizing as he said it that it would cause a problem.

"I'm sorry, sir. We do not give out information on our customers," the Hispanic man said, beginning to get irritated.

"It wasn't a customer. It was a woman named Rosa," Edward said, trying to explain.

"Only customers are allowed on the tour busses. I am sure you are mistaken. I need to get back to this customer. If you would like to have a seat..." Just then, the woman sitting at the desk cut him off. She had gotten up and came over and said, "Mateo, I'll take care of this." She pulled Edward away from the counter and over to a corner. In a harsh whisper, she said, "You need to stop this. Do you know how much trouble Juliana will get in if they find out?"

"Find out?" Edward said, confused and trying to match her hushed tone.

"Juliana brought her back from Uxmal as a favor and against company policy. If they find out, she will get fired," the woman said. "What are you trying to find out?"

"I need to know what happened to Rosa," Edward exclaimed.

"Well, I can tell you that. I drove her from here on another bus. I'm Yesenia and a friend of Juliana's. When she got here with Rosa, she asked if I could take her further north to save her some money. Usually, I work in the office, but when we get swamped, I do tours. I returned late last night from the tour Rosa was on with me," Yesenia said.

"Where did you drop her off?" Edward asked.

"Who are you?" Yesenia inquired in a protective tone.

"I'm sorry. I'm Edward. I'm the one she is trying to find," Edward explained.

"You're Edward?" Yesenia said, now looking Edward up and down. "I can see why she was chasing you," she then looked sternly at him and slapped him on the shoulder. "This is for abandoning her," Yesenia said. "And if we weren't here in front of everyone, I'd smack you silly."

"I didn't know she was pregnant, and I didn't know she would leave to come find me," Edward said, holding his shoulder where he was hit. "I love Rosa. I'm trying to find her."

"Well, she got off the tour bus in Naica after we toured the Cave of the Crystals. Speaking of which, the guy giving the tour up there had a strange tale to tell after Rosa went through. Strange things happening to the crystals, he said."

"Where was she going from there?" Edward said, feeling anxious.

"She said she was going to take a bus up to Chihuahua that afternoon and then another bus the next morning up to the U.S. border," Yesenia answered, still wondering if Edward was worthy of the information.

"Thank you so much!" Edward said genuinely. "Do you have any photographs of Chihuahua that I can see? A travel guide or something?"

"Well, we have this," Yesenia said as she walked to a turnstile postcard rack, moving it around in a circle and stopping after it went three-quarters the way around. She pulled out a postcard that said "Chihuahua" across the top at an angle with a picture of a beautiful market area and a Chihuahua dog that reminded Edward of an old Taco Bell commercial. Edward studied the picture, handed it back to Yesenia, and said. "I owe you one," as he turned and headed out the door.

"Well, you can pay me back if you have a brother," Yesenia said, half under her breath.

Edward returned and found an alleyway two doors from the corner convenience store. He pulled out his tetrahedron, which only had two ovals filled in with light orange energy. He thought about the market in the Chihuahua Mexico postcard and blew on the artifact. What seemed like an orange breeze materialized a circle portal before him, and he walked through.

Edward was now in the very marketplace he had seen on the postcard. It was now lunchtime, and several people saw him materialize through an orange circle floating in the air. Two old men eating at a table nearby fell over, pulling the table and their lunch with them. Edward used the distraction to run around the corner. He didn't know much Spanish but knew how to say "Estación de autobuses" to ask a few people where to find the bus station. He was pointed in a direction, and he headed that way. After asking a few other people, he went to the bus station. Once there, he found a map of the bus routes. Edward's heart sank when he realized there were three different bus stations and he didn't know which Rosa would have gotten off at. He was about a 10-minute walk away from one of them, so he took off at a sprint. When he arrived, he went to the ticket purchase window and pulled out the picture of Rosa that Angel had given him back at the hotel in Uxmal. He asked if anyone had seen her. As he went from person to person, each shook their heads and said, "No. No la he visto."

The afternoon was pressing on, so Edward hopped in a taxi and went to another bus station. He got out and went through the same process of showing each employee at the bus station the photo of Rosa to see if anyone recognized her. No one did. Edward sat down on a bench next to the bus route map. On one side of the glass, he noticed the local bus routes in and through Chihuahua. On the other side was a map of the long-haul bus routes to other cities across Mexico. Rosa heading up to the U.S. border, would likely have had to make other bus transfers, so she would be impossible to track. Then Edward realized that no matter which bus she took, she would have had to pass through one of the U.S. Customs and Border Protection offices to enter the United States. He looked up at the Mexico/U.S. border and found that other than some unlikely routes. She would have needed to go through one of 3 locations in Arizona or 2 in California. But which one? He pulled his tetrahedron out of his pocket. There was only one charge left, and he hadn't had any time to recharge it. He only had one chance to get this right. Rosa was heading to his address in California. Still, the border patrol offices in California were so far away, and you had to pass other border patrol locations. Edward believed she would have crossed the border when she had the chance to leave the three locations in Arizona. The nearest one was in Douglas, and there was a middle one in Nogales and the furthest one away in Lukeville. He didn't know what logic Rosa used to pick where she would cross. Each had its appeal.

He decided against the Douglas entry point because once in the U.S., you would have to backtrack some to go north to Phoenix. He went into the bus station, where they had two coolers of drinks and a rack of magazines next to the purchase counter. He looked for anything with a picture of the border patrol offices. There was a pamphlet on the bottommost shelf with requirements and steps on immigration into the United States. Edward couldn't read it, but on the back was a picture of the Nogales border patrol station where you could present filled-out documentation. There was no photo of the facility in Lukeville, so the pamphlet decided for him. He went outside, found a public bathroom, and focused on the image of the border patrol office; while he blew on his poly, a portal appeared, and he walked through it.

The photo he used was taken far enough away that no one was around as he came through. He ran to the office, into the doors, and waited in line. Once his turn, he asked the man behind the glass if Rosa Garcia had passed customs. It was now 7:00 pm, and the agent indicated that she had not, not at that site nor any other site. Edward breathed a sigh of relief. He had cut her off at the pass. He was in front of her now. He would be reunited with her here at the border shortly. He left a note with the border agents to let Rosa know Edward awaits her. Edward passed into the U.S. himself and went and got a bite to eat. He ensured he was within viewing distance of the border office to see when she made it through.

8:00 passed, then 9:00. He didn't know how far back she would have been. He knew she could have made it here with a relatively long day on a bus, but maybe she decided to stay somewhere overnight. Knowing she would have to find a hotel once in the U.S. and that they were more expensive, he figured she would choose to remain in Mexico one last night. He would get some sleep and check in at the border office the following day. He also desperately needed to charge his tetrahedron, which would take at least 12 hours for each charge under the right conditions. Thankfully there was a steady breeze. Edward opened his hotel room first floor window and let the air current flow over the poly. By the following day, he should have at least one charge.

He also realized that tonight was the eclipse and he was lucky enough to have a south-facing room which meant he could place some other stones out to be charged. He grabbed the leather bag and placed three gems and crystals on the window seal. He then fell asleep exhausted from his very long day.

~

EDWARD SAT STRAIGHT UP IIN BED in a cold sweat. He looked over at the phone, which showed 1:17 am. He couldn't shake a dreadful feeling that something was wrong. He got up and went to the window. He could now see the full blood moon eclipsed directly above him. He found he couldn't go back to sleep, so he stayed up pacing the floor. When the earth's shadow had fully passed over the moon, he collected the various stones he had set out and placed them back in his leather pouch. He needed to wait until the poly was fully charged before leaving. When the tetrahedron had a single cell filled with orange light, he grabbed the poly, left the hotel room, and returned to the border office. He went through the line again and asked if Rosa had come through. The officer typed it into his computer and said. "Well, no, but," he paused "... she attempted to cross into the U.S. at the Lukeville station but was denied entry."

"Denied entry. Why?" Edward asked

"It says she was denied due to the possibility of giving birth while in the U.S. We have a policy to deny entry to lone women close to their due date." The agent answered.

"But she isn't that close to her due date," Edward said, confused.

"I don't know. It just says that she was denied entry. You would have to talk to them to know more." The agent said.

"How long does it take to drive there?" Edward asked, thinking of the single charge on his poly.

"About three and a half hours," he said.

"Well, that answers that," Edward thought. "Do you, by chance, have a photo of that office I could see?" The guy looked confused, paused, and then said, "Yes. Right here." He pulled a photo off his wall. I used to be stationed in Lukeville, and this was last year's Christmas party. The picture had 8 or 9 agents in it taking a photo in a lobby with a Christmas tree and through the windows a parking area. Edward studied it carefully, thanked the man, and left the building. Edward found a Welcome to the United States sign and walked behind it. A few moments later, Edward was in the parking area on the U.S. side of the border in Lukeville, Arizona.

He dashed into the border patrol office and impatiently waited in line. Once at the window, he asked about Rosa. He told them she was denied entry and wanted to talk with someone about what happened. The officers on duty at 8:00 p.m. last night were not yet working, so there was no more information than what the system had previously told him. He found out they would be there at noon. So he passed through the border and decided to search for Rosa until noon.

He returned with no luck finding her and was directed to a curly red-headed woman who recited what had happened the night before. Unfortunately, this wasn't helpful. They didn't know what happened to her after she left. He sat down in the lobby area, not knowing what to do and hoping perhaps she would try to go through again when all border agents except two got up and went into the back room. Within a few minutes, several patrol cars left the parking area and headed east on the c13 border road. Edward hadn't thought much about it until about 15 minutes later, one of the two remaining agents got on their radio and then walked over to Edward. "I need you to come with me," the agent said.

Edward, confused, followed the agent. They got into his vehicle and drove in the same direction as the other vehicles. The agent offered no answers to Edward's inquiries. Within 10 minutes, Edward saw many vehicles which had encircled a small adobe structure with a sheet lying over a body.

The next hour was extremely difficult for Edward, with so much missing information. So much he couldn't understand. Had she come into the U.S. by way of a tunnel? She had given birth and then died? Was their foul play? Who was she with? Where is the baby? Did the baby survive? The officers said that was unlikely based on how far out her due date was. As Edward gave more details, it became clear that Rosa should have been let into the U.S. using her passport the night before, and her story was all true.

An agent approached the car Edward was sitting in, opened the back door, and asked Edward to follow him. They got to another vehicle where there was a man on the radio. He turned to Edward. "We just got word that a tiny newborn child was dropped off at the Sells Hospital, a town about 45 minutes from here as the crow flies," he said. "The baby is in critical condition."

Edward fell to the ground, his legs no longer able to bear his weight. The agent said, "I'll drive you there now if you like," Edward absentmindedly nodded. He got into the other vehicle, and soon they were driving down a small path through the desert. You could tell it could only be used by someone who knew the area well, and this agent had driven it before. He asked the agent to use the radio to determine whether the baby would make it. The agent reluctantly grabbed his radio and began speaking into it. A few moments later, the message returned that the baby was not expected to make it. Edward then asked if any belongings had been dropped off with the child. The answer was that only a white stone and nothing else was with the child. Edward asked, "You mean like a sandy, glass tube?" the agent repeated the words into the radio, a bit confused. The answer was that there was nothing like a glass tube—only a stone. Edward asked if they had any record or video of who dropped the baby off. They came back saying they parked outside the view of the cameras. A Hispanic woman came in and handed them the child. They asked her to stay, but when they came out, she was gone.

Just then, the front of the vehicle launched into the air and landed on its roof as if it had hit a land mine. A moment later, Edward began to come to his senses. He saw the agent in the front seat limp with his head askew in an unnatural position. Edward felt something warm creeping up his chest and over his face. His hand wiped it, and he found it to be blood. He was dizzy and couldn't focus well. He then saw two sets of feet walking toward the vehicle. A face bent down and peered in. It was the short bald man from the Redwoods. The last thing Edward remembered was the other man saying, "Der you are. You are a hard man to track," with a thick Russian accent and seeing the outline of his triangle tetrahedron sitting on the underside of the car roof as his eyes went dark.

Edward woke up in a dungeon cell where he had now been for the last eight years, where someone came in every few days and tried to force him to say where the Emerald was. He has repeatedly told them he doesn't know. He honestly didn't know. It wasn't with Rosa's body (he sobbed, thinking of her again). It wasn't with the baby. What happened to it? Of course, he hadn't told them all those details, only that he genuinely didn't know. They had even used a druid that specialized in extracting information and manipulating people's minds. He confirmed Edward was telling the truth, but Thomas was still convinced Edward knew more than he was letting on, so in the dungeon, he had been held with every passing day losing his will to live.

Chapter 6

I T WAS THE END OF THE MONSOONS in Arizona, and Aura sat in her bed in the congregate care center in Tucson, Arizona. She didn't have a window near her bed, but she could see out the window at the end of the room. It was cloudy but had not rained today yet. She felt her room was one of the best because it was a little smaller, so only 14 girls shared it. The room had 14 cots with red bedframes that only stood about 6 inches off the floor. The beds were lined up on both sides of the wall, six on one side and six on the other, with two running down the middle where there would generally be a walkway. Aura's bed was in the far back corner, which was nice because only one girl was beside her. It gave her double the space to hang up pictures she had drawn on the cornflower blue walls with white painted trim in the form of clouds.

On the opposite side of the room from her was the door to the room. Not all of the beds were full all of the time. Sometimes the room was only about half full; other times, it was pretty crowded. There was one time when they had to bring in two additional cots, which made it so they had to walk on the beds to get in and out of the room. This month was light, with only 9 of the 14 beds being used.

Kids would rotate in and out pretty regularly. Well, everyone except Aura. Sometimes kids needed to be put in temporary housing until their parents could have them back. Sometimes it was drug use. Other times it was physical abuse. But most of those kids would either return to their parents or, within a short time, go to another extended family member.

The longer-term kids didn't have direct or extended family. They would be accepted into foster care homes or adopted permanently by families. They were usually there longer than the others: weeks and sometimes months, but only that long.

They often told Aura she was a "special child" because she didn't fall into those categories. She didn't have any parents. She was left at a hospital shortly after she was born. She was told her mother was trying to enter the U.S. illegally and died in childbirth shortly after crossing. Her mother's name was Rosa, and she knew nothing about her father except that her mother wasn't married. With no immediate or extended family, no one had ever returned for her in all the nearly eight years she had been in congregate care.

She hadn't been accepted into foster care, nor had she been adopted. They told her that most families and foster parents are not equipped to handle a child with severe health issues. This is why she held the record for the most extended stay in congregate care and would likely "age out," they called it. She was old enough now to realize that when foster parents or couples came in to look for a child to bring into their home, she wouldn't be leaving with them. This made her feel good because if she were accepted into a family, it would prevent another child in the facility from going with them.

Aura had some severe health issues due to being born so prematurely. She was told that it was a miracle that she even lived. From what the doctors could tell and what she had heard as the adults talked about her, she had been born about three months early, weighing 2 lbs and 4 oz, 14.1" long. As a result, her lungs were severely underdeveloped, which resulted in long-term severe asthma. As a newborn, she had feeding problems, hearing problems, blood pressure issues, some internal hemorrhaging in her brain, respiratory distress, anemia, low blood sugar, and immunity problems, which also persisted. Aura seemed to get sick anytime anyone in the facility as much as sneezed. Of course, this was in her chart and viewable to prospective adopters or foster parents.

She liked to think that each time she wasn't chosen, it was helping another child. She sometimes felt more active in helping certain children get adopted. Three weeks ago, a couple came in looking for a girl between 4 and 8 to adopt. The process always was such that the prospective parents were given the files on all the girls meeting the desired criteria. Aura was screened out due to health issues, but her friend Olivia was chosen to do an in-person meeting. They didn't call them interviews, but that is what they were. Usually, only 2 or 3 children make it to this final stage.

It was raining that day, really hard. Although Aura was young, she had seen so many couples come through during her life that she knew that their mood made a big difference in whether they chose a child and which one. Aura liked to believe that she could subtly influence this process. For example, on that day, when it was Olivia's turn to meet some prospective parents, Aura could see into the meeting room through her window, looking across the courtyard and swing set. Rain was pelting the window, which felt sad and cold to Aura. So she concentrated hard, and soon the rain stopped, and the sun shone through the meeting room window. She saw the prospective mother stand up, go to the window, looks up as if seeing a sign, turn, and nod at her husband. Olivia had been selected to be adopted. She didn't know if she had helped, but it felt like she had made a difference.

Of course, each time she felt like she helped a friend, she also lost a friend because they would be adopted and no longer with her in the congregate care center. Sometimes she got letters from old friends, but they usually stopped writing her within a few months. She believed they were so happy in their new life they didn't want to think about what it was like here with Aura. Deep down, Aura did want to know what happened to her mother. She wanted to know who her father was. She pulled a stone out from under the bed. It looked like a giant popcorn ball with dark caramel stains. It was with her when she was dropped off at the hospital. It was her only possession in the world, and she didn't even know what it was. At that moment, she felt sad and cold. She looked up and saw the clouds had become very dark, and it had begun raining.

~

HUI LIN WAS SURPRISED when she answered the phone; it was her son's school. "Yes, I'll come right down," she said and hung up. She walked to the school, which only took 9 minutes; a walk she and her son Liang did most mornings. He was seven and would turn eight in just a couple of months. Hui Lin had been working only part-time since she had her baby boy. She had just returned from work like usual, just a few minutes before Liang came home from school. While she would walk him to school in the mornings, he would usually walk himself home in the afternoon.

As she neared the school, an ambulance loaded a small person into the back. When she got the call from the school, she didn't realize it was an emergency like this. She ran, but the ambulance pulled away and drove in the other direction before she could get there. The principal, Mrs. Gāo, was standing at the doors to the school. Hui Lin ran up to her and asked, "Is Liang okay? What happened?"

"Liang is inside, and he is fine. Please come with me," she said in a stern tone.

Hui Lin followed the principal through the hall and into an administrative area with a large counter. Adjacent to the counter was several seats. Liang was sitting on one of the chairs, tears rolling down his cheeks. Hui Lin dashed to Liang and asked. "Are you okay? What happened?" Liang didn't say a word and never looked up. The principal opened her office door and said, "Hui Lin, please come in."

Hui Lin was about to take her son by the hand, but Mrs. Gāo said, "It would be best if Liang stays here for a little bit."

With confusion mounting every minute, Hui Lin said, "I'll be right back" to her son and followed Mrs. Gāo into her office. It wasn't large; a small desk with two chairs in front of it, two filing cabinets in the corner, and a series of educational certificates were framed and hung on one wall. A window overlooking a playground that was currently empty. "We had an incident today involving your child," Mrs. Gāo began.

"An incident?" Hui Lin said, concerned.

"Yes. Are you aware that your child has been the victim of bullying behaviors here at school, Mrs. Zhang?"

"Liang is a quiet boy. He keeps things to himself. He has come home with some bruises but insisted he just fell during recess. What has been happening? How long has it been going on?" Hui Lin asked, her tone intensifying.

"It recently came to my attention from Liang's teacher, who has been attempting to manage the situation herself. Until recently, it wasn't anything out of the ordinary. This behavior happens frequently, and we pull in the kids and discuss it. If necessary, we also pull in the parents of the child who is doing the bullying. A young lady has been somewhat aggressive with many of the students. She has been held back a year due to some learning issues, so she is quite a bit taller and larger than the other students in her same grade. This young lady's attention has turned to your son in the last few weeks. I just learned about his bruises, which seem to have been sourced from this student I am talking about." The principal began pacing and continued, "Then today; there was a severe incident on the playground. This young lady was aggressive with another smaller student, and your son attempted to stop the bullying. The young lady turned her aggression on Liang pushing and shoving him down to the ground several times. I am sorry to say there were no teachers in the playground to witness what happened next. The other children say that your son stood up and shoved this other student back, and when he did, well, they say a burst of light came out of his hands."

"What?" Hui Lin said, aghast, "That doesn't make any sense?"

"I agree," Mrs. Gāo continued. "We didn't find any weapons or devices on Liang, so we don't know what to think."

"Weapons? Devices? What are you talking about? My son is seven years old!" Hui Lin was beginning to wonder about what type of school her son was in.

"We are trying to understand what happened because the girl that was bullying your son is headed to the hospital right now in that ambulance you saw. The girl is blind. Well, that is to say, she was blinded and now can't see. The paramedics are unsure if it is permanent. No one can explain what happened. All we have are the stories from the other children about a flash of light.

Later that night, when Ju-Long got home from work, Hui Lin spoke to him privately about her visit with Mrs. Gāo and the incident at school. Hui Lin said, "Do you remember that time about a year ago when Liang was outside, and there was that mean dog that was always aggressive around the neighborhood?"

"Yea. It was Feng Li's dog. That guy was as nasty as his dog."

"Right! Remember how we heard Liang crying outside one day, and we went out, and Liang said he was being chased and attacked by the dog? But then later, our neighbor found the dog in some bushes, dead and burned. Almost cooked?" Hui Lin asked

"Yes, I remember. I can't say I miss that dog, though," Ju-Long said.

"Do you think Liang had anything to do with that? I mean, now, with this other incident today. Could they be connected?" As the words came out of Hui Lin's mouth, they sounded even more absurd.

"What do you mean?" Ju-Long asked, confused.

"Oh, I don't know. Do you remember that old man who gave you that stone I wore during pregnancy? He told me that Liang was special. I always thought he meant that he was supposed to be born without arms, but the old man insisted he was unique in another way. What do you think he meant?" Hui Lin asked.

"I don't know, but I think you have had a very long day and need rest."

When the two asked Liang what happened, he said he didn't know. He said he was trying to stop the girl from hurting him and the other kids, and then a moment later, she couldn't see, and no one knew what happened. They didn't know what else to say to him.

Hui Lin kept Liang out of school the following day. It was the last day of the week anyway. She asked a friend to cover her shift at work which opened up the day for Hui Lin and her son to be together. She decided to take him to the Giant Panda Sanctuary. He always loved it there. They went often. They decided to go through one of Liang's favorite fast-food restaurants, Kentucky Fried Chicken. He loved American food. Each had a small box with their chicken wrapped in tin foil.

Hui Lin had never seen the old man since that day when she was pregnant. She had never been able to thank him for what he did for their son. The doctors had decided that the ultrasound machine had been faulty and produced erroneous results. Hui Lin knew what happened, but she didn't understand it. She had hoped to find Min again.

Liang was stretching a long bamboo pole over the fence, allowing a panda to eat the end. The panda fell backward and rolled into another panda, eating as well. None of the docile creatures seemed to mind what was happening, although all the visitors were laughing.

Hui Lin looked to her right at another enclosure and saw Min and a young girl walk out and then turn down the walkway in the other direction. Hui Lin pulled the bamboo from her son's hand, handed it to the woman next to them, and she ran to not miss Min. For a moment, she lost him in the open market behind some oversized panda stuffed animals a store had on display but then caught the sight of his long white beard again and followed. She caught him right as they were about to leave the sanctuary.

"Min. Hello," she cried, and the old man and young girl turned. "I don't know if you remember me, but.."

"Hui Lin. Of course, I remember you. How are you? And how is your husband Ju-Long?" he asked. Hui Lin was shocked he had remembered her and her husband. "Is this your son?" Min asked.

"Yes. This is Liang. If you remember, I was pregnant with Liang when we first met," she said. Liang was getting a piece of chicken out of his box and began eating it.

"Yes. That seemed like a particularly challenging day for you," he said.

Hui Lin continued, "I have often looked for you to thank you for all you did. I still wear the stone you gave my husband" Hui Lin pulled the black jet stone from under her shirt, the two engraved wings in perfect balance. "I have not had the chance to thank you for what you did for me and Liang. Thank you so very much. I don't know how you did it, but I know it was you. Look, he was born completely normal."

"Your boy is anything but normal. As I told you before, he is extraordinary, much like this young lady." He put his hand on the shoulder of the young girl. The girl was Indian with a dark complexion, broad nose, and long brown hair that went past her waist. Her eyes drooped on the outer edges. She had soft cheekbones and a reserved smile. She wore black jeans with a bright yellow top with extended sleeves and flared with overlapping sheer material at the ends. Yellow bows pinned the sleeves at the elbows. She wore bracelets on both wrists. "This is Avani," introducing her to Hui Lin and Liang.

Liang looked about the same age but was quite a bit shorter. He was wearing a dark blue hoodie with an anime character on it in a fighting stance. Liang had short black hair that needed to be combed. "Say hello, Liang," his mother said. He gave a bashful "Ni hao" to Min and Avani. On the other hand, Avani stuck her hand out to Hui Lin, and they shook hands.

"Avani doesn't know much Chinese. We have been speaking in both of our secondary languages of English," Min explained. "Avani is a relatively new student of mine."

"I didn't know you were a teacher. What do you teach?" Hui Lin asked.

"Many of the ancient arts," Min replied.

"Both today and when we first met, you mentioned that Liang was special, but you weren't referring to his condition during pregnancy. What do you mean?" she asked. This is the question she had been hoping to be able to ask him since that first day more than eight years ago.

"I don't expect you to believe me. Most people don't. Everyone is born with special abilities. Unfortunately, few people develop those abilities. Some are born with an added measure of these abilities making it easier for them to use than others. Does that make sense to you?" Min asked.

"You mean like a guzheng prodigy?" she asked, referring to the traditional Chinese string instrument that sits like a harp in front of the player.

"No, not that type of ability," Min tried to sense how Hui Lin might react to what he was about to say. "I mean abilities that can interact with or control nature or the world around us. You believe your son was healed while you were pregnant?" he asked.

"I do. Although I have no idea how you did it," she replied.

"That is the type of ability I am talking about. Do you remember the first day we met and you helped me heal one of the Pandas?" Hui Lin nodded. "I used my ability to help heal the bear just like I used my skills to heal your son. That is my ability. There are different abilities people have. Avani here, for example, has an earth-bound affinity. While we don't share the same affinity, there is much I can teach her about her skills and how to use her powers. Show them, Avani.

Avani reached over to Liang's box of chicken and took out a piece of tin foil. She held it flat in her hand. She then closed her eyes and concentrated. The tin foil began to move and bend. Edges were folding over themselves and then folding back. The back folded inwards, and then the top extended. Hui Lin and Liang couldn't believe what they were seeing. A few moments later, the tin foil hand transformed into an origami dragon. She handed the tin foil dragon to Liang with a smile.

While watching her, he forgot he was holding a chicken leg, dropping it, and taking the dragon from her. "How did you do that?" Liang asked, speaking more than a whisper for the first time.

"Master Min taught me how," she answered, looking up and getting a proud grin from the old man. "Unicorns are my favorite, but I thought you would like a dragon."

"So when you say she is special…" Hui Lin spoke slowly, trying to understand what she was about to say "…do you mean to say that my son is special in the same way?"

"Not in exactly the same way. I do believe your son is very powerful and has tremendous potential. Still, I do not believe he shares either the affinity I have or what Avani has," Master Min said.

"You think I have powers like her?" Liang asked with eyes as big as saucers.

"Different ones but yes, like that," Master Min replied.

"How do I learn?" looking at the tin foil dragon as if the most remarkable thing you could learn is how to make tin foil dragons.

"You have very different abilities, but that," Min pointed at the dragon, "is nothing compared to what you could do. Avani's powers are growing, and so could yours with proper training.

"So you have a school?" Hui Lin asked.

"Not exactly like what you are imagining. No. I last taught a very long time ago. Due to this young woman's special nature and family background, I took on part of her training. No one teacher can teach everything they need to know. Special children like these can be taught by some of the greatest masters in the world. But to do it, they must travel worldwide for several years. Avani will be with me for a time, and then she will move on to another teacher in another part of the world. Each teacher helps them reach their full potential. I am just one part of that process."

"Can I do that, Mom?" Liang asked his mom like he was asking for egg tarts.

Hui Lin, not answering her son and a bit flustered, said, "Wow. I have so many questions right now. What powers do you think my son has? Would you be willing to teach him? And if so, he wouldn't live with us any longer?"

"As I said, I have not taught in a long time and am not accustomed to taking on new students. They have to be pretty unusual circumstances. I have sensed that your boy is special, but that doesn't mean I should be the one that teaches him. I would need to test him. They are straightforward, noninvasive tests. Would you be available to come to my home tomorrow evening? I also want your husband to come, perhaps after he is done with work," Master Min asked.

Hui Lin agreed and got directions from Master Min. When Ju-Long got home that night, Hui Lin and Liang told him about the encounter with Master Min and Avani. Liang was excited to show his dad the tin foil dragon. They continued talking about it all through their dinner of Beijing roasted duck.

After Liang was down for bed, Hui Lin sat with Ju-Long for a serious discussion. "I can't imagine not having Liang with us here at home. I can't even believe I am considering this, but my mind keeps going back to these incidents that have been happening. The one just yesterday with the blinding of that girl and then the dog incident. I can't help but feel those are part of what makes Liang unique, and without the help of someone like Master Min, perhaps worse things could happen in the future. What if that girl is blind forever? What if someone gets hurt or worse?

"Can we even trust this Master Min? We barely know him. You have met him twice and me only once. Two of the three encounters with him were over eight years ago, and now we will give our son over to him? Doesn't this sound unbelievable?" Ju-Long insisted.

"I agree, but I can't shake the feeling that there may be something to this. Also, I guess it can't do any harm if he gets tested tomorrow. Let's see how that goes, and then we can decide if there is anything to this," Hui Lin suggested. Ju-Long nodded, and they went to bed.

The following evening, after looking at the directions, Hui Lin and Liang met Ju-Long at work, which was far closer to where they needed to go. It appeared that Master Min lived somewhat near the Longfeng Community, a small mountain village near the Zhaogong temple. When they arrived, they were shocked to find a large two-story traditional Chinese-style home with a curved roof. The structure was a large square with another smaller rectangle section protruding from the back and front, giving the roofline eight corners that each flared upwards to a peak. From the eves of the ornate curved tile roof hung red lanterns. Perched on the roof were eight stone dragons. The upper level was almost completely covered in windows with a gold-colored railing around the entire balcony. A large walk-around porch with ornate wood columns made them feel like they were walking into a museum more than a home. Master Min opened the door before they had the chance to knock.

"Huānyíng" he said as he welcomed them into his home. The inside was just as ornate as the exterior, with intricately carved furniture, including several small tables and benches against two walls. The ceiling was traditional exposed wood beams and a Large tile stone floor with different earth tones. The walls were antique wood covered with various carvings. Lights hung from the ceiling to look like large lanterns from which a warm glow filled the room. There was a staircase behind one wall leading to the upstairs. Off to the right was a small room with a tall bench with a cushion on it. In the center of the large middle room were several ornate rugs, each set on top of the other, about a span smaller than the one it rested on. There was a small table in the center of the carpets with tea cups set out. Avani came out from behind a wall separating another area with a teapot, and she set it on the small wood table. Master Min invited everyone to sit with him on the rugs. The Zhang family was not usually this traditional and sat on chairs and an upright table. They lived more Westernized, but Master Min came from a very ancient and authentic Chinese way of life.

Ju-Long said, "How long has this building been here? It is in perfect shape. No damage whatsoever, and no buildings survived the great earthquake ten years ago. This looks to be more than 100 years old. Is that possible?"

"This home predates me, and I have been alive a very long time," Master Min answered.

"Then how did it survive the great earthquake?" Ju-Long asked. Hui Lin did not discuss the great earthquake. Avani began to pour tea for everyone and then set the pot down in the center.

"Thankfully, I was able to protect and preserve the home through the earthquake," Min answered, picking up his teacup and taking a long sip. "We are here to talk about you, young man," Master Min directed his statement to Liang. "First, you have to understand this if you qualify. This is different from the school you have been attending. This is very different. You will learn very different things, but what you learn will be far more helpful for special people. The style and approach will also be different. I do not stand in front of you all day lecturing, and then you go home to a meal your mother has made you. No. This is an apprenticeship—the traditional way of learning. We work and live and learn together. When it is time for a meal, we all work until we eat and work until it is cleaned up. When the house needs to be cleaned, we all do it together. But sometimes, when I am entertaining guests, you may be required to serve the tea just like Avani did for you. If I must be gone for a few hours, you may be expected to do laborious tasks while I am gone." He takes another long sip of tea. "In other words, it is not as easy or as simple as life has been for you."

Liang looked a little disappointed at this but was still attentive. "But before we get too much into all that, we need to check some things," Master Min continued. "Liang, can you come here and lay on this table for me?" With a nod from his father, Liang got up, hopped up on the table, and laid down. To one side of the table was a tall chest with six drawers. He pulled open the top drawer and pulled out a small, primarily white, flat stone with black markings on it.

The stone almost appeared to have a background scenery of trees, flowers, and birds in a nearly Rorschach ink blot painting way. "What's that?" Liang asked.

"This is a scarce stone known as Dendritic Opal but comes from a single mine deep within New Mexico, in America. This particular variety is known as Merlinite. You can identify its rarity through the leafy plant and fern dendritic inclusions," Master Min said, holding the stone up for Liang and the others to see. "It is known as a shamanistic stone, and I'm hoping it will tell us a few things." Master Min proceeded to hold it over various areas of Liang's body. Master Min was concentrating. Hui Lin and Ju-Long looked at each other, wondering what they were doing there. A few moments later, Master Min returned the stone to the cabinet and opened the bottom drawer. He pulled out a black rock that looked like petrified wood. He asked Liang to hold it in his hand. While he did, Master Min held his hand over Liang's and again concentrated.

"This stone feels good," Liang said to Master Min. "What is it?"

Master Min opened his eyes and said. "You can feel it?"

"Yes," answered Liang.

"What does it feel like?" the master asked.

"It feels warm, but not just warm; it feels happy." The young man's voice sounded more confident than before.

"Liang, I want you to keep your eyes closed for a minute." Master Min went back over to the bottom drawer of the cabinet and pulled out another stone, but he did it so no one could see the stone. He walked over to Liang, and with the boy's eyes closed, he placed it in his right hand. "Now, Liang, I want you to concentrate on the stone I just placed in your hand, and I want you to tell me what color is the stone?"

"Red," he answered.

"Open your eyes, Liang," Master Min said, and he showed him the stone and then held it up for the rest of the room to see. "That is red aventurine, a type of common mica. A mineral of sorts. You can sit with your parents." Liang jumped off the table and sat next to his mother. "I believe your boy is a freq."

"What? We come all this way just for you to insult us? My son is not a freak!" Ju-Long blurted out.

"Oh, no. You misunderstand me. I forget that is a derogatory term in modern pop culture. He is a F-R-E-Q—a freq. It means he has the power of frequency. The universe has six total affinities, and your son is aligned very strongly with the frequency affinity. It means that if he trains, he can control frequencies such as light and heat. Let me explain further. Avani, could you bring those chrysanthemums, please?" Avani got up, went to the window seal, and pulled down a pot of significantly wilted chrysanthemums. "Thank you," said Master Min. "See, my affinity is that of life. He put his hand over the wilted flowers, and as they watched, they began regaining their posture. Their stems and heads became firm and full of life. A rich yellow filled the firm petals.

Turning to Hui Lin, he said, "This is how I healed that panda the day we met. This is how I healed your son of his deformity while in the womb. This is my power. My gift." Avani's gift is that of earth energy. She can control matter like the tin foil you saw yesterday." Liang remembered the tin foil dragon. "Your son's gift is that of frequency energy." Master Min walked back to the chest of drawers, pulled out a small glass ball, and returned to the table. "Avani, can you dim the lights?" Avani moved and turned down the lights very low.

"Liang, open your hand." Liang did so without looking at his father, and Master Min placed the object in his palm. "This is a clear quartz crystal. It has many general uses but works well for what I will show you. Well, what Liang is about to show us," he said. "Liang, close your eyes, and I want you to concentrate on the object. I want you to see the light shining out from it. I want you to imagine the light from this crystal filling the entire room. Concentrate until it fills the room and you with light."

Nothing happened. Liang's brow furrowed as you could see him strain and clutch the stone as hard as he could. "Not intense like that. Relax. It doesn't take physical muscles. It takes the brain and energy muscles. Relax your face and hand. Now try again. Just project your thought to the center of the crystal in your hand and imagine it lighting up the entire room." Just then, a spark flickered in the center of the crystal that grew and grew until it was the brightness of a light bulb. "Excellent, Liang. Keep concentrating but open your eyes." He did and couldn't believe what he was doing. His parent's jaws dropped as he was able to have the crystal get even brighter. "Now, I want you to imagine the light changing to another color. Tell us what color you will change it to, and then imagine that color coming from the crystal."

"Red," Liang said in a firm voice; slowly, the light began to change until it was a dark crimson red. "Blue," he said next; the crystal changed from a red to purple to a dark royal blue.

"Hand it to your father." Liang put it in his father's hand, it still glowing blue. "Now, I want you to imagine the crystal getting very hot."

Ju-Long said, "Ouch!" and dropped it, which landed in his cup of tea. He began blowing on his hand. They all looked at the crystal, and the tea started to boil within a few moments.

"Outstanding, Liang," said Master Min. Well, what do you all think?

With a myriad of expressions on his face at once, Ju-Long said. "This is quite amazing and impressive. But what good will light shows and tin foil origami do in the real world?"

"Well, for one, your son will make scalding tea," Master Min said with a smile. "I am joking. These are ancient skills, and you see the seedlings of what they can become. If he can do that on his first night, can you imagine what he may do if he continues to develop? Growing up to be an accountant or a dentist or anything is a fine pursuit. But anyone can be in those careers. Very few can make the impact that your son could. He could be one of the most powerful people that has ever lived. You are seven years old, right Liang?"

"Yes," answered Liang

"What day were you born?" he asked.

"December 21," he answered.

"What year?"

Liang looked at his mother. "2010," she said.

Avani was startled, and a smile grew on Master Min's face. "So you were born on December 21, 2010, is that right? Wasn't that the night of the full lunar eclipse?"

Hui Lin nodded. "Yes, it was. We remember it well."

"You were born on the same night as Avani here." Avani and Liang shot glances at each other. "Twins of destiny, perhaps? I don't know," Master Min said to himself. "I took Avani as a student and would be willing to take your son because there is something exceptional about children born during that eclipse. It may be due to a very old prophesy that many believe foretells of a unique child born during a winter solstice lunar eclipse. Do you know the last time there was a winter solstice lunar eclipse? Almost 400 years ago. Yes, your son is very special, just like Avani here is very special. I would be willing to help teach him about his gift, but that is your decision."

~

"CHILDREN, TODAY I WOULD LIKE TO TEACH you about polys," Asha began her session. They were on the top east floor of the Thomas Blood mansion. The mansard roof caused the ceilings in the upstairs rooms to be shorter and curved near the tops. The rooms were also narrower due to the roof framing, which left wide dormers with benches to look out the windows over the beautiful grounds in central England. The walls were plain; however, Asha had hung up many posters, maps, and other teaching tools to help the children learn. Most children that learn to become a druid do not begin training until after their Becoming Day at the age of eight. However, Thomas insisted on his children getting a head start, and so for the last two years, Asha had late morning sessions with them teaching the basics. The twins were both very bright, but their learning styles and attention spans varied widely.

As usual, Denebula was stoic and attentive as she sat with perfect posture in the chair with her dark walnut desk in front of her. She had short brown hair with bangs she combed down to her high cheekbones. She had perfect brown eyes and flawless skin. On the other hand, Kai was slumped in his chair, looking out the window, only half paying attention. His hair was about the same length and color as his twin sisters, but it was messy, being combed with his hand. He had similar high cheekbones but pale blue eyes.

Teaching the children was difficult, as it is with all kids their age. Asha could take a more traditional "lecture style" approach with Denebula. At the same time, Kai needed more hands-on learning if she wanted something to sink in. Denebula was very serious and rigid with little sense of humor. Whenever someone spoke to her, you could see her analyzing every word to determine whether she could trust them. Kai couldn't have been more opposite. He was outgoing, friendly, and smiled a lot. He didn't take things very seriously, including schoolwork.

"Kai. What is a poly?" Asha asked. "Kai?" she said louder to get his attention.

Kai pulled himself from his daydream out the window and said, "What?"

Denebula answered, "A poly is that little device my dad and other druids have that allows them to travel by way of a portal.

"That's right. Why do we call it a poly?" she asked. Denebula's facial expression showed she didn't know the answer.

"I don't know for sure, but all the ones I've ever seen are different polygon shapes. Is that why they call them polys?" Kai asked.

"That is right," Asha said. She pulled from her pocket a copper object with eight sides that looked like two pyramids connected at the bottom. Each of the eight equal sides had an open oval. A small round ball on each corner would act almost like a stand when the object was sitting on a flat surface. This device had light green energy filling 5 of the eight openings. "This is my poly. It is called an Octahedron because it has eight sides. Who can tell me how many different types of polys there are?"

Kai answered, "I'm guessing six," he said confidently.

"That's right," Asha said. "Why?"

"I think there is a different one for each affinity. Plus, that is how many different types of dice are in my online Dungeons and Dragons game. They totally look like gaming dice," he said.

The light went on in Denebula's eyes, and she said, "That makes sense; each different type of druid has a different type of poly."

"Excellent children. As a review, what are the six types of affinities?" Asha walked to a dry-erase board and picked up a blue marker.

"I'm a liq," Kai said with pride.

"Liquid. Yes. What else?" Asha continued

"Earth, Life, Frequency, Atmosphere, and Cosmos. The last one is mine," Denebula added.

"Again, very good. So, if I am a life druid with an Octahedron for my poly, what type of poly will each of you one day have?" Asha asked, wondering if they had any idea. After a moment, Denebula said, "I have the same affinity as my father, so I think I'll have the same type of poly as he does. I'm trying to remember how many sides his has." She sat there for a minute, searching her memory. "I know it is more than yours. 10 or 12 sides, I would guess?"

"Cosmic druids use a 12-sided polygon called a Dodecahedron. You are right. That is what your father has. Kai, what type of polygon will you have one day?"

"I don't know," Kai shrugged.

"A liquid druid gets a 6-sided poly," Asha explained

"Ah, bummer," Kai exclaimed, throwing his head and arms back. "That is the most boring type of dice."

Asha went to the board and put the number 6 next to liquid, the number 12 next to Cosmos, and the number 8 next to Life. "Children," she continued, "Let's fill in the rest of the chart here. What polygon shapes do the remaining three affinities use?"

Kai sat straight up, this being the type of puzzle he liked to solve. "Okay, we are missing a 4-sided, a 10-sided, and a 20-sided," he said out loud. "Nephrite wears hers as part of her jewelry, and hers looked like a 20-sided dice. What type of druid is she?" he asked.

Denebula said, "Earth."

"That is right," Asha said as she wrote a 20 next to Earth on the board. "That only leaves 2."

"Atmosphere is 10," Kai guessed, knowing he had a 50/50 shot.

"No. Frequency druids use the 10-sided poly," Asha said.

"I should have known that," said Denebula. "Grandpa was a freq, and Dad has Grandpa's poly on a stand in his office."

"And that leaves a four-sided poly which is for atmospheric druids." Asha finished wring them on the board. Now, let's go over their names. I will test you on this at the end of the week, so when we are done, I expect you to write this chart down in your notebooks. This is very important," Asha said as she began writing the formal names down next to the affinity and number of sides the poly has.

Liquid – 6 - Hexahedron

Earth – 20 - Icosahedron

Life – 8 - Octahedron

Frequency – 10 - Decahedron

Atmosphere – 4 - Tetrahedron

Cosmic – 12 - Dodecahedron

"Now, do you both see how my poly has several ovals filled in with green energy?" Asha continued. "Will each of your polys have the same green color?"

"No," Denebula answered. "Dad's is purple. So the 12-sided dodecahedron will be purple. That is what I am going to have. It's my favorite color!"

Asha wrote green next to the octahedron and purple next to the dodecahedron. "Kai, what color will your Hexahedron be?"

"Blue. Because I'm a liq, and it is also my favorite color," he said with a touché to his sister.

"That is right," Asha wrote blue next to the Hexahedron. "What about the others?" The children didn't know. "Atmospheric with the 12-sided poly lights up orange," she wrote these on the board as she spoke. "The 20-sided earth poly lights up yellow. And the frequency 10-sided poly lights up red". These colors are meaningful to each affinity for artifacts, stones, and relics."

"Now, why does my poly have only 5 of the eight ovals filled in with green energy?" Asha asked.

"Because you have used 3 of the eight charges," Kai said

"That is right. Well done, Kai. You are doing well today," Asha said with a certain surprise.

"Thanks for teaching an interesting lesson," Kai said. "Dungeons and Dragons is cool!"

Asha shook her head a little, realizing she would need to pull this away from online gaming. "Kai is right. This is how you know how many times you can use your poly before it will no longer work."

"Can you recharge your poly?" Denebula asked.

"Great question. Yes, you can. Each affinity has a unique way of charging the poly based on their magical affinity. As a liq, Kai, you will charge your poly very differently than Denebula will. I will not get into all that today because we will need to do a whole lesson on that another time. But for example, when I charge my octahedron, I have to find something with a life force. A person, an old tree, or an animal, for example. Something living. I place my octahedron there overnight, and it gains one charge. As you can imagine from the configuration, mine only has a maximum of 8 charges," Asha explained.

"I have a question," Denebula raised her hand. "My dad took us to the United States once using his" she paused, thinking of the word "dodecahedron. Did that just take one charge, or does it take more if more people travel through the portal?"

"I was wondering that same thing, D," Kai said.

"You are asking excellent questions today, children," Asha confirmed. "It takes one charge for each person who uses the portal. So if your father, brother, and you go through a portal to America and then return the next day, you would have used six total charges: three to get there and three to return. As you can imagine, you want to keep your poly as fully charged as possible. You never know when you might need it."

"When do I get my Hexahedron?" Kai asked.

"You must be trained by six master druids, each teaching a different affinity. This will happen over the next several years. I am one of those masters, and I'll focus on the magic surrounding life affinity. When you have completed my training, you will be trained by another master, one by one, until complete. Each master will give you a magical token that signifies you have completed that course. Once you have all six tokens, you can present them to a Gabha, a druidic blacksmith. He takes your tokens, verifies they are authentic, and then forges your poly. Once you have it, you go through a ritual that will make it soul bound to you. That way, no one else, even with your same affinity, can use your poly unless they go through a portal with you," Asha said, trying to reinforce this lesson.

"So once we get our polys, we can go anywhere?" Kai asked.

"Well, not exactly. We can get into the details another time because I don't want to oversaturate you with too much information today. However, just like each poly has different charging requirements and charges, they also have travel limitations. For example, Kai, your 6-sided Hexahedron can only be used when you are at a waterway, and you can only go to a connected waterway. So if you are by an ocean, you can go to many places but not an inland desert. But if you use it at an isolated lake, you could only go to another part of the lake," Asha continued with her lesson. "Denebula, your 12-sided dodecahedron will allow you to portal anywhere you have been before. So wherever your father took you in the States, you could portal there using your poly, but if you have never been to Africa, your poly can not take you there."

"Well, if I can't get anywhere, how will I increase the places I have been?" Denebula asked.

"Two ways. One is the old fashion way. You take traditional travel methods such as planes and cars and so forth. Once you have been someplace, you can always travel back using your poly. The other way is to team up with someone like your brother. This is very effective for druids to work together because you could travel with your brother on any waterway to a place you have never been. Then you could use your poly for the both of you to return," Asha's explanation seemed to satisfy Denebula. Kai began staring out the window again. She knew she had saturated them for the day.

"I expect you to copy this chart from the board for the rest of class. Be sure it includes the affinity, the number of sides to the poly, the name of the poly, and the color. At the end of the week, I'll give you a test where you must fill all that into a chart from memory. You can go for the day once you are done copying it down," Asha finished her speaking as the children furiously wrote in their notebooks.

~

October 2018

IMPERIAL PEARL, INC. was starting the 10 am tour of their facility right on time. The company based in Rhode Island offered two tour times each day to see a wide range of pearls from across the globe. The tour group was small, nine people, including a family of 4 from Indiana that all had matching red Indianapolis 500 T-shirts, an elderly couple from Wisconsin that had parked a pin-striped Winnebago across three parking spots, a businessman traveling from Florida, and what appeared to be a father, daughter pair. Their similar height and complexion made them look related. Still, their age difference caused people to assume that the girl in her 30s was the daughter of the much older man. Their dress couldn't have been more different. He wore a thick black coat and hat, while she wore her usual all-white leather pants and jacket. It was Alexander and Bryne sent here by Thomas Blood.

The woman offering the tour did her best to be excited and energetic. Still, she had bags under her eyes, and the way she walked, it was evident that her newborn was not allowing her much sleep. With both hands holding the 24oz black coffee, she began. "Ladies and Gentlemen, I welcome you to Imperial Pearl, the world's leading pearl distributor. We ask that no photography of any kind be used while in the showroom. Thank you. Pearls have been a source of fascination for thousands of years. They are considered to be the most magical and feminine of all gems. Pearls are the only gems that are created by a living organism. As a result, they have a warmth and glow not found in any other stones. Pearls have been prized for their beauty and rarity for over four thousand years, from ancient China, Egypt, and India to Imperial Rome and the Arab world and even right here with Native American tribes. Cultures worldwide and throughout recorded history have valued these rare biologically based gemstones longer than any other. You are standing in our pearl gallery. If you will follow me over here to our first display case," she said as she walked backward, beckoning everyone with one hand while the other held tight to her coffee.

Just above the case on the wall hung a 55" screen. The caffeine-injected tour guide pulled a remote control from behind the counter and pressed play which began a video describing how pearls are formed. "The pearl is the only gemstone grown inside a living organism. Pearls are formed within oysters or mollusks when a foreign substance (most often a parasite and not a grain of sand as most people believe) invades the mollusk's shell, entering the soft mantle tissue and picking up epithelial cells." A woman with a British-Asian accent narrated the video as images of oysters flashed on the screen, which turned into an animation of the process of pearl formation. "In response to the irritation, the epithelial cells form into a sac which secretes a crystalline substance called nacre. Nacre is the same substance that makes up the interior of the oyster's shell and builds up in layers around the irritant, forming the pearl."

The video described how rare pearls are when formed from a completely natural state, how only a tiny fraction of oysters ever produce a pearl, and how even fewer ever create one of a size, shape, and color that would ever be desirable. The video then went on to describe how in the late 19th and early 20th centuries, Japanese researchers discovered a method to artificially stimulate the development of round pearls by inserting a foreign substance into the tissue of the oyster or mollusk and then returning the creature to the sea and allowing the resulting cultured pearl to develop naturally. This process was patented in 1916 and was used to create Akoya pearls. The video said that since then, the process has been improved and extensively used throughout the pearl industry, not just for Akoya pearls but also freshwater, South Sea, and Tahitian pearls. The video display showed pearl farms and the process of creating these various pearls.

The video narration changed to a distinguished man's voice who began describing the pearl grading process. He described the pearl luster with the screen showing four variants of luster of pearls from very shiny to dull. He went into the various pearl colors, each displaying on the screen beginning with silver, silver pink, white, white pink, golden white gold, and finally Tahitian. Pearl shapes were next described as round, drop, button circle, semi-baroque, and baroque, near round and oval, each displayed with a close-up on the monitor. This was followed by size and surface quality, indicating that pearls are available to those of any size budget. The narrator mentioned how pearls were the perfect gift for that special someone in your life, how pearls are the birthstone of June and the appropriate gift for the 3rd and 30th wedding anniversaries and symbolize a happy marriage. The elderly woman looked expectantly at her husband. Clearly, he had missed the proper 30th wedding anniversary gift by a decade or two. The video ended with an oyster shell open with a perfect pearl on display. The video screen faded to black.

The tour guide who had moved behind everyone had sat down, laid her head in her arms, and was now back up and moving. "In the case in front of there, you will see a selection of Akoya Pearls. These are considered the classic among cultured pearls. They are primarily round or oval in shape and most commonly measure 5 to 8mm. They are cultured in many parts of the world, but most commonly in southwestern Japan and China. Their colors range from pinkish white to creamy shades of silvery blue. Our Akoya pearls extend on the first 6 cases on this side of the showroom." She moved to the other side of the showroom and gave everyone a few moments to look in on the Akoya pearls before starting up again. "The pearls on this row of display cases have our Chinese freshwater pearls. These pearls are grown in an amazing variety of delicate shapes, ranging from round and oval to button, drop, and baroque. Their colors vary from pure white to orange and rosy violate." She again moved out of the way as the couple from Wisconsin moved in excitedly.

She moved further down the showroom to a set of display cases. "This is our collection of Tahitian pearls. These gems are synonymous with magic and perfection. Most come from the atolls and lagoons of the South Pacific. They tend more toward drop shapes than round and vary in size from 9 to 14mm, and some can occasionally reach 16 or even 18mm. They can be black, silver, dark, or light gray. The rarest color is "peacock green," the greenish-black color of a peacock feather."

"This final set of display cases behind me exhibits our South Sea pearls. These are unquestionably the rarest and finest cultured pearls in the world. No other pearl can equal its natural beauty and size. South Sea pearls range from 9mm to 20mm and come in various shapes and colors. The Australian are especially prized and generally more valuable among all the South Sea pearls."

The tour guide then walked into what looked like a small antechamber off the main showroom, where a single podium stood in the center. Four lights from the ceiling are shown down on the case. The walls were adorned with pictures and a story of the pearl in the central case atop the podium. An engraved plaque above the display case said, "The Imperial Hong Kong Pearl."

"Imagine the rarity of what you are seeing," the tour guide said as everyone crowded around the display case. "Long before cultured pearls were available, natural pearls were so rare and unique that they were often reserved only for royalty. This baroque pearl, nearly the size of a bird's egg at 26 by 39mm, is among the world's largest and most rare pearls. It is called The Imperial Hong Kong Pearl. During the Renaissance Period of the late 16th and 17th centuries, jewelers valued baroque pearls because of their unique shapes and colors. While the date of discovery is unknown, it is believed to have originated in a saltwater oyster, Pinctada Maxima, commonly found between Southern China and Northern Australia. This pearl is one of the world's largest natural pearls and is famous for its fantastic luster and deep coloration. As a result, this pearl was originally called the 'Miracle of the Sea.' As you can see, the pearl is a beautiful silvery-white color, baroque with an irregular drop shape. It has an astounding weight of 127.5 carats which is 25 and one-half grams. With an average pearl of about 7mm, The 'Miracle of the Sea' is about 18 times larger. The pearl is set in a platinum and diamond pendant designed as a foliage leaf intended to express jewelry's designs during the Renaissance Period."

The tour guide took a long sip from her cup and then continued. "This pearl was once owned by Chinese Empress Dowager Tz'U-Hi, who ruled China from 1861 to 1908. Her prized jewel was among her vast treasure of diamonds, emeralds, sapphires, rubies, and more. She wore it around her neck most days from 1875 until her death. She believed it would grant her good fortune and extended life."

Several on the tour pushed in to see the famed pearl.

The Indy 500 family walked away bored very quickly, but the old couple drew in closer to study the pearl for a very long moment.

"After she died in 1908, her tomb was filled with pearls and gems from her vast fortune. This pearl was placed in her mouth, which the Chinese believed would preserve her body. Twenty years later, in 1928, the tomb was raided, and all the gems, including the Miracle of the Sea, were taken. The pearl resurfaced in the British colony of Hong Kong in the 1940s and was purchased by our company. That is when it took on its current name, 'The Imperial Hong Kong Pearl.' While we have gone through several mergers and acquisitions ever since, we have had it in our possession." The tour guide looked around, almost not realizing she had finished her script.

Just before the tour guide asked if there were any questions, Bryne said. "Isn't there more to the story than that? All the tombs of the Chin dynasty were looted in 1928 by General Sun Dianying after decades of revolution. After ripping the pearl from her mouth, they violated the empress's well-preserved body. It was then taken to Hong Kong and sold to your company. Correct?"

The tour guide began to be uncomfortable but said, "I believe that is correct."

"So let me ask you a question," the Scandinavian woman said a bit louder now. "Wouldn't this qualify as a Chinese national treasure that was stolen?"

"I assure you that our company acquired it through completely legal means," said the tour guide.

"So, if some Americans broke into the national archives and stole the Declaration of Independence and then sold it to a Chinese company, that is a legal sale?" The woman in white said as she took something out of her pocket and placed her other hand on the top of the display case.

"I'm sorry, miss. We ask visitors not to touch the display case," the tour guide said while pointing to the plaque that said, "Please do not touch the display case."

What happened next was recorded in detail on the official East Providence police report, which listed the date, time, and location at the top of the page with a large "Crime Information Bulletin" centered at the top of the page. The description section of the report read as follows:

At or around 10:20 am at the Imperial Pearl headquarter (an importer of pearls from around the world), the suspect stole their most prized and oldest pearl at the conclusion of a guided tour which included the display of the stolen pearl. No other items from the vast collection of pearls or other valuables are reported missing. Near the end of the tour, which was about 10:20 am, everyone in the showroom heard a loud 'pop,' as all the lights went out, followed by a shattering sound. Upon investigation, an electronic surge blew all the lightbulbs in the building. While many windows should have provided adequate light to the room, those interviewed said that they couldn't see anything and that it was pitch dark. Light did eventually fill the area a few minutes later, everyone could see that the display case holding the pearl was broken and the pearl gone.

While security footage should have been available, at 9:45 am, the CCTV system became inoperable in what appears to be a coordinated system attack allowing the perpetrators to enter the building and join the standard 10 a.m. tour. The external and internal surveillance cameras recorded a bright light as if a flashlight was shown into the camera until the building lost power at 10:20 with the surge that blew the lights. No weapons were seen by any witnesses, and it is unknown how they broke through the ½" Plexiglas security case or removed the pearl without the security system being tripped. Early investigation indicates heavy equipment would have been needed, although no one saw either suspect with anything on their person.

The suspects are described as a tall male, white, almost 65 years old, 6'1", 195lbs, wearing a black coat and hat, and a tall female, white, early to mid-30s, 6' tall, 145lbs, short white hair with brown eyes wearing all white. With CCTV down and tourists not allowed to use photography in the showroom, there are no photos of the suspects. No one saw which direction they went.

The victim describes the pearl as a one-of-a-kind relic that dates back centuries, with the latest value by appraisers set at over 4 million dollars.

Chapter 7

December 21, 2018

I T WAS AN EXCITING DAY. It wasn't often that the kids at the congregate care center got to go on field trips and to top it off, it was Aura's 8th birthday. It was a Friday, and she had been looking forward to this day since they announced it a month ago. At 10:00 a.m, they boarded a yellow school bus loaned from the local school district for the day. They were going to Kartchner Caverns, about an hour's drive southeast of Tucson. Aura had never been inside a cave before, and it sounded exhilarating. Getting to leave the congregate care center for any reason was exciting. They were even going to be able to stop at an authentic Mexican restaurant on the way for lunch. The ride was fun; although Aura couldn't sit next to the window since she was quite a bit taller than the boy next to her, it wasn't difficult to see the orange desert landscape with cacti everywhere as it rolled by.

They stopped in a small town named Benson which was only about 7 minutes from the 90 turnoff, which led to the caves. They pulled into a dirt parking lot, and all the kids exited the bus. There was a small yellow building with a white door and a sign above it that said "Su Casa Restaurant." Next to the white door was a lit-up "OPEN" sign. Behind the building was a connected structure that appeared like a home, likely for the family that owned and ran the restaurant.

As they walked in, they saw only about eight tables, so half the kids would need to eat outside on some folding tables and chairs that had been set up. Aura overheard two of the employees of the congregate care center talking about how the facility manager was friends with the restaurant owner. Aura was one part of the group set down inside the small restaurant. The walls were the same mustard yellow as the exterior of the building. Each table had orange tablecloths and matching orange napkins. Covering the walls were multi-colored sombreros, and even the lights were converted into sombreros hanging above each table.

The lunch was designed to let the kids pick hard or soft shell tacos. They brought out the food platters and set them down in the middle of each table. As soon as the food was on the table, many little hands grabbed the tacos and put them on their plates. Aura was seated at the furthest back corner table, so their tacos were brought out last. Aura pulled a breath from her inhaler that she carried with her as a woman that looked considerably older than what had to be her actual age came towards the table with a large platter of tacos. The woman had bright eyes and a kind smile. As she was about to place the tacos on the table, she saw Aura. She gasped, and the platter of tacos fell to the floor, the plastic platter bouncing and then coming to rest against Aura's chair leg. "Eres tu!" she said, putting her hands to her mouth. While walking away with no thought of the tacos strewn over the floor while looking and gesturing to Aura, she gasped, "Espera aquí, espera aquí" as she walked into the back.

Everyone inside was confused. A restaurant server and an adult from the care center began picking up the tacos from the floor. Another platter of tacos soon replaced the fallen ones, and the kids started eating. Then both adults went to the back to get some cleaning supplies. The woman that dropped the tacos came back with a bag. She knelt in front of Aura and began to talk. She put a bag on Aura's lap. Aura didn't understand Spanish, but a boy named Diego, who was sitting at the table, began translating. Diego said, "My name is Isabella. What is your name?" she asked.

"Aura," she answered.

"I knew it! I knew your mother for a very brief time. I recognize you from your amber eyes, and your mother wrote your name on you before she passed. Such beautiful eyes you both have. You look just like her. She was a kind and caring woman. It was a terrible tragedy what happened to her. These are yours," the woman said, pushing the bag further into Aura's lap. "They were your mothers. I have been hoping since that dreadful night that I would someday be able to return them to you. I never knew if you lived or where they had taken you." The woman had tears pouring down her face. Then something came into her mind. Diego translated again, "Oh my. It is your birthday today. I didn't realize until now that it was eight years since your mother passed—8 years since I have seen you. I am so sorry for your loss. Please. These are yours. I have been saving them for you." With that, the woman stood back up, wiped the tears away from her eyes, bent over, kissed Aura on the forehead, and returned to the kitchen.

Aura and everyone else didn't know what to think. The rest of the lost tacos were cleaned up a few minutes later, and everyone finished their Mexican food except Aura, who was in shock. "That woman knew my mother," she thought. Aura wanted to go in the back and find the woman, but she was gathered up with the rest of the children and forced back on the bus. She told the congregate care worker that she needed to return and speak to the woman, but they said they couldn't allow her to do that. Aura, disappointed, took her seat on the bus with a small grey duffel bag on her lap. They were entering the Kartchner Caverns National Park parking area a few minutes later. The kids filed off the bus. Aura took the grey duffel bag with her. She didn't want anything to happen to what she had been given.

The children were in line, and they followed the care center worker across the parking lot, passing several outdoor booths with Native American Indians selling trinkets, jewelry, and stones. They walked through the small building where the care worker presented their tickets. They then walked out a back door to a platform with a green metal ladder going down to the cave entrance. An Arizona State Park Ranger walked to the front of the line of children while another stood at the back. The ranger at the front, a medium build man with a goatee, thick wire frame glasses, and a cowboy hat, began talking about the discovery of the cave by two college students who desperately wanted to preserve the cave. He discussed this history, including the purchase of the land by the state of Arizona and its eventual opening for cave tours. With that, they walked through an opening. The floor changed to a paved walkway that led to a hallway that ended at what looked like a giant freezer door. The ranger turned again and said, "As you all know, we live in a desert. It is dry. It was about 38% humidity when you got off the bus. That means how much water is in the air. A lot of people think this door looks like a freezer. No, we don't have any ice cream for you behind this. The ranger laughed, but no one else did. This door is here to protect the humidity level inside the cave. You will feel a big difference between the humidity level here and once in the cave. Does anyone want to guess the humidity level in the cave?"

The ranger looked around, but no one raised their hand. "It is 100% humidity, which means it is very moist. You will see lots of water, and everything will glisten. As we go in, be sure to use handrails in slippery areas. Also, this is very important. Do not touch any of the formations. This cave has been deemed one of the most mineralogically important caves in the world. What you see in there has been forming for hundreds of thousands of years. Let's not end its growth and progress today, okay boys and girls?" The children nodded.

The ranger opened the big stainless steel door, the children walked through, and the ranger closed the door behind them. Aura couldn't believe what she saw. There were stalagmites and stalactites everywhere. There were columns where the two had met and grown together. She could watch water drip from the formations on the ceiling to the ones on the ground. The guide described microscopic minerals in each drop that would be deposited onto each design, one after another. This would go on every minute, every day, every year for thousands of years to form the beauty they were seeing.

They entered one cavern, and the guide asked the children to describe what they thought the cave was made of. "Carmel Icecream," said Diego, the same boy that helped Aura at the restaurant said.

"That is probably the most common answer we get in here," said the ranger. He went on to describe the types of mineral deposits they were. They went into another chamber that looked like it had spaghetti hanging from the ceiling. "This is helictite. Over here," he pointed at another formation using his flashlight, "is what are called soda straws." Aura thought they did look like soda straws being perfect tubes hanging from the rocks and walls. The ranger described how these were very delicate and hollow inside. The water would go down the middle of them and deposit new minerals on the ends of the straw, making it longer and longer over time.

The tour continued, and they went into another chamber and then another, each connected by hallways that were as beautiful as the rooms themselves. They then entered the most prominent chamber. There were cement benches that the kids were encouraged to sit on. Aura was at the end of the bench, and she put the bag on her lap. The ranger again used his flashlight to point out various limestone formations. He showed one large section taking up the entire corner of the room, which looked like vast strips of folded bacon glistening and sparkling like it was being cooked.

"Now, who here would like to see how dark it is in a cave?" said the ranger.

The kids responded with nods and "Yeah!" Aura never liked the dark. She started to get nervous. She unzipped the bag and let her hands move through it to take her mind off what they were doing. Mostly she felt clothes, but at the bottom of the bag was a cardboard tube with a lid. She pulled it out, and it looked like one of those things that hold blueprints but much shorter. She was curious about what was in it. She removed the top and let the contents slide onto her clothes. It was bizarre. It was like a long, thick, snarled glass tube, but it wasn't entirely hollow, as something blocked the middle. The glass wasn't clear but rather dark and rough, with bits of sand stuck in and around it.

"Okay. No screaming when the lights go out. Stay calm and quiet. Promise?" he asked. The kids nodded, the other ranger flipped a series of switches, and the cave went completely dark. The children waved their hands before their faces and couldn't see anything. Aura began to get a little scared. "Neat, right?" said the ranger. "Okay, we will turn them back on now." With that, they heard clicks where the other ranger was, but no lights came back on. The clicks went back and forth but no light.

"They aren't coming back on," said the other ranger.

Murmuring and sobbing began to come from some of the children. Out of fear, Aura grabbed whatever was in front of her for comfort, which was the sandy glass straw. When she touched it, a soft glow emerged from the cave walls. The light was different from the lights that were on before. The light spread across the walls and ceiling until the entire room was full of light. The care workers and children were amazed at the light show displayed as part of the tour. The tour guides looked in wonder and amazement, having never seen anything like it. The room began to shimmer, and the light moved across the walls and ceiling like slow rolling waves across the surface of the bacon and down the stalactites and up through the stalagmites. It flowed down the soda straws with a bright sparkle of light as it reached the end. After several minutes of the light show, a pulse of energy radiated out that was more felt than seen. Then the regular lights returned, and the soft flowing lights dissipated into the limestone. The ranger working the switches looked up at the other guide, who looked stunned. The tour group cheered and clapped. Not knowing what to say, the front guide cleared his throat, "Well, we hope you enjoyed that. We are wondering if they just installed a new light system and forgot to tell us about it. That was new to us as well."

Not knowing what to think, Aura dropped the glass tube into her bag and zipped it up. "That is the end of the tour," the first guide said.

"Children, can you say thank you for the tour today?" said one of the care workers.

"Thank you," the children said in near-unison. The guide led the group up another green metal ladder and back to the parking area. All the kids and adults talked about how amazing the light show was in the cave. The two guides were at the desk with two other park rangers. Aura couldn't hear what they were saying, but both used their hands to describe what had happened. The other two were shaking their heads and not believing them.

As the children returned to the bus, Aura passed one of the roadside tents where Native American jewelry was being sold. The old woman behind the table had been watching Aura from the moment she left the ranger station. Aura saw this, just smiled, and did a small wave as she passed.

"Come here, child," the old woman said. Her deep wrinkles and a sunken mouth made Aura a little uncomfortable. "It is okay. I have something for you."

Aura approached the table, looking at the care worker loading the kids on the bus. Aura wanted to make sure she could call her if she needed help. "You are a very special child," the Indian woman said. "I noticed you when you got off the bus a little while ago. Did something happen in the cave? I felt something happen when you were in the cave."

"What do you mean?" Aura said

"Did the energy manifest itself? It only does that for extraordinary people. Did the cave light up? Did you see the sign?" These were mostly rhetorical questions, as the old woman seemed convinced of what she was saying. She reached to her left into a box on the ground next to her chair. She pulled out what looked like a white seed of some kind. The rosette formation looked like white pine needles wrapped around a large marble, giving it the look of rose petals. "This is called a desert rose, my dear. It is made from selenite. Some people call it a gypsum rose, or a sand rose. It is said that warriors who passed away during battle would return from the spirit world and place these to protect themselves and their loved ones. They are meant to guide you. I want you to take this." The old woman placed the desert rose in Aura's hand. "This will lead someone to you. Trust this person. They will help guide you. You are exceptional. Always remember that."

"Aura!" called the care worker from the bus door. She was the only student not in the vehicle.

"Thank You," Aura said, and she ran and got on the bus.

~

WHEN HE FELT IT, Edward was lying on his side, head inside the stone grate. "The emerald!" He could feel that his flesh and blood had touched it. His child! He didn't understand.

A few minutes later, he heard them coming down the stairs, through the stone hallway, and unlock and open the heavy metal door. "You almost had me convinced, Edward. You almost convinced me that you didn't know where it was," Thomas Blood said as Syrpens and Alexander came walking in behind him. "Syrpens felt it. We have a good idea where it came from. Does Arizona sound familiar? Is that why you were there when we captured you? And on winter solstice too. This is your last chance. Tell us where the emerald is, and we will spare whoever has it. If we find it without you, I will make it extremely unpleasant for the one who has it."

"How did you do it?" Edward said in slow, labored words. "How did you know I was in Arizona when you captured me? I have gone over it again and again in my mind. I had used my poly. You couldn't have followed me or known where I was going. I had gone through several portals before that. How did you know I was there?"

Thomas pointed at the picture of Rosa on the wall. "After your tour in Uxmal, we investigated and learned about your romance with her. To make a long story short, that hotel manager was allowed to keep his family alive if he gave you this picture. I had Nephrite cast a tracking spell on it. Brass frame," he said, tapping on it.

"She died that day. There is nothing more you can take away from me," Edward lied.

"Yes, we heard about your girlfriend. Tragic," Thomas replied, "But whoever you sent the emerald to will end up far worse than she," again pointing at Rosa. Edward turned back towards the grate and showed no interest but was very worried. For the first time in a very long time, he knew he needed to escape. A feeling that had long been dormant due to time and oxygen deprivation. He needed to find his daughter. He needed to protect her. He had assumed all this time that she either hadn't survived or the emerald was lost, keeping everyone safe. With the emerald being united with his baby girl, she was in danger, and he needed to protect her.

Edward heard the door to the dungeon slam closed and the lock click. He didn't have any artifacts or relics, and they had stripped the room of anything that could be used. Then for added measure, the oxygen reduction was to keep him from being able to get fully creative. Being creative is what being a druid is all about. Then he remembered what Thomas had just said about the picture of Rosa in the brass frame, and he got an idea. "This is going to be painful," Edward said to himself.

They didn't want to leave anything in the cell that could be used by a druid to enable magic use. Good druids can be very resourceful. His food tray was plastic, as was his plastic utensils and cups. Such things can hold little energy; in fact, they often absorb and dissolve magic. The more manufactured or artificial something is, the less magic it can hold. The only thing in the cell that wasn't stone or plastic was the chain inside the toilet that pulled up the plunger. Edward was grateful he had a toilet rather than a box with a hole, as would have been the case when the castle was initially built. Each time he went to the bathroom, he would begin to get dizzy within a few seconds gasping for air. When he heard that Thomas and his cronies had climbed the stairs, he moved quickly over to the toilet, opened up the back, and pulled out the chain. He moved back over to his spot where he could get full oxygen. He knew the quality of the metal would not be able to hold any significant magic. Edward wasn't sure if this was going to work. He reached into his mouth and wrapped the chain around the gold tooth in the back of his mouth. It was just a crown, so he hoped to pull it off the stem with the proper pressure. This idea came to him just a week ago when he felt it slightly loose, but he put it aside in complete despair. But now, he knew it was his only shot.

In his mind, he counted backward from five. At one, he pulled as hard as he could. To his surprise, the gold crown did fly off the stem, ricocheted off another tooth, flew out of his mount, and bounced along the floor and outside the iron bars against the far wall out of reach. Additionally, the metal chain had bent two links. One caught Edward's cheek while the other scraped along his gums while he pulled the gold tooth. Significant drops of blood began flowing from Edward's mouth.

He went over to the toilet paper, rolled up a big wad, and put it in his mouth. He approached the bars and stared at the gold tooth three feet out of reach. The toilet paper in his mouth became saturated quickly. He pulled it out and threw it in the toilet. When he got the idea, he wadded up another bunch and stuck it in his mouth. He pulled most of the rest of the paper off the roll. He laid out 4' lengths and then folded it over on itself, making a large loop. He took the loop and returned to the grate for a few minutes, getting more oxygen. He then got up and took the toilet paper loop, and swung his arm out with the loop, trying to catch it on the tooth. It took several tries, but he finally landed on the tooth and tried to pull it to him. The toilet paper was too light, so he took the bloody wad out of his mouth and put it in one end of the loop. He threw it again and landed just over the tooth, and with it, he could pull the tooth back through the bars leaving a small streak of blood on the stone floor.

He put another wad in his mouth, returned to the grate, and looked carefully at the tooth. This was his way out, but he needed to activate and charge it. He could assume that Thomas had bought this place on a ley line, so he could count on that. Thomas had said that today was the winter solstice. Edward realized it was eight years since his beloved Rosa was gone and the day he almost got to see his daughter, whom he now knew was still alive. And she had somehow gotten the emerald.

Gold needs to be buried. It should be buried in the darkest spot on the year's darkest day on a ley line. Edward had seen several floor stones where the grout had pulled away. He went to one of the chairs and took it to the rock that looked the most loose. He took one of the legs and scraped it at the edges of the stone. "This could work, but I need leverage," he thought. He lifted the chair and smashed one of the legs against the floor, and the leg broke off. The broken end came to a point. He jammed the pointed end into the side of the stone and tried to get under it. After a few attempts, he caught the edge and pried the stone up. He went back over to the grate and took several deep breaths. He went back, took the same chair leg, and dug into the dirt until he had a hole and a channel to the edge to pry it quickly again. He placed the tooth in the spot and covered it with the stone. "This has to work," he told himself.

~

AFTER AURA HAD RETURNED to the center and eaten dinner, orange chicken with rice, which was one of her favorites, she raced back to her room and pulled the bag out from under her bed. Everyone else was still eating, so she had the space to herself. She had been waiting all day to look at what was inside. This had already easily been the best birthday and day of her life. In some strange way, she felt like she got a birthday present from her mother.

After using her breather and setting it aside, Aura unzipped the bag and began to look at what was inside. She first removed the strange dirty glass pipe she had touched in the cave earlier that day. It was ugly, to be sure, but at the same time, it felt significant in some way. She tried to look through it, but it didn't go through. She saw something else and pulled at it with her finger. She pulled out a ripped piece of paper which said:

12848 CA-254, #12 Myers Flat, CA 95554

She set the glass tube on the bed and dug into the bag again. She pulled out the desert rose stone the American Indian woman had given her. She set that next to the tube. She then pulled out the clothing items one by one. As she pulled out a pair of pants, a passport fell out. She opened it and saw for the first time in her life a picture of her mother. The woman was right; she looked very much like her. She had the same amber eyes, which she had been told times were very rare. She had a passport. She wasn't illegal like she had been told. Although she flipped through the other pages, nothing was on them. After staring at her mother's picture for several more minutes, she placed the passport next to the other items.

She continued to pull out the rest of the clothes. On the bottom, Aura found an envelope with money. It was Mexican money, and she didn't know how much it was. She stood up and held up each item of clothing to her imagining her mother in them. Then she carefully folded each one and placed it back in the bag. She put the money in the bottom of the bag. She then took the cardboard tube and set the glass pipe back in. There was just enough room to put the desert rose and her other stone in the lid and could still close it. Then she put that in the bag and hid it under her bed.

~

FOR MONTHS, Hui Lin and Ju-Long debated whether to send their son to train with Master Min or leave him in regular school. On the one hand, Master Min seemed to have performed a miracle for Liang, and their son had shown some unusual talents when they were at Master Min's home.

On the other hand, it seemed like they were sending their son off to some crackpot old man they barely knew.

But Liang had been having issues at school, and they feared something could happen again. Thankfully, the girl causing Liang problems left the hospital after a few days. Her blindness was temporary, but what if something happened to someone else and wasn't temporary? Someone could really get hurt. That someone could be Liang himself. If he did have special powers, as Master Min said, maybe he did need to learn to control them.

But what pushed them to allow him to be trained with Master Min finally was that Liang wanted to do it. When he was being tested, he could feel the power, and he wanted to learn how to control it better and use it to help people. It would have crushed him to tell him no, so they agreed to one year of training to see how it would go, and then they would reassess. Master Min also agreed to allow Liang's parents to see him occasionally. This was, of course, encouraged. They could visit Liang anytime they wished. So on Liang's birthday, they went back to Master Min's home. As they dropped Liang off with two suitcases full of clothes and everything else he would need. His mother unhooked the necklace from around her neck, holding the jet stone that had changed the course of Liang's life. She placed it around his neck and said, "You wear this now. It will bring you luck and power." After a short visit, Liang's parents left him with Master Min.

"You must know of the tradition," Master Min said to Hui Lin.

"Tradition?" she said, bewildered.

"You gave your son a traditional gift on his becoming day," he said. When someone joins the order on their 8th birthday, they are given a gift to begin their journey. The traditional gift is a family heirloom passed down. You gave your son the jet stone. A very fitting gift."

"I just wanted him to have it. I'm glad you approve," Hui Lin said.

Master Min then walked over to the cabinet, opened the top drawer, and pulled out something covered in a red and gold silk cloth. "Avani" for your becoming day today, your family sent this." Master Min uncovered an intricately molded silver bracelet. A lotus flower bloomed from the center with a broad display of designs as it went around. "You may recognize it as the one your grandmother wore. It was given to her by your grandfather as a wedding present. Your grandfather got it from his grandmother, who was said to be very special like you. I believe over time, you will find great protection by wearing it."

Avani took the bracelet with tears in her eyes of memories of her grandmother. She placed it on her wrist and held it to her heart.

The Zhang's said their goodbyes to Liang, his mother kissing him many times on the head before Ju-Long had to pull her away. "We will be back soon to check on you," Hui Lin said. "Be safe," and they left.

Master Min showed Liang to his new bedroom, which was upstairs across from Avani's. Master Min's room was at the far end of the same hallway. "We will begin tomorrow morning. We will try to catch you up to where Avani is," Master Min said. Avani had a grin. She liked feeling like she was ahead of others, especially a boy.

~

THE TWINS WERE BROUGHT into their father's office. They weren't allowed in there very often. Thomas Blood was sitting behind his desk. Their stepmother, Jessica, was standing beside him with her hand on the shoulder of his navy suit. Her other arm held their baby brother Alaric who was just over a year old. Of course, the twins called her mother, but they knew she wasn't their birth mother. They didn't know much about their birth mother. But they knew Jessica wasn't their mother because their father had only met and married her three years before. Denebula remembered the wedding well as it was on an island with lots of sand that got all over her dress.

Asha was also standing in the office on the far side of the desk near the tall cascading windows. Thomas had two silk handkerchiefs covering two different objects on his desk. One was ocean blue, and the other was dark purple, nearly black.

"Happy birthday, children," he said to Denebula, who was alert and attentive but always seemed to have an untrusting look, and Kai, who was yawning and looked very tired. "More importantly, today is your becoming day. Birthdays come and go, but you only have one becoming day. For you two, this day is even more special. Do you remember the prophecy? I'm sure Asha here has taught it to you.

Denebula began 'When the moon passes," Asha shot a look at her. "When the red moon passes through shadow and blood on the darkest day, the druid of destiny will be born of death on the final archer where energies cross to create tension between the heavens and the earth which will begin when the ancestor stone is gifted on the day of becoming.'

"Very Good, Denebula," said her father. "That last part is vital today. Every druid has their becoming day on their 8th birthday. But one of you is the druid of destiny, and starting today, according to the prophecy, you will slowly begin to develop all of your gifts across all the affinities. It says, 'will begin when the ancestor stone is gifted on the day of becoming.' Today, both of you get your ancestor stone. Who would like theirs first?"

"I do," Kai said, suddenly looking wide awake. He approached the desk, and his father pulled the blue silk handkerchief off a 3" long stone tower with six sides and a pointed end."

"Oh, bummer," Kai said, "I was hoping for a drone."

"Son, this is much more powerful than a drone," Thomas said disappointedly. "This is a very rare blue fossilized coral. Looking at it carefully, you can see the fossilized coral markings. This type of coral comes only from the Indo-Pacific oceans. It was harvested over two hundred years ago. Your great-grandfather purchased this from a man on the island of Koh Ta Team, a tiny island off the coast of Cambodia. Koh Ta Team is a powerful ley line crossing."

"We were just about to begin learning about Ley line crossings," Asha said.

"Well, you will soon learn about these locations in the world where powerful energy is released, and when something forms there, such as this coral, it becomes a potent magical artifact. Fossilized coral takes over three hundred and fifty million years to form. When it forms on a ley line, it is a very powerful artifact. Over time you will learn how to use this, but be very careful with it. I am giving you this Kai because you are a liq. You will learn to have power over water and all other liquids. This was formed in water and, with its rare blue color, should allow you to channel very potent magic. As the only liq in the family, this should be yours. I present this to you on your becoming day, my son."

Kai took it and began looking at it. He did start thinking it was cool when he heard it was 350 million years old. That is way older than even dinosaurs. "Thanks," he said to his dad as he stepped back. Denebula then walked up to her father's desk.

"For you, my dear…" he pulled the purple silk handkerchief to reveal a ring with a white and blue stone with an adularescence quality, making it seem to change color and move slightly as you look at it, like lunar light floating on water. "… this is a moonstone ring. This was your great-grandmother's ring on my mother's side. It originates from Sri Lanka, where the purest moonstone comes from. Volcanos from 2 billion years ago spewed great amounts of lava which cooled uniquely, creating moonstones. As you learn about ley lines, some are based on a planetary grid system that is very ordered. There is another type of ley line that is more chaotic. These energy lines follow earthquake fault lines and where volcanos rise through the earth's crust. So your relic comes from a more chaotic polarity while your brothers come from an ordered polarity." Kai's face began to sour as he heard that his sister's gem was older and came from awesome volcanoes.

"This ring will help you detect magic. It can help you find objects and test artifacts, gems, and relics to see if they have magical qualities or have been activated or charged. You will find it very useful throughout your life. I present this to you on your becoming day, my daughter," and he placed it on her finger. Unfortunately, it rolled over because her finger was too small. "I thought that might happen." Thomas said, "Be careful, and don't lose it."

"Thanks, Dad," Denebula said, genuinely excited about her gift.

"From this point forward, you must take your studies very seriously. Much will come to you naturally, but much more will need to be learned. Finish your training with Asha, and then you will be sent to the other masters. Learn as much as you can as quickly as you can. Do you both understand me?" Thomas said firmly.

"Yes, Father," both children said in unison.

Tomorrow, the three of us will be going on a quick trip. Your ancestor relics have been previously activated but need to be charged. Tomorrow, we will charge Kai's in addition to something I need to do. We will leave around lunchtime tomorrow. Plan on nasi goring for dinner.

Chapter 8

December 22, 2018

L IANG WAS NOT USED to getting up nearly this early. Avani seemed perfectly alert. Master Min had woken the children early, promising an exciting day. The children were expected to prepare the congee, which they did. Both children liked rice porridge, especially when allowed to sweeten it. While it was cooking, Master Min began his lesson.

"Children. Today will be very unusual. Liang, being your first day, you won't have anything else to compare it to. Still, I need to teach you some crucial things quickly because we can witness something rare today. But you will only understand what is happening if you have some background. Usually, what I am about to teach you would take many weeks. This will be a rapid course because we are going on a field trip. Please pay close attention because there will not be time to repeat myself. We can go back and review this material on another day. Now, please, follow me," Master Min said in a rather rapid tone. Liang and Avani both liked the sound of today. They got up, left the house, and followed a pathway. It was a brisk morning but warmer than usual for the time of year. Master Min stopped near a small pond.

"First," Master Min continued, "You have been blessed with abundant power. That power can be used for any number of purposes. Some use it to help others, to heal the world, and make it a better place. Some use it to become wealthy, powerful, or to gain fame. It is up to you to determine how you will use your power. My job is to teach you that you have a choice and that all choices have consequences. The only way to control the consequences of something is by making choices that lead to the outcomes you want. You also need to understand that often, with this type of power, the repercussions of your actions, those consequences, will be felt by many other people. In other words, if you aren't careful, you can create a wake of destruction behind you that you may not face, but you force others to pay the price for you. Some with this type of power love that others face the consequences of their actions. Let me illustrate. Liang, will you pick up a single piece of sand and drop it into the pond?"

Liang did as he was told. "Children, notice how small ripples are moving away from the sand. Even the smallest actions have effects on the things around us. Now Avani, could you please throw this rock into the middle of the pond?" Avani took it and threw it. As it landed, a great "kerplunk" sound was heard. "Children, now notice the size of the waves. The larger the action, the greater the impact is on the world around us. Now, Liang, throw this rock into the water near where you stand." Liang was a little disappointed. He wanted to throw it further into the pond, but he followed the directions Master Min had given and dropped it just out of arm's length.

"Now, notice what is happening. The ripples from Liang's rock are beginning to clash with the waves from your rock Avani. What happens? Do the ripples get bigger?" Master Min inquired

"No. They cancel each other out when they clash. They are getting smaller," Avani said.

"That is right. A counterforce can neutralize some of the effects. But that is on this side of the pond. What happens on the other side of the pond? On the other side of where Avani threw her rock?" Master Min asked Liang

"It looks like there are twice as many waves over there, all going in the same direction. They aren't clashing like over here," Liang said.

"Exactly. So even when we do something to counteract the effect of Avani's stone on this side, we could be adding to the effect somewhere else. As a druid, it is imperative to understand this principle. We must always understand the ripples we are making around us and try to minimize any negative impacts on others. If others do things that create negative consequences, they should be stopped. We should strive for balance—net neutrality in the universe around us. Children, these gifts we have been given are powerful and can do enormous damage if we are not careful. I didn't learn that lesson until it was too late.

Master Min began leading the children back to his home where they were a bit confused as they thought they were going on a field trip. Master Min continued, "As druids, we must be honorable stewards of the energy and power we have been given." As Master Min was talking, he walked back to his home. The children came inside and sat on the carpet in the center of the room. Master Min went to his chest of drawers and pulled out a large medallion.

"I am sure you have seen this before," Master Min said. A yin and yang symbol the size of a hockey puck with the black teardrop on one side and the white on the other. A dot of the opposite color is in the center of each side of the image. "What does this symbol mean?" Master Min asked Avani.

"Opposites?" She said.

"Yes. This represents interconnected forces. You can't have one without the other. Order and chaos. Light and Dark. Right and wrong. Maintaining the balance between them is vital, for many people can be hurt when things are out of balance. Magic is not making something out of nothing. That is what we see on television or in movies. True magic, the magic that you wield, comes from energy. Energy forces should remain in balance all of the time. When they aren't in balance, natural disasters occur to one degree or another." The children looked at Master Min with an expression of understanding.

"Where does the energy come from?" Asked Liang.

"Good question. Avani, what did I teach you about that last week?" said Master Min.

"You told me that energy is all around is. You said there are energy sources from all six affinities," she said.

"What are affinities?" Liang asked.

"The world is made up of 6 different types of energy. While most people think of them in silos, they blend more than people think. We can get into that another day. Usually, each person is associated with a single energy affinity. For example, Avani here is an earth druid. It means her energy is associated with that of the earth. When it comes to earth energy, most people refer to ley lines. Ley lines are sources of energy in the earth. They are physical locations that you can see on a map." Master Min went to the side

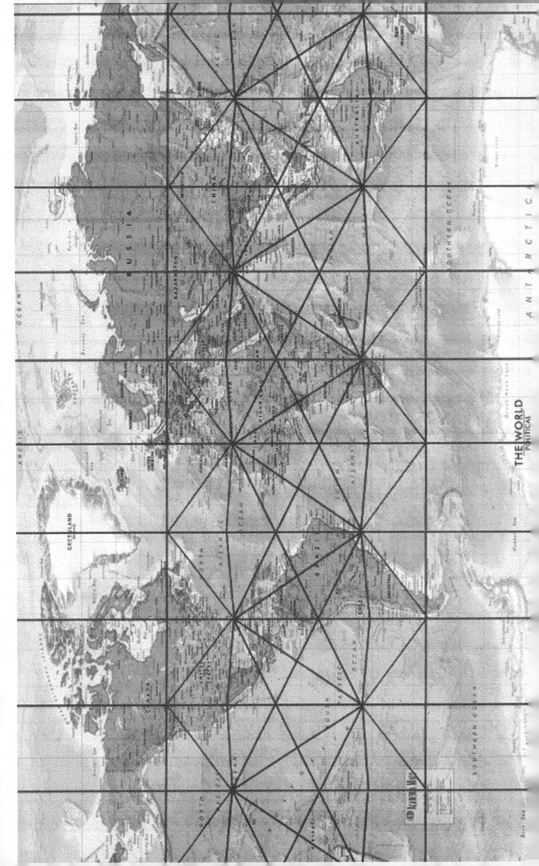

THE WORLD
POLITICAL

of the chest of drawers where there was a bin with tall rolls of paper sticking out. He pulled one of them and returned to the floor, unrolling it. Avani had seen this same map the other day. "This is a map of one type of ley lines worldwide. Where the lines intersect, it is called vortexes. Where a vortex occurs, it creates an energy radius that can be felt far from the epicenter of the crossing. These gridlines would make more sense if we looked at a globe, but you get the idea.

Look at the places on the map where ley line crossings occur."

Liang and Avani began to study the map. "The great pyramids of Egypt are one of the vortexes," Liang said.

"Stonehenge is another," said Avani.

"Easter Island. Oh, look, the Bermuda Triangle," Liang said excitedly.

"Yes. These sites are among many that are well-known to be energy vortexes and have been for thousands of years. You can absorb vast energy on these lines, especially on the vortexes. But remember the yin and yang symbols. This is one half of an earth energy equation. Another side is the opposite of this 'ordered' energy gird." Master Min returned to the rolled-up papers and pulled out several others.

"Show him the volcano one first," Avani said. Master Min began unrolling another map.

"This map, again based on earth energy, plots all the different volcanic activity on the planet. As you can imagine, Liang, volcanos have tremendous energy from the earth. Master Min began unrolling several other maps. One with tectonic plates. Another is with the fault lines in earthquake-prone regions. "These other maps show energy locations that we call 'chaos energy.' The opposite of the ordered energy lines you saw on the first map. Both are ley lines but with different polarity," Master Min said as he began rolling the maps back up.

"What do you mean by polarity?" Liang asked.

"Polarity is the term used to describe the opposing energy. Like yin and yang, chaos energy works oppositely from ordered energy. But this is just the earth's affinity with ordered and chaotic energy. Each affinities have the same yin and yang regarding energy," Master Min said, walking back to the rug. "Liang, there is a wonderful balance with you. Your name means 'bright light,' yet you were born on winter solstice, the darkest day.

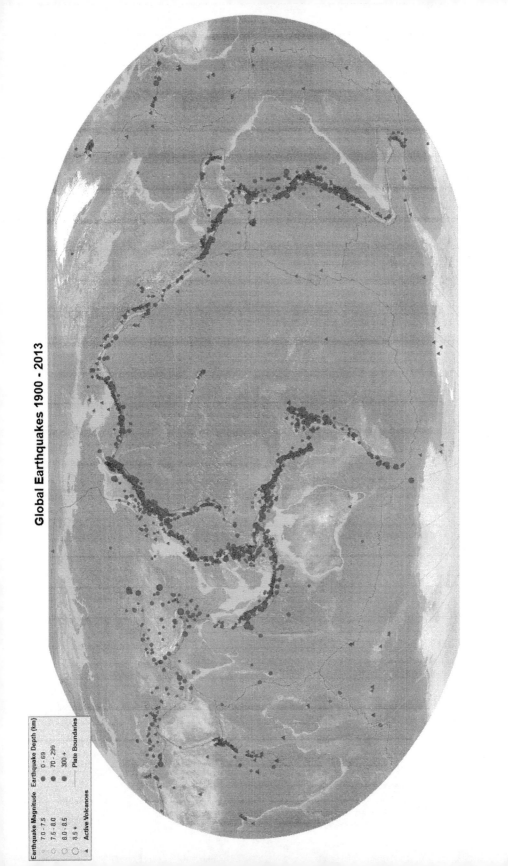

Global Earthquakes 1900 - 2013

Earthquake Magnitude   Earthquake Depth (km)
    7.0 - 7.5   0 - 69
    7.5 - 8.0   70 - 299
    8.0 - 8.5   300 +
    8.5 +   —— Plate Boundaries

▲ Active Volcanoes

"What affinity do I have?" Liang asked.

"Based on our testing, you are a frequency druid," Master Min said. He then went to the kitchen, dished the congee into three bowls, and brought them to the children. They all began eating.

"What is a frequency druid?" Liang said, wiping his mouth on his sleeve while getting even more interested in this discussion.

"Frequencies are the term we use for the entire spectrum around light. That is why you could make the crystal change colors. Light is also associated with heat, like on the infrared spectrum. But the frequency spectrum moves way past what we can see as visible light. X-Rays are a frequency, for example."

"You mean I'll be able to see through stuff?" Liang asked, cutting Master Min off.

"There are some frequency druids that have developed their abilities far enough to indeed see through objects. Yes," Master Min said while holding his hands up to calm Liang down.

"Cool!" Liang said. Avani hadn't heard about X-Ray vision before and was a little jealous of Liang for the first time.

"Avani, what are the other affinities?" Master Min said, looking over at her.

"Liquid, Cosmos, Atmospheric, Earth and Life," she answered as if reading from a script.

"Very good," he continued. "I am a life druid. Each of us plays a different role in how energy is used in the universe. We must be responsible for our part to maintain balance across the energies where we can. But you must understand that not everyone understands or cares about maintaining balance. Many feel the world and everyone else in it are beneath them. Entire civilizations have fallen as a result of this type of thinking. Some of those rulers throughout time were druids, and some had druids as their closest advisors."

"So, do you have to stand on a ley line or a vortex to use magic?" Liang asked. Avani laughed, and Liang got a little embarrassed, thinking maybe he had asked a dumb question.

"Do not laugh, Avani. Liang has a great question and shows he truly understands the basics of druidism," Master Min said, shooting a look at her. "Liang, you are right. It wouldn't make sense for magic to only work at these locations. That is why druids use objects to store and manipulate energy—such as the crystal you held when you were tested. An endless variety of stones, gems, crystals, rocks, and other objects can be used. Each type of object may work better or worse with different affinities. So, for example, a shark tooth would work better to store and control water or life energy than earth or frequency energy."

Suddenly, Liang wished he was a life or liquid druid to have a magic shark tooth. "One of the main purposes of your training over the next few years is to learn about various objects and how to best use them with your affinity. Come here, both of you," Master Min said as he walked back to his chest of drawers. "Here are some of the objects I have collected throughout my life." As he spoke, he pulled open drawer after drawer, filled with gems, crystals, stones, and many other things, all in perfect order. "Each of these has a different use and purpose. Some are stronger than others. Some have abilities not available with any other object. Over time you will collect things that you can use to help you control magic."

"So I just need to collect some rocks and stuff, and I'm good?" Liang asked.

"There is a bit more to it than that," Master Min said, closing the drawers and walking back to the rug. "First, not all objects are created equal. For example, gemstones' cut, clarity, color, and size can make a difference in their magical capabilities. Additionally, where it came from and what has happened throughout time can dramatically increase or decrease its magical capabilities. The more unique and special an object, the more energy it can store and manipulate. Unique objects are referred to as artifacts and relics. But just having a thing isn't enough. An object must be activated and charged before it can store or manipulate energy."

"Like a battery?" Liang asked, looking over at Avani to see if it was a stupid question.

"Exactly like a battery," Master Min said. "Activation is initially setting the energy parameters of an object. Imagine an energy scale from 1 to 100, with one being shallow energy like a AA battery and 100 being a nuclear power plant (although some artifacts can be far more potent than that). When you activate an artifact, gem, or whatever, you define how much power the object can store or manipulate. So if you take the world's most perfect diamond and activate it on a ley line vortex under other special conditions we will discuss later, it would make that diamond a mighty artifact. You will have a reasonably worthless object if you activate an included, cloudy, small diamond on a random Tuesday afternoon with no special vortexes, ley lines, or anything else. So activation is crucial. What you use, where, and how you do it, and many other conditions are essential when activating an object. Once activated, you need to charge the object with energy occasionally to continue using it. So activation only ever needs to happen once on an object. Charging will happen many times depending upon how often it is used." Master Min paused and looked carefully at the children. "We have been covering a LOT of ground today, kids, but we have no choice based upon our afternoon. Does this all make sense?"

Both kids nodded, although they felt some of the information stuck and may have missed some. "Can you over-activate or charge an object," Avani asked.

"Let's go back to our example of the low-quality diamond. Put that diamond in an energy-rich place under extremely powerful circumstances. One of two things will happen. Either the object will activate with limited power levels due to its imperfection, or in some cases, it will shatter or break under the energy surge," Master Min said while illustrating an explosion with his hands.

"What is happening this afternoon that is so important?" Avani asked.

"An extremely dangerous man who does not care about the balance of energy will activate a one-of-a-kind relic later this afternoon. We are going to go and watch what he does. We aren't going to stop him or get involved. This is the beginning of something far more sinister, so we must learn today. But the background we have covered today will help frame the context of what you may see later," Master Min said.

"How do you know it is going to happen today?" Avani asked.

"I was told this man would steal a particular precious gemstone. I cast a tracing spell on it to know where it went. It was indeed stolen. It is a precious pearl. One of the largest in the world. As a result, I know who has it, and I saw earlier that it is on the move again today. So when it stops, we will know where we need to go. This is the type of object that depending on how it is activated, could cause severe imbalance. Children, finish getting ready and prepare for travel."

~

THE FOLLOWING DAY, Edward felt a slight "thump" in the ground, almost as weak as a heartbeat. "The tooth is activated," he thought. He went over, pulled up the stone floor piece, and lifted out the tooth. The activation process here would provide little charging, so he would need to do something more. While waiting for the tooth to activate, he had been calculating the moon's phases since imprisonment. Knowing it was a full moon for the eclipse on December 21, 2010, he figured 28-day periods for the next eight years. He used a small rock and made scratch marks on the wall. He took 365 days and multiplied it by 8, one for each year. He then divided it into 28-day lunar cycles. He adjusted for leap days and added one more day since yesterday was the winter solstice. The calculation came out to an even number.

"It is going to be a full moon again tonight," Edward said out loud. He thought about the moon's position on a full moon in the sky. He could see in his mind that for the moon to appear full, it must be opposite from the sun relative to the earth's position. So, at sunset, you would see a moonrise of the full moon. Likewise, at sunrise, the full moon would be setting. He knew the science wasn't perfect here, but it was close enough for what he needed. He took a deep breath, went over to the window, and looked out through the bars and glass as best he could. It was near sunset, which meant it was getting into late afternoon. There was a good chance the moon was now rising.

Edward took the same chair leg he had been using to pry up the floor stones and put the end through the iron bars, and hit the solid window. "I can't believe I'm doing this in winter," he said as the glass shattered. He used the leg to clear away the broken glass on the edges. Taking the gold tooth in his right hand, he put his arm through the bars and into the window well and tossed the tooth into the air. It came falling back to the ground, where he grabbed it again. He threw it up just above the edge of the window well at ground level, allowing the moon's light to strike the gold tooth. It came falling back down. "Now I only need to do that about 1000 more times without losing it," Edward said as he threw it back up to catch the full moon's light again.

~

AT NOON, the twins walked into their father's office. Thomas Blood was wrapping some items in cloth and placing them inside his dark green suit pocket. "Kai, do you have your artifact?" Thomas asked.

"Right here." Kai lifted the petrified coral from the pocket of these worn jeans.

Thomas pulled out his gold dodecahedron, all 12 ovals cast in glowing purple electric waves. He lifted it to his forehead and projected thought through it, and a purple portal opened in front of them in the blink of an eye. Thomas went first, followed by Denebula and then Kai.

One by one, they stepped out onto the sand of a beach in Pantai Wisata Tanjung Tua, Indonesia, the southernmost tip of the largest island in the island chain, where it was dusk with only a dark orange glow of a sunset remaining over the horizon. The kids hadn't traveled by portal many times. Kai's favorite thing to observe was where the sun was when they left and where it was when they arrived. Nothing seemed to imprint the power of using a poly, as did that. Denebula watched as three circles on her father's poly extinguished their light. "Dad, doesn't your dodecahedron require you to have been to a place before to go there again?" asked Denebula.

"Yes," answered Thomas. "I came with some friends during my college years," he said in a tone letting her know it was an unimportant question. "Kai, where your fossilized coral came from was north of here. Exactly where you are matters greatly for many reasons when you activate an artifact. When you charge an artifact, it doesn't have the same strict requirements to get the maximum benefit. In other words, we could charge your coral point anywhere with naturally moving water. Still, since I needed to come here anyway, it will be more than adequate, although I don't know if we have enough time to charge it fully."

"Why did you need to come here?" Asked Kai as he watched some kids about his age jump from some stone cliffs down further where the beach ended, and rocks protruded out of the shoreline.

"To activate a newly acquired relic," answered Thomas as the two children followed their father 100 feet to the shore's edge. Many people were still on the shoreline, enjoying the water, but most were packing up and walking back inland. Their father kept walking and seemed to know where he was going because he led them to a little inlet cove where almost no other people were. It was rockier than the beach they had crossed. "There," Thomas pointed to Kai. "See how the water comes in and sits but isn't strong enough to pull anything away. This would be an ideal place to charge your blue coral."

Kai took the fossilized coral from his pocket and placed it on what almost looked like a stone pedestal. The tide was such that the water coming in would gently lap up on the stone altar, bathing the coral until it slowly drained. "Let's get something to eat. No one will bother it while we are gone," Thomas said. "There is a great restaurant not far from here."

Their father wasn't kidding about nasi goring for dinner. The restaurant, which was half indoors and half outdoors, was only about 200 yards from where they had left Kai's artifact. They sat down on bamboo stools as their father ordered for all of them. The young waiter, a thick young man with dark brown straight short hair, obviously didn't get guests that looked like them, so he was very active regarding drink refills. The food came out only a short time after. As best Kai and Denebula could tell, it was a fried rice dish with pieces of meat and various vegetables. Kai picked out most of the vegetables. Denebula put some of her meat on Kai's plate, which he appreciated.

~

GOING THROUGH MASTER MIN'S PORTAL was the coolest thing Liang or Avani had ever done. Liang thought he would never think about anything again until he smelled the food from the nearby restaurant. Just around the corner from the restaurant, Master Min, Avani, and Liang stood watching the twins eat dinner with their father, Thomas Blood. Liang's mouth began to water. "Do we get to eat?" he asked Master Min.

"Not right now," Master Min answered, not taking his eyes off Thomas.

"What are we doing?" Asked Avani.

"Do you see that man and the two children with him?" Master Min asked the children. That is Thomas Blood.

"Thee Thomas Blood?" Asked Liang. Even only eight years old, he had heard of the wealthiest man in the world. "He is the guy that owns the biggest space rocket company in the world."

"Yes. And with those riches comes a tremendous amount of entitlement. As I told you earlier, recently, he acquired one of the most fabulous pearls in history by less than honorable means. He intends to activate it tonight. Do you remember what I taught you earlier about activating relics?"

"Yes, you said it needs to be a unique object. You said it should be done on a "Liang paused, trying to remember the word.

"Ley line" Avani chimed in.

"Yes. Ley line. You said they could be either ordered or chaotic ley lines. You also said other conditions could be important or add strength," Liang finished.

"Very good. Now, look around and tell me what you see," Master Min asked as he continued to watch Thomas Blood.

"Well, we are at the beach. Is this where the pearl came from?" Avani asked.

"I am not sure," said Min, "But often a master druid will take an artifact or relic to its place of origin to maximize the activation, so I guess that you are right."

"Are we at a ley line crossing? A vortex?" Liang had almost forgotten the word but said it just before Avani jumped in again.

"Yes. This area is highly volcanic. Some of the world's most active volcanos are near here," Min answered.

"So super powerful artifact. Check. Ley line vortex. Check. The original location of the artifact. Check. Oh, and look a full moon. I'm guessing that is significant," Avani said.

"Yes, it is. Full moons are always a great time to activate or charge artifacts," Min said, still watching Thomas closely.

"Check," Said Avani.

"But don't druids activate things all the time? What does it matter, and why are we spying on him instead of eating dinner," Liang asked, still focused on his empty stomach.

"Something isn't right. I sense that Thomas Blood has deeper plans than just tonight. A man like him does not do small things. A man like him is notorious for bringing things far out of balance at the expense of everyone else. If he is up to something, we need to understand better what it is," Min replied.

~

"THIS IS WHAT WE ARE HERE FOR KIDS," their father said as he pulled one of the wrapped objects from his pocket. It was a misshapen, creamy white pearl hanging on a silver necklace. "This is called the Imperial Hong Kong Pearl and is one of the largest and rare natural pearls in all the world. It is believed to have been originally found somewhere in this region. I picked this location because out there in that water…" Thomas was pointing out towards the ocean "is an island newly formed in the last 100 years. There is an underwater volcano, one of the most powerful in the world, sitting right out there. Lava erupts from it frequently. It began building a volcano cone from the ocean floor, as you see in pictures and movies. In 1929 it emerged from the ocean and continued to build and grow higher and higher. It is now almost 1000 feet tall and is still growing. Understand and always remember this, kids; often, the best place to activate a relic or object is where it was created. The pearl was created inside a gigantic clam of some kind around here, and we are going to activate it now."

Thomas stood up and left cash on the table, which by the look on the boy's face, was more than he had seen that month. They walked back down to the small cove where the coral was left. Tide was a little higher but still just lapping over the blue coral. The beach was now nearly empty. A little after 9:00 pm local time, Thomas walked into the water until it reached his thighs. He seemed to have no thought he was doing this in a $4,000 suit. With the Imperial Hong Kong Pearl dangling from the silver chain, he dipped it into the water, concentrated, and said the incantation to activate a stone. "Lig don chruinne an chumhacht a thabhairt duit chun do chumas iomlán a bhaint amach agus go ndéanfaidh na lámha ar a bhfreastalaíonn tú a ndícheall chun cothromaíocht agus comhchuibheas a bhaint amach." As Thomas concluded, they all heard a deep thumping sound as if a drum the size of the island had been struck. They heard a loud crack from a long distance away in the water. Thomas froze, listening and watching. Then they all felt the earth under their feet move. It was an earthquake. It was so strong that Thomas fell over in the water and almost let go of the pearl. The kids fell over, and the blue coral fell off the rock altar. Almost half a minute of shaking happened before it stopped. Everything was silent. Thomas relaxed a bit and began walking back to the shoreline.

"What was that, Dad?" Screamed Kai.

Thomas' feet reached sandy ground sooner than expected. At first, he thought the children had moved back from the shoreline by about 30 feet, but Kai was still standing next to the cove where the coral was sitting, which was bone dry. Thomas looked behind him and saw the water on the beach receding into the ocean at an alarming pace. Thomas looked down the beach with the bright full moon hanging in the sky as all the water pulled back into the sea. "Oh no," Thomas whispered to himself. "RUN!" Thomas yelled to his children. The kids froze, not knowing what to do. The other adults began to look around and noticed what was also happening, dashing inland, and grabbing children along the way.

They were all searching the dark landscape for the highest ground as they ran. A small roadway on a ridge behind the restaurant increased in elevation quickly and was illuminated by the full moon. There was a path leading up to the road where almost everyone was beginning to converge. Kai pulled away from his father's hand and said. "Wait, I left my blue coral," and returned to the now desolate beach. Thomas screamed for Kai to stop, but he couldn't be heard over all the yelling and commotion.

With Denebula still holding his other hand, Thomas turned around to follow Kai. Thomas had just returned to the sand when he could see it. The full moon's glow cast a beam of light across the water, which seemed to grow and grow. It was a tsunami wave heading toward shore. Think clouds in the distance quickly filled the sky with an ominous darkness that seemed to follow the wave like a shadow of death. Thomas looked towards Kai, who was still running and hadn't noticed the oncoming surge.

~

MASTER MIN SEEING THE COMMOTION and receding shoreline, told the children to follow him quickly. He sprinted up the trail behind the restaurant to an upper ridge with a split north and south road. To the south, the road turned into a small path that ended at the cliffs the young children were jumping off of earlier. Going north, the road continued to climb in elevation to a ridge where it leveled out. Most everyone else from the beach and restaurant was heading up on the road to the higher ground as the wave came into sight.

Master Min walked a few steps south, opened his robe, and pulled out what Liang was sure was a sand dollar you can find on many beaches. He placed it in the palm of his right hand just as the wave hit the cliff-side and began consuming the rocky outcropping as it raced towards them.

~

THOMAS AND DENEBULA CAUGHT UP TO KAI just as he picked up his coral. He then looked up, and the wave was only a half-breath away from them. Thomas grabbed both children, and Kai pushed out his hand, holding the blue coral in an instinctive defensive position. It cut the tsunami wave right in half. Two invisible dividers forced the wave to the left and right of the twins and Thomas and passed them unharmed. Their eyes followed the wave as it folded back in on itself, filling the void just as the water picked up the restaurant off its foundation like a child's toy and began to carry it back into the ocean directly at Thomas and the twins. Thomas pulled out his dodecahedron and quickly projected thought through the purple glowing spheres. A purple-colored portal appeared brighter than usual as the dark clouds had now covered the full moon. They stood on the beach as the water rose like a high tide in hypersonic motion. Thomas yelled, "GO!" to the kids, who all dove through the portal.

Thomas Blood's portal had opened up back in his study. As it opened, water poured in on the parquet floor as Thomas and the twins landed on the floor. They looked back through the purple circle portal when they saw the entire patio section of the restaurant heading for them. Thomas closed the portal just as one of the bamboo chairs was halfway through the portal, cut off, and landed broken on the office floor.

"Did we do that?" Kai asked his father.

Thomas didn't answer.

~

MASTER MIN WATCHED CLOSELY as the tidal wave began rolling across the coast and up on the rocky cliff straight in front of them. He looked to the left as he saw the wave part just before Thomas Blood and his two children. He looked forward again as the enormous wave got closer to them. "Children, do you remember when Avani dropped the big stone in the pond this morning, causing the ripples?" He asked rhetorically. "What did Liang do to counteract the force of those ripples?"

"He threw another rock," Avani said.

"Exactly," said Master Min as he pushed his hand, holding the sand dollar outward like throwing a great bolder. A significant energy surge pulsated outward from Master Min towards the tsunami. It hit it, causing an explosion of water that went hundreds of feet into the air. The rocky cliff split in two, and the cliff diving area fell sideways into the water. As a result, the oncoming water had been stopped saving those racing up the hill.

Master Min turned back toward Liang and Avani. "Children. That concludes today's lesson," he said as he thought about other areas of the surrounding islands that were being hit by the wave at that very moment without warning or defense.

Chapter 9

THE LARGE CAFETERIA where all the children eat their meals at the congregate care center in Tucson, Arizona, had a large television in the corner on SNN where a man holding a microphone was onsite on a beach with lots of debris. He said, "Yesterday, a modest amplitude but devastating tsunami struck Indonesia's Sunda Strait from 9:27 to 10:00 pm local time." The screen went to a map view of the affected areas.

"leaving at least 437 dead and tens of thousands injured. The tsunami swept onto the coastlines of southeastern Sumatra and western Java without warning from any alert system. The source of the tsunami was along the southwest coast of Anak Krakatau, an active volcano on the rim of the caldera of the great 1883 Krakatau eruption." Aura nervously rubbed the desert rose stone in her pocket. She kept it with her since it was small enough to fit.

"Aura. Aura. Can you come here, please?" said Mrs. Walsh, one of the center's workers, as she changed the channel to a nature station. Aura was nearly finished with her breakfast anyway. She popped the last piece of waffle in her mouth, threw away her trash, stacked her tray, and followed Mrs. Walsh to her office. She would get called to her office once a month to discuss her health and medication needs, although this was a bit early this month. As she walked into the office, in the chair across from the desk was a very old Native American woman with dark leathery skin that was stretched and shiny. She had piercing blue eyes that seemed to look through you rather than at you. Her hair was white, with a broad forehead and a thin braid down her back. She wore a bright red, almost ceremonial outfit with a thick necklace full of blue beads and animal teeth, a medallion hanging from her neck, and a wide black belt with many blue and red stones.

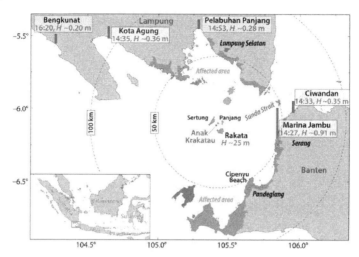

"Aura, this is Makawee. Makawee is a foster parent for many of the tough, um, I mean, she is an ideal foster parent for children with unique circumstances. She lives on the Hualapai Native American Reservation, west of the Grand Canyon. She wanted to talk to you about living in her home. How would you feel about that?" Said Mrs. Walsh.

"Um, I don't know. I don't know anything about it or her, but I'd like to hear about it. I've always wanted a chance to be adopted or be in a family or something. I've only ever been here. I don't know what anything else is like," Aura said softly.

"May I speak to Aura alone for a few minutes Mrs. Walsh?" Makawee asked in a broken and labored tone.

"Is that okay, Aura? Would it be okay if you two chat alone for a few minutes? If not, I can stay here," Mrs. Walsh asked Aura.

"I think that is fine. You can go," Aura said. Mrs. Walsh left the room and shut the door, but the footsteps stopped immediately. She was obviously sitting right outside, although Aura didn't think she could hear them even with the door open Makawee spoke so softly.

"I have heard about you," Makawee said to Aura. "The special girl. Were you given something and told that someone might come to see you?" she said. Aura reached into her pocket and pulled out the desert rose. "Ah, yes. You are the right girl, then. Listen, there is a lot you need to know—a lot you need to be taught. I can help in part. I can help put you on the path. But to begin your life, you can't stay here. Would you give me that chance? I promise you, if you don't like what I have to offer, you can come right back here. But I think you will like it. I really think you are going to like it. What do you say?"

Aura got butterflies in her stomach and thought about this for a minute. She didn't expect ever to get adopted or put into foster care. She didn't know what it would be like to live on a reservation, but she didn't know what it would be like to live anywhere. "I have health problems, so no one has wanted me before. They say it may be hard to help raise me. I have fragile lungs," Aura said to see what the woman would say.

"Oh, yes. That won't be a problem," Makawee said. "You will see."

"Okay. I'll try it. I want to try something new," Aura said.

Makawee got up, went to the door, and opened it, and Mrs. Walsh practically fell through. "Oh, there you are," Makawee said to Mrs. Walsh. "We have discussed it, and Aura said she would like to come with me. I know this is highly unusual regarding the expeditious nature of this. Still, I am just so excited to have Aura. I wish I had known about her years ago. Would it be possible for her to get her things while you and I finish the paperwork?"

Mrs. Walsh said, "Oh, it normally takes some weeks to get the approvals and prepare the paperwork, but since I got a call from the chairman who said we can do all of that in parallel, I see no reason why Aura can't leave with you if she would like."

"Wonderful," Makawee said. "Aura, why don't you collect your things, and we can head to my home together? Sounds good?"

"Okay," Aura said and headed to her room. It only took a minute to collect her things, most of which were already in her mother's duffel bag. She returned to the cafeteria and said goodbye to several other kids. They had looks of bewilderment on their faces. She returned to Mrs. Walsh's office, who walked Makawee out with Aura. In front of the building was a black Chevy Tahoe with another Native American man who got out of the driver's seat, came around and opened the door and helped Makawee in, and then helped Aura in. He got back in the front and drove away.

~

EDWARD HEARD SOMEONE walking down the long hallway. He put the tooth back under the stone and repositioned it carefully. He repositioned the chair's broken leg against a wall so it didn't look damaged. He returned to the grate and lay on his stomach as the door opened. It was his meal brought down by Mercurous. "You know I ate comin' down ere," he said as he slid the tray through the opening on the bottom and stepped back, not to be affected by the lack of oxygen. He then looked around, noticing how cold it was.

"Something broke the window," Edward said from his prone position on the stone floor.

"I won elp ya nun. Dat spell works either way. It is cowd in ere dow," Mercurous said as he closed the door behind him and walked back up the stairs.

Edward took the leg from the chair again, pried the stone floor, and took the tooth. He placed it behind one of the bars on the window and spoke the incantation. Nothing happened. Edward did it again, and still nothing. Then Edward looked closely at the bottom of the iron bar; it had the first signs of rust. "It is working. Just very slowly because this tooth isn't very powerful," he thought. "I need to just give it time."

~

AURA DROVE FOR ABOUT 2 HOURS before they stopped for lunch, a quick drive-thru on the north side of Phoenix. They all got burgers and fries. Aura enjoyed an Oreo shake, one of her very favorites which was a rare treat for her. Then after a quick bathroom break and the young man filling up the gas, they drove another 3 hours before the black Chevy Tahoe pulled up to a two-story white house shaped like a large log cabin. It was mostly enclosed by short bushy trees which bordered a high desert forest. There were no other homes nearby. Aura couldn't see any homes or other buildings as far as she could see. Only the front porch overlooked a low-lying grassy hill with six straight trees at the top, forming a circle. The back of the second story had an oversized wooden deck nestled into the forest.

The young man got out and opened the door for Makawee, who got out, and Aura followed. Makawee, only about 4 inches taller than Aura, looked down at her and said, "Let's take a walk together." She took her by the hand and began to follow a path into the forest.

It was now mid-afternoon and mild in the late December Arizona air, with the sun far in the southern sky. "Aura, tell me about yourself," Makawee began.

"What do you want to know?" Aura asked.

"Well, how old are you? You look like you are about eight years old," Makawee surmised.

"Yes, I just turned eight just two days ago."

"A winter solstice birthday. How unique," Makawee responded more to herself than to Aura.

"What is a winter solstice birthday?" Asked Aria.

"You don't know what solstice is? Let me tell you," Makawee began as they walked further into the forest. "Winter solstice is the year's darkest day because there is the least sunlight. Do you see how the sun is far to the south right now, and yet it is in the middle of the day?"

"Yes," Aura answered

"If it were in the middle of summer, the sun would feel like it was almost directly over our heads. See, as the earth is tilted, and as it goes around the sun, it makes it so that for us, in the summer, we get more sun, and in the winter, we get less. It would be the opposite if you were in the southern hemisphere," Makawee continued.

"Where is the Southern Hemisphere?" Aura asked.

"Well, that is the bottom half of the world. We are on the top half of the earth. We live in the northern hemisphere. Those that live in the southern hemisphere just began summer while we just began winter, on your birthday. See, winter solstice begins winter, whereas summer solstice begins summer. Winter solstice in the northern hemisphere is the same day as the summer solstice in the southern hemisphere. I'll explain more about that later," Makawee said, realizing that Aura had a lot to take in. "How was your birthday? Did anything special happen?"

"It was my best birthday ever!" Aura exclaimed. "I got to go on a field trip. A stranger gave me some of my mother's things. I saw a light show in a cave. It was wonderful."

"Someone gave you something on your 8th birthday? What was it?"

"Just some old clothes, a stained white stone, and a weird glass tube," Aura said, not wanting to mention anything about the money. She had seen that people act strange when it comes to money.

"May I see them?" Makawee asked.

Aura paused momentarily, not knowing if she should or shouldn't but then decided she would. She crouched, opened the grey duffel bag, reached under the clothes, and grabbed the cardboard tube. She opened it up, and the cauliflower calcite fell out from the lid, and then the sandy glass pipe fell out of the main body of the packing tube. Aura picked them up and held them out for Makawee to hold. Makawee looked at the items curiously without touching them. She took her hand and held it over the sand-infused cylinder for a full minute with her eyes closed before saying anything. Then she did the same with the cauliflower calcite. Aura didn't know what to do, so she kept holding them.

"Remarkable gifts. This one is a fulgurite wand. You said it was your mothers?" Makawee asked.

"The woman that gave it to me said it was my mothers. She didn't say anything else. What is a fulgurite wand? Aura asked, still holding it in her hands.

"You are holding fossilized lightning, my dear," Makawee said. When lightning hits the ground, it is so hot that it instantly vaporizes and melts the materials in the ground. When it happens, it sometimes forms a clump or just a crust, but in exceptional cases, it creates a tube such as this."

"Lightning made this?" Aura asked.

"Yes. The other is called cauliflower calcite, another powerful stone. Still, I sense energy and life force have been added to it, which may explain the strange discoloration of the stone. Both hold power and can be wielded by a druid to create magic," Makawee said in a solemn tone.

Aura didn't know if she was being silly or joking like adults sometimes do to children. "What is a druid?" Aura asked with embedded skepticism.

"We both are. We both have special abilities. That is why you saw that light show in the cave on your birthday. The world around you is bursting to let you know that you have magical abilities. That is why I wanted to bring you under my care. You must learn the ancient ways," Makawee said slowly.

"Prove it," Aura said defiantly. She didn't like being treated like a baby. She needed to know if the Native American elderly woman could be trusted, and this would tell her.

Makawee put her hands over the medallion on her chest, just above the large beaded necklace. She closed her eyes, and the ground began to shake. Lightly at first and then rather violently, Aura fell over. Still, Makawee stood firm, almost like she wasn't feeling it. A few seconds later, it stopped, and Aura stood back up, dusting off her pants. "You did that?" Aura asked.

"Yes. I am an earth druid."

"So I can make earthquakes?" Aura asked excitedly, fully believing the old woman.

"I sense that you are an atmospheric druid. That is why the fulgurite wand came to you. There are different types of druids, and you and I are not the same, but I can still teach you many things. Your magic is very different but also very powerful. You probably can only express small manifestations of your power right now. Small electrical charges or a light breeze, for example, but over time, your power will grow. Would you like to try it?"

"YES!" Aura said, bursting with excitement.

"Magic requires energy and control. Energy is all around us, and you can tap into that energy as a druid. So the energy is the power to perform magic, but what will the energy do? What magic will you perform? That is where the mind and focus come in. You need to have an understanding of what you are trying to do. This requires a knowledge of how the world and universe work. The more you understand science, physics, nature, the environment, and so much more, the more types of magic you can perform. This is important! Knowledge is the key to magic. The more you know, the more magic you can do. So to perform magic, you need to focus on what you are trying to do and understand it. In this case, you want to create a lightning bolt. A lightning bolt is caused by having positively charged clouds and negatively charged ground. When they build up enough, lightning connects them, creating a balance. So focus on using the energy to make a positive charge in the air and a negative charge in the ground. Your mind is the idea and control; the artifact is the access to or focus of power. Artifacts and relics such as your wand and even your calcite stone are helpful to tap in, magnify and focus the energy," Makawee said, pointing first to the fulgurite wand and then to the dark red stained calcite still in Aura's hands. "These help you tap into the energy that is all around us. So focus the idea through the artifact. Your mind projects the idea, and as the focused idea passes through the artifact, you will have a manifestation of power, which most people call magic.

"Since it is your first time, don't expect much. It takes years and years of training and practice to control the forces of nature. Do you see that old stump there in the middle of that clearing? I sense that your cauliflower calcite has been activated through unusual means. Let's practice with that one. I want you to hold it in your right hand, think about that stump, then I want you to imagine what you want to happen. Can you do that?"

Aura held the calcite and focused on the tree stump about 20 feet away in an open clearing with tall grass around it. She imagined lightening having seen it so many times from her window at the congigate care center but nothing happened. "Nothing is happening" Aura said, more than a little disappointed.

"You must concentrate and clearly imagine what you are trying to do. Close your eyes and imagine what lightning looks like and what you are trying to do. Remember you are creating positive energy above and negative energy below the stump."

Aura held the calcite and focused on the stump. She then closed her eyes and imagined the lightning. A massive lightning bolt struck the stump out of a clear blue sky. Makawee's beady eyes became the size of saucers as she and Aura were knocked back several feet. Both landed on their backs in an oversized bush with red berries. When they looked up, the stump was split into four parts, all burning.

"I did not expect that," Makawee said hoarsely, looking at Aura through the branches of the buckthorn bush. With eyes wide like Makawee's, Aura drew out her inhaler and drew a deep breath using it.

The next several weeks were quite an adjustment for Aura. She was living in a new home with new kids and a new schedule, but all that was nothing compared to learning that she had magic powers and was a Druid. Most days, she would walk with Makawee in the forest and discuss many things. Aura got a lot of individualized attention from Makawee even though nine other kids were in the large seven-bedroom home. Aura learned that all of the children were druids. All the kids were older than Aura by at least a few years.

The home was two stories. On the main level, it had two bedrooms, a living room, a connected library, and a kitchen with a broad granite island in the center. The basement had a family room and several bedrooms. A staircase led downstairs from the main level near the front door. Aura's bedroom was downstairs. She shared it with an eleven-year-old girl that had been there for almost a year. Her name was Halona, and she didn't seem to like the amount of individual time Makawee was spending with Aura.

Aura learned that there were schools (for lack of a better word) set up for kids taught by elder druids. Druids travel by way of portals that are created by things called "polys." A druid could only get a poly if they graduated from all six schools of magic (each school is dedicated to a different affinity). When you graduate (as objectively set by the elder druid), you will get an artifact from that elder. You needed all six artifacts to get your poly, and having a poly was critical for any druid. Not having a poly would be like being a regular human adult without a driver's license. Do you have to have one? No. Is your life going to be a lot harder if you don't? Yes. Aura wanted to earn her earth druid artifact as quickly as she could from Makawee.

Makawee mainly taught one on one with students. The general classes were led by Nane, a younger woman who lived in the house. She was in her early 40s, thin, with black hair. She dressed very similarly to Makawee, often in traditional Native American garb. Nane taught two or three classes each day on a variety of subjects. The classes were designed for older children, but Aura attended them and understood the material well.

The rest of the time was divided between individual study and leisure time. Personal study for Aura usually meant going to the library and reading. When she first learned about magic, she assumed she would be memorizing books of spells. At least, that is what it always showed in movies she had seen. As it turned out, magic was more about the creative use of science than anything else. Rather than spell books, she was expected to read about earth sciences and geology. Much of druid magic revolves around endowing objects with energy. Many things that are most conducive to holding, manipulating, and focusing energy are made naturally from the earth, like crystals, rocks, and gemstones.

Makawee and Nane, as earth druids, talked a lot about rocks. Aura had no idea there were so many kinds. They taught all about rocks, crystals, and gemstones. Aura learned that some gemstones or crystals are suited to particular purposes. For example, if you want to heal someone from an infection, the best stone to use is a bloodstone. Sure, a quartz crystal would be okay, but it would only provide a fraction of the benefit the bloodstone would. Understanding stones was all about the potency of energy for a particular purpose. If you wanted to maximize your magical powers, you needed to understand which stone to use for which purpose.

Then, with that information, Makawee and Nane (and several books in the library) taught how to activate and charge the stones. This was just as important as picking the suitable stone or object in the first place. So many factors went into activating and charging stones. Nane talked about what she had learned from Makawee. One day she said, "There are many ignorant druids that think all you need to do is find a ley line crossing on a full moon, which maximizes energy absorption. That is not true. Many subtle things can dramatically increase or decrease energy during activation and charging." Nane taught the six aspects of charging, including what object is being charged, where, when, and how it is being charged, for what purpose it is being charged, and for what type of druid.

"Children, here is an extreme example," Nane said one January morning during a class. "A Cosmic druid that wants to activate and charge a stone that stops time needs to be perfectly balanced, just like the present is balanced against the past and future. An optimal activation may come from the cosmic druid using a perfect crystal such as one used in a watch. The more included the crystal (meaning the number of flaws, cracks, or other imperfections), the less precise the spell's outcome will be. You would want to charge it under optimal circumstances to create balance. While there is no one way to do this, an example might be to activate the crystal somewhere on the equator during the spring equinox when the sun is over the earth's center. If you could align all that with a waxing half-moon, it could enhance the energy concentration. Notice the theme of balance here. If activation occurred at noon, with the sun at its most balanced point during the day, and all those other conditions met, the potency could be even higher."

Nane went to the board and began writing. "Each factor that contributes to the potency of energy has a doubling effect. So in the example I just gave, the right crystal in the hands of a competent cosmic druid may produce an artifact with an energy value of Z," she wrote 'Crystal' and then a 'Z' at the top of the board. "Activated on the equator could mean Z x 2." Nane wrote 'Equator' and then 'Z x 2'. "Add the equinox" She then wrote 'Equinox Z x 4'. "Add the right phase of the moon," she wrote 'Moon Phase Z x 8'. "Add activation at noon, and you could have a crystal with 16 times more powerful power than one activated without special conditions." She finished saying as she wrote, 'Noon Z x 16'. "There is no one way to activate and charge an object, but each factor will determine the potency of your relic."

Nane would give many examples like this to drive the point home, and they would be entirely different for each type of druid. For an earth druid, she would talk more about ley lines, a diamond's hardness, and the deepest cave on a new moon on the winter solstice. For a frequency druid, she spoke of the bottom of a powerful waterfall in the cleanest part of the world when the sun is shining, causing a rainbow to appear with clear quartz in the shape of a pyramid. She said, "It is difficult to maximize energy efficacy, but more care should be taken to do all you can. With a little thought, much more powerful relics are possible," she would say, "potent activation of artifacts was a lost art, and most objects used in the world today had only a fraction of their original potential."

She directed the students to the many maps they had in the library with ley lines. Some of an ordered polarity with standard gridlines, and some with a chaotic polarity based on tectonic plates, fault lines, and volcanoes. A disproportionate amount of maps and books focused on earth druidism due to Nane and Makawee being earth druids.

Aura and the other students had to memorize the Mohs scale of hardness, which measures how hard rocks and gems are. Everyone knows a diamond is the hardest stone in the world, so it has a ten on the Mohs scale. But Aura had to memorize many rocks and where they fell on the scale. They had to remember mineralogy classification charts and know which minerals contributed to the colors of various precious gems and semi-precious gemstones.

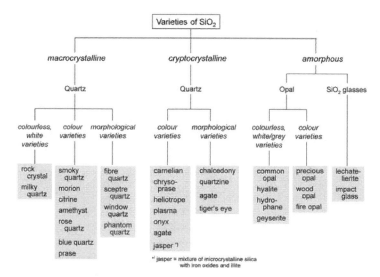

Nane taught about the earth's formation, the layers within the earth's magma, and the chemical reactions that create the various types of stones. She discussed precious metals but said a future cosmic druid teacher would likely cover them as the source of things like gold is inside massive stars that explode into a supernova.

Aura enjoyed one book with many pictures of various artifacts throughout time. These often had many gemstones inlaid with gold, silver, or other precious metals. Some were powerful and highly versatile because a single artifact could hold the energy for various uses. Druids wanted to avoid digging into a bag of rocks each time they wanted to do something different. Having a staff, scepter, crown, shield, necklace, or other artifacts with multiple magical objects embedded was very popular.

This learning went on for weeks and weeks. As March rolled in, the children spent more of their leisure time outside, practicing their magic or playing games with the other kids. The game the kids most often played was what they called Ardu, a Druidic word meaning "the Rise," both referring to where they play and rising to greatness. It was played on the grassy hill in front of the house. The top of the hill was rounded slightly, with an even slope on all sides. Six trees had grown around the perimeter of the ring equally. Opposing trees were 30' apart, making the diameter of the top of the hill 30' without any obstructions. Six students would play at a time, standing just behind the imaginary line between the trees. A ball would be placed on the top of the hill, slowly rolling down towards one of the openings between the trees where a player would be. The student would then need to redirect the ball from his area toward another player. Each player starts with 6 points, and they would lose a point if the ball passes through their set of trees. When a student gets to 0, the game ends, and the player with the most remaining points wins. The trick was you couldn't touch the ball. You had to use magic. The magic could not be used on any other player. If you did, you were immediately disqualified.

Aura wouldn't play but would watch the other kids use magic as students would be eliminated one by one. One afternoon in mid-March, Aura was on the front porch reading a book entitled "Mineralogy. It Rocks! A study of chemistry and crystal structures" Six other kids began a game of Ardu. This game was unique because each of the six students had different magical affinities. These games often became unofficial ways of showing your affinity was the best. It wasn't required, but when they wanted to get serious, each player would dress in the colors most often associated with that affinity of magic. The life magic druid, a girl named Rebecca, wore green. The frequency druid wore red. Her name was Hope. The atmospheric druid was a boy named David, who wore orange. The cosmic druid wore purple. His name was John, but he went by Eos. A third boy was named Jordan, wearing blue and was a liq. The final spot was filled by an earth druid named Brynn wearing yellow. Brynn felt the most pressure at an earth-druid school and wanted to represent her affinity well.

The ball was set in at the top of the hill, all six players between the six trees as the ball began rolling down towards David, the atmospheric druid who was using turquoise carved as a flat round stone. He was casting a spell that brought about a breeze strong enough to push the ball over the hill towards Jordan, the liq. He seemed to struggle to conjure anything, and the ball passed through his set of trees, and his points went from 6 to 5.

The ball was set again, and the next round started. The ball headed towards Eos, who opened a portal using a short, thick labradorite stone. The other end of the portal was just up from Rebecca, the life druid who blocked the ball by causing a tree root to pop out of the earth, which directed the ball again towards Jordan, and it passed by him again, casing his score to go down to 4.

Round three began with the ball heading towards Eos again, but this time he used a time manipulation spell to reverse time on the ball, which took it back up the hill. It then headed towards Brynn, the earth wizard who launched a stone at the ball, sending it back towards Eos. However, this time, Hope used her obsidian to cause the ball to become invisible by manipulating the light reflecting off the ball. Because Eos couldn't see the ball, it passed by him, and his score went from 6 to 5.

The game went on for some time and ended with Rebecca causing a swarm of bees to push the ball towards Jordan, who was finally able to pull enough moisture from the ground to force the ball towards Brynn, who upheaved some earth blocking the goal and then sent the ball back towards David who attempted to increase the atmospheric pressure on the ball at an angle to send it towards Hope. Still, the pressure was too great, and it popped the ball, which took David from 1 to 0 points ending the game. Brynn had 4 points remaining and won the match.

Even with the coaxing of the kids and Nane, Aura wouldn't play. She was not yet ready for that kind of pressure. She preferred going into the forest alone and practicing her spells which she was beginning to get a grasp on. She realized that spells were about the degree of mental control and focus you have which creates the outcome. You must concentrate but also stay grounded and centered. If she didn't stay balanced as she focused, nothing would happen, or the result would be intense and out of control.

Makawee helped her understand this as they took their walks which happened most days. More kids began to get jealous of Aura because she seemed to get more of Makawee's attention than anyone else. During these walks, Makawee would talk about odd things that she never heard in class and never saw in any of the books in the house library. She spent an entire morning telling Aura about how diamonds can be colored. Aura learned that lower-quality diamonds can take on various colors due to defects combined with nitrogen, hydrogen, or nickel impurities. High-quality diamonds with almost no imperfections rarely have color except under conditions produced by radiation exposure. These scarce, high-quality colored diamonds are some of the most powerful gems in the world.

Even being the youngest of all the kids, she seemed to remember everything she was taught and read. She was able to recall all this information at a moment's notice. As a result, she was progressing faster than most of the other students.

Aura continued to struggle with her health, especially her breathing. Her inhaler was becoming less and less helpful. Makawee said that the dry air in Arizona, especially as they were moving into summer, was probably irritating her airways and causing more asthma attacks. They had a humidifier at the care center, but not only did they not have one at the house, she was spending so much time outside it wouldn't have mattered. As a result, Makawee began looking into transferring Aura to another elder druid to continue her learning. Aura didn't want to leave until she had earned her earth-druid artifact. Most dedicated students earn them in about six months. She had been with Makawee for over four months and thought she was ready.

The requirements for graduation were different if your affinity matched the school. For example, an earth druid would have to demonstrate proficiency in many areas to graduate from an earth druid school. Since Aura was not an earth druid, her exam (a face-to-face interview with Makawee and Nane simultaneously) consisted of a barrage of questions involving many aspects of geoscience. There were questions on the earth's lithosphere with a deep dive into geology. They spent a lot of time on mineralogy, including the physical properties of many types of rocks. She was asked to draw the structure of a perovskite crystal. She struggled for a few moments trying to remember if it was magnesium or iron in addition to the oxygen and silicon and then remembered it could be either. There were even questions about the earth's magnetic field, which she got right but couldn't remember where she learned it. The test took over an hour. She could see why her roommate Halona had been there now for over a year and wasn't ready to test. Makawee and Nane spoke for a few minutes with Aura out of the room and then called her back in.

"You passed!" Nane said. Makawee had a big grin on her face. "We are very proud of you. Did you know that no one as young as you has ever graduated this fast or this early? You are quite the druid prodigy, Aura."

Aura blushed, not knowing what to say. "So what happens now," she asked.

"Just because you passed the test doesn't mean you can graduate. There is one other requirement we have here at this school. You have to win at least one game of Ardu," Makawee said. Aura's heart sank. She hadn't played a single game and saw how good the other kids were at it. "Once you win a game of Ardu, you will go to your next school, which I have arranged and believe will be much better for your health."

Word spread quickly throughout the house that Aura had passed her exams. Many of the kids felt like she had shown them up, being the last to come into the school and the first to pass. Brynn was especially irate as she was an earth druid, and Aura had shown her up. But when the children realized that she needed to win a game of Ardu and she hadn't even played a single match, they decided they could gang up and keep her there a very long time by not allowing her ever to win.

Aura decided she would try Ardu the next day because she knew she would never progress as a druid without winning a match. She had watched many games and had come to learn the strategies and tactics that most of the students used during a game.

During breakfast, several students, notably Brynn and Halona, were heckling Aura about when she would compete at Ardu. She said, "How about right after breakfast?" The students took a look at each other and started laughing as they cleaned up their plates and headed out towards the hill. Aura borrowed an orange shirt from Nane and headed out towards the field herself. She had pulled out her discolored cauliflower calcite to use during the match. Six players took their positions with everyone else, including Makawee and Nane, watching from the patio. Three players were the most frequent champions, including Rebecca, Hope, and Brynn, representing life, frequency, and earth, respectively. Also joining was a boy named Caspian, a liq. Halona, her roommate, who was a frequency druid, and herself. All players were wearing their affinity colors.

The ball was set at the top, and the game began. It rolled towards Halona, who put a reverse time spell on it, and it rolled back up the hill and then over towards Caspian, who had the benefit of it raining the previous evening. So with plenty of moisture on the ground, he controlled the water to hit the ball toward the border between Brynn and Aura. Brynn raised a dirt mount which deflected the ball through Aura's trees. Aura was now 5 points.

The ball started again at the top, this time rolling towards Aura. She held out cauliflower calcite and cast a spell to create a rain storm to direct the ball between Brynn's trees. Still, when Caspian saw the rain, he could redirect it, knocking the ball back towards Aura and through her trees. She was now 4.

The ball started again from the top, heading towards Halona, but Aura knew she would try the time reversal spell again. She cast a wind gust spell at just the right time, so as soon as the ball reached the top, the wind caught it, and the ball sailed over Halona's head between her trees. Halona was now five and noticeably perturbed.

The ball started at the top again, this time heading towards Aura. She saw Hope cast a spell out of the corner of her eye. She knew it was meant to make the ball appear in a different spot than it was. Typically this caused the defender to miss the ball and lose a point. Still, Aura, anticipating this, immediately cast a mist spell, causing the entire mound to be covered in a light stratus cloud. This diffused the light making Hope's mirage disappear. It also gave Aura a split-second advantage which she used to push the ball between Caspian's trees.

In the next round, the ball headed to Rebecca, who had several squirrels come out from a nearby log and push the ball toward Aura. The squirrels were slow, making it funny to watch. The squirrels were getting near the top where they could push the ball down towards Aura. She lifted her cauliflower calcite and focused on lightning. She had been practicing her marksmanship with lightning bolts and could direct it right at the top. Sure enough, the squirrels ran off, and everyone, including Rebecca, was so surprised that the ball rolled past her.

Brynn caught the ball rolling toward her during the next round by opening a crevice. Aura took advantage of this by creating a dust devil right over it, which pulled the ball out of the aperture and shot it at Brynn, hitting her in the chest, causing her to get the breath knocked out of her and lose a point.

The game went on with Aura out-thinking each other player's strategy. She was able to anticipate their quite obvious moves and counteract them. It was easy to scare off Rebecca's animals or insects with lightning. The Mist largely stopped Hope, who relied on light, optics, and shadows to score. Halona only had a couple of tricks up her sleeve between the time manipulation and portals. Both could be used against her easily enough. If she opens up a portal just before a ball goes between her trees and sends them towards Aura's area, Aura would do a massive gust of wind, sending it right back for which Halona had no defense. Caspian was initially tricky with so much water. Still, Aura realized that if she froze the water by dropping the temperature on the hill, it wasn't a liquid any longer, and he couldn't control it. As a result, he was down to 1 point the soonest. The ball kept rolling right past him as he couldn't think of anything else to do. Brynn was the most difficult as she had both defensive tactics pulling up earth to block or crevices to stop or redirect the ball. She also had offensive maneuvers by using rocks to hit the ball in her desired direction, usually toward Aura.

It was now Rebecca 2, Hope 3, Aura 4, Halona 2, Caspian 1, and Brynn 4. Brynn shot the ball using a rock toward Aura. Still, because Brynn was next to Aura, it was a shot she could deflect using a dust devil up toward Caspian, who was defenseless on the icy ground. It passed between his trees, and his score went to 0. Usually, that would be the end of the game, but because Brynn and

Aura were tied with 4, a final round had to be played. Aura saw Brynn make a gesture at Halona. She realized they would try to work together to make Aura lose in this sudden death round.

The ball immediately began rolling down towards Brynn. She had been waiting for this. Halona opened up a portal just after the ball was halfway towards Brynn, with the other end of the portal above Aura's head just 1 foot away from the tree line. Brynn cast a spell picking up a medium-sized rock and planning to hit the ball toward the portal. In a flash, Aura realized there was no defense against such a cheap shot. She concentrated on making the ball not move. The ball began to get squished against the ground and became somewhat oblong. Brynn launched the stone at the ball, but rather than hitting the ball through the portal, the rock bounced off the ball and hit Brynn, who was knocked backward. Aura released the pressure against the ball, which slowly rolled down and through Brynn's trees. Aura had won the game!

Later that night, there was a small ceremony, as was customary when a student graduates and obtains their school relic. All the students were seated in the living room as well as Nane. Aura was called up. Makawee took out a hand-carved, ornate stone box the size of which could hold several books. She used a stone Aura couldn't see to unlock and pull off the lid. She reached in and took out a deep red garnet stone. It was cut to be a 20-sided polygon. She took the stone in her other hand and placed it on the garnet. A moment later, she removed it, and Aura saw an etched seal on one of the 20 faces. The seal was a globe of the world with etched North and South America and a dot where the Native American reservation was in Arizona. Makawee handed it to Aura and said. "You should be very proud of how far you have come in such a short time. You are truly gifted."

Chapter 10

THE FOLLOWING DAY, Makawee covered the classes while Nane helped Aura prepare to travel. Nane said "The way a druid travels when we aren't driving the black Tahoe is by portal. To do this, we use these," she pulled out a metal object about the size of a small apple. It had 20 equal triangle-shaped sides. In the center of each triangle was a cut-out oval so you could see through the object, which was hollow in the center. Each oval had a yellow energy that filled it. "This is called an icosahedron," Nane said. "but we call them Polys, which is short for polygons." Each of the six types of druids uses a slightly different poly. Once you get your poly, only you can activate it. So you can't just take mine and use it, but if I use it, you can come with me.

Nane then pulled out two maps from a large flat drawer that Aura knew were ley line maps. "We are here," Nane said as she pointed to the Hualapai Indian Reservation in Arizona on the United States ley line map. This was an ordered polarity map, so the ley lines were in a repeating grid pattern. Aura could see that Nane's finger was on one of the longitude-like ley lines that went from North to South. This line crossed through the Gulf of California, entered the U.S. in the Organ Pipe Cactus National Monument, went up through the Hualapai Reservation, and then up through Utah, the bottom part of Idaho, western Montana, and Canada. "Our home here is directly on this ley line which has many benefits for us as earth druids. Earth druids can only travel on the Ley lines when we travel by poly. Thankfully that includes both ordered ley lines and chaos ley lines." Nane overlaid the other map on top of the grid map. "So your next teacher lives here in the Redwoods in northern California," she said as she pointed to the other map. "So to get from here to the Redwoods, we must travel this ley line here." Her finger followed the first map's ley line from the reservation south into Mexico. She then went to the same spot on the other map and began tracing up into California. "Then we can connect to this ley line, a series of connected fault lines up through California until we get to the Redwoods. That should get us close," she said.

Aura had studied ley lines and heard about polys, but she was excited to see how everything worked. "Do you have everything?" Nane asked.

"Yep," Aura said, holding her mother's small grey duffel bag. She had carefully packed her belongings, including her fulgurite wand, cauliflower calcite, desert rose, and new red garnet.

"Traveling through portals can be tricky, especially for an earth druid like me. Icosahedron portals form flat on the ground. The other side is also on the ground, so imagine this in your mind for a moment," Nane holding Aura by the shoulders. "If you just simply jump in straight, you would come out and land on your head on the other side. That is if you are lucky enough not to fall back through the portal back to here. So it would be best to dive through the portal head first at an angle so that you come out and land on your feet. It is a bit of an adjustment. If you don't do it right and fall back through, it will cost a charge on the poly. Some druids have been known to burn through all their charges in a single attempt, so let's be careful. I'll go first. You come through right after me, and I'll grab onto you. Okay?"

This sounded scary to Aura now, but she didn't know what to do other than say, "Okay."

Nane lifted her icosahedron to her head, focused then blew on it, and on the floor right in front of her opened a round yellow circle through which you could see the blue sky. "Follow me," she said as she dove through head-first at an angle.

Aura could see her land on her feet on the other side of the hole. Feeling very nervous, she dove head-first through the yellow portal. She immediately felt vertigo as the gravity shifted as she passed through. She didn't do quite the proper dive and was at a 45-degree angle and falling back into the portal when Nane grabbed her duffel and pulled her upright. She looked over her shoulder, where she could still see the library in Makawee's home, and then the portal closed.

"That was pretty good for your first time," Nane said.

"Are we in the Redwoods?" asked Aura.

"No. Remember I said we needed to travel south on the ordered Ley line? Then we could travel north through California on the chaotic fault lines. That requires two separate jumps using this type of poly. A portal rides both types of ley lines, but you must make two separate jumps to do it," Nane said.

"You mean I have to do that again?" Aura asked.

"You did fine. Just take a moment and orient yourself, and then we will do it again."

Aura looked around. They were in the middle of the desert. Cacti, sand, and dust as far as she could see except to the west, where it looked like water was in the distance. "Is that the Gulf of California?" she asked.

"Yep. Are you ready?" Nane asked.

"Let's get it over with," said Aura.

Nane again put the twenty-sided copper relic to her forehead, concentrated, and then blew softly on the poly and another yellow circle just like the last one opened in front of her. As Aura looked through it, she couldn't see the sky but a canopy of green leaves extending from tall trees. It was so strange to look down, up into the sky. Aura got a little dizzy. "Okay. The same as before, okay?" Nane asked. Aura nodded. Nane dove through head-first at an angle again and seemed to land perfectly. Aura dove again and did a little better on the pitch. Still, vertigo with the whole world flipping so fast and the gravitational shift as you passed was very disorienting. Nane grabbed her arm and steadied her as she came through, and the portal closed. Aura bent over and threw up. "That is also very common for people's first time."

"Are all polys like this?" Aura asked.

"Liquid polys are even worse, I have heard, because you have to do it in water, which is scary. There are pros and cons to each affinity. That may be disorienting and multi-stepped, but at least I have twenty charges," Nane held up her icosahedron, which now had 4 of the ovals without yellow energy. "You are an atmospheric druid. Your poly (if I remember right) only has four charges. So even with the extra difficulty, I like mine."

"Where are we?" Aura asked as she wiped her mouth with her sleeve.

"The Redwood forest. I know the way from here. It is very close," Nane answered. She was right, within 2 minutes she said "We are here" although to Aura it looked like the middle of a forest. "It will be good to see Daniel again," Nane said with too much enthusiasm as she walked towards a vast tree with an opening big enough for someone to walk through, which is precisely what Nane did. When she was through the tree, she turned, and Aura could no longer see her. "Come on," she heard Nane's voice say. So Aura also walked through the tree, and as soon as she passed through, she could see wood steps ascending nearly vertically around the tree trunk.

"Why couldn't I see these before?" Aura asked.

"Daniel lives in a tree house, and he had a frequency druid cast a spell that keeps his home hidden from others. In reality, it is only an optical illusion, but it keeps unwanted people away; or so I am told," Aura remembered Halona's ball during the Ardu game. They ascended around the tree three times before seeing a narrow bridge from the tree with an opening to another tree with a huge house. Aura couldn't call it a tree house because it was as big as a regular house, just at the top of the trees. At ever-increasing heights, three large platforms were wrapped around the enormous tree. The platforms extended away from the trunk by at least 25' with solid reinforcements holding them in place. Rooms wrapped around the tree sitting on the platforms, leaving a walkway around the perimeter with staircases going up to the other levels. The bridge led to a front porch and a door on which Nane knocked on eagerly. A moment later, the door opened, and it was a tall, beautiful woman with long blond hair and blue eyes. She wore an oversized black T-shirt with long legs extending from the bottom. In a bubbly voice, she said, "Hi. Can I help you?"

"Uh. Is Daniel here?" Nane asked as Aura could see all the anticipation and enthusiasm leave her body like a wind sock on a still day.

A man even taller than the blond woman with medium-length brown wavy hair came up behind her and said, "Nane! How are you doing? Come in. Come in," he said genuinely.

"I can't stay," Nane said with her cheeks flushing, "But as we discussed, this is Aura. Aura, this is Daniel Silva, and um," she said, looking at the blond.

"This is Kimberly," Daniel said. "She is a frequency druid from Southern California helping me fine-tune the illusions around the house. Nice to meet you, Aura," shaking her hand. "Are you sure you can't stay, Nane? I was planning on you both for lunch."

"No, I need to get back. Makawee is covering my classes, but you know how she gets," Nane said as she turned to Aura. "It was very nice getting to know you. You always have a place with us on the reservation if you need." Aura hugged her. Nane then walked back across the bridge and down the stairs as Aura waved goodbye and Daniel shut the door.

Daniel wore a loose white knit button-down shirt with only the bottom three buttons clasped with his sleeves rolled up to just under his elbows. He had a thick beard that matched the thick hair on his exposed chest. Hanging from his neck were at least a half dozen necklaces of various types. One was silver with a medallion at the end. Another was made from red glass beads. Another was a stone in a cage hung from a black rope. Still, another looked like tiny white seashells all strung together. For pants, it almost looked like he was wearing a wool dress. Still, the material came down from a very loose crotch hanging below his knees and then connected and tapered around each ankle. Daniel seeing Aura eyeing the pants, modeled them and said, "Do you like them?" he said while turning around. "They are my new harem pants. Super comfy! Tell us about you, little lady. It's Aura, right? Love that name!"

The three of them sat down on a simple sofa in the first room as Daniel and Kimberly asked question after question of Aura.

"So you just discovered four months ago that you are a druid? Whoa! I can't remember a time I didn't know. And you have lived in a foster care facility your whole life?" Aura nodded.

"Do you know what happened to your mom and dad?" Daniel asked. Kimberly elbowed him a little, letting him know it was an inappropriate question to ask but only out of social graces as she wanted to know the answer herself.

"I don't know anything about my dad, and the first I heard about my mom was when a stranger gave me a bag of her things just a few months ago," Aura said as she lifted the grey duffel bag and set it back on her lap.

"What was in the bag?" Daniel and Kimberly said, both riveted.

"Just some clothes, her passport, a fulgurite wand, and a brownish stone," Aura said.

"Can I see the passport?" Daniel inquired, holding out his hand. Aura opened the bag and began reaching under the clothes for the passport when the fulgurite wand became exposed on the top of the heap. Daniel jumped back, tripping over the sofa and falling over. "Holy, Shhhhh-where did you get that?!" he said, pointing at the glass tube.

"It was in my mom's bag," Aura said, startled, having found the passport.

"I know whos that was. Oh my! He took the passport, opened it to the first page with the picture, and looked at the name. Rosa. Rosa from Uxmal. I can't believe it. I knew your father!"

Daniel spent the next half hour talking about Edward Blood, his close friend who he hadn't seen since late 2010. "Yeah, it has been almost nine years since I saw him. He would talk about your mother all the time. He was so in love with her. He was doing everything he could to protect her."

Aura was in tears, and Kimberly had moved over, sitting next to her, holding and rubbing her arm. They were putting the pieces together that Rosa had gotten pregnant and must have been trying to find Edward. Aura pulled the piece of paper out of the end of the fulgurite wand and handed it to Daniel. "This is his handwriting, all right. It is for an address down in Myers Flat where his house is, but this isn't his address. I've been to his home many times, hoping to find him, The dude just vanished."

"So something happened to both your father and your mother, and you ended up abandoned at a hospital since birth. HEAVY!" Daniel said with glazed-over eyes. Aura reached into her bag, found her asthma inhaler, and breathed in as she thought she felt an attack coming.

"Asthma?" Daniel asked.

"Yes, I have many health problems, but the worst is weak lungs because I was born three months early. At least, that is what they told me. I am also very anemic," Aura answered.

"Well, little missy, that is something I can help with. Come with me. Kimmie, would you make some sandwiches while I work on Aura here?" Daniel took Aura by the hand, and they walked out onto the walkway and scaled the wood steps up to the second level. Aura looked down over the railing over a drop of at least 50 feet and decided to use both hands on the wood railing. They entered another room with a small wooden chair in the center. It had four legs fixed on the ground but angled back like a permanent recliner. "Sit right there," Daniel said, pointing at the chair while he went over to a wooden chest and opened it up. He pulled out a small cloth bag synched at the top with a string resembling Daniel's pants but without the legs. He then took out a small ivory tusk and a dull grey stone. He came over and sat down before Aura, opened the bag, pulled out the contents, and placed them on the floor before the chair. There was a yellow oval semi-transparent stone, a ping mostly clear crystal ball the size of a walnut, and a white stone with markings on one flat side. He held the tusk up in front of Aura. "This tusk is from an elephant in Africa. I got in a scuff with some poachers years after seeing them do this to a magnificent creature. I cast a spell on them that anything they did to another animal would immediately happen to them. Let's say it only took them once to learn the lesson," Daniel said with a satisfied grin.

"Tell me about these items you have," Aura said, being very interested in stones from her previous school.

"Well, this yellow one is amber," Daniel said.

"Amber formed from tree resin. I read about it, but I have never seen it," Aura said as she took it from Daniel and looked at the pale milky yellow stone.

"This one is rose quartz," he said, handing her the pink round ball.

"I thought that is what it was," she said.

"And this is a fossil. You can see the impression of the ocean critter from millions of years ago. Have you ever seen one of these?" He asked.

"No," Aura said, looking more closely at it before handing it back to him.

"And this is a chunk of iron showing her what looked like a grey rock. Aura, I am a life druid. My magic revolves around living things. Most relics a druid like me uses come from or are associated with living things. The amber from a living tree, the fossil, and the tusk," Daniel said, "The rose quartz is just a crystal, but it is known as the heart stone, and its frequency aligns well with life druid magic," he said, anticipating Aura's next question. "Life relics are meant to heal us." He returned the tusk to Aura and asked that she hold it with both hands. He took the necklace with the cage from around his neck, removed the stone, put the amber in it, and fastened it around Aura's neck. He pulled the chain until it was centered on her chest and did a quick knot to hold it there. He then took the fossil and placed it on her head. "Don't move," he said. He held the rose quartz in his right hand, closed his eyes, and began to focus. She then felt a warm burning in her chest, like she had been sprinting but wasn't out of breath. "Let me know when the warmth subsides," Daniel said.

The sensation continued for some time before Aura said, "It's done."

"How do you feel?" asked Daniel as he removed the necklace and fossil from Aura.

She took a deep breath through her nose, deeper than she ever had, and blew it out through her mouth. "That feels so good," she said.

"We will have to fix your anemia in a couple of days since this iron ore here needs to be activated and charged, but you can throw that inhaler away, girly girl. Your lungs are perfect," Daniel said with a smile.

She jumped up and hugged him with one arm while holding the tusk with the other. "Thank you, Mr. Silva!"

"Your father is like a brother to me. You call me Uncle Danny."

~

EDWARD BLOOD WAS COLD. It had been hard for the four months since he had broken the glass of the barred window in the dungeon of his cousin's castle, where he had now been a prisoner and tortured for over eight years. At first, he wasn't sure his idea would even work, but it was working; it was just painfully slow. Edward took a deep breath from inside the grate near the floor, then walked over to the bars on the window and looked behind them. Severe rust and corrosion had almost entirely eaten through two bars on the bottom and one on the top. It had taken four months to get this far. The gold tooth that he had activated and charged the best he could was now wrapped around the top of the second bar with toilet paper holding it in place. The gold tooth was accelerating the process where oxygen and humidity interacted with iron to cause it to rust. The corrosion had worked its way through most of the bar. He was nearly there; only a little bit more time. Then he heard two voices approaching. He quickly removed the toilet paper, put the tooth under the floor stone, and had just enough time to dive towards the grate when the heavy metal lock clanked and swung open, and Alexander and Mercurius walked in.

"I told you e said e was going on da 15th," Mercurius said.

"Himself?" Alexander responded. He doesn't get his hands dirty very often these days. Maybe he wants to go because it is in Paris."

"Dat is what e said. Ah mean da thing is nearly 2000 yeaws owd," said the short, rounded man who seemed only to have one pair of clothes as he wore the same brown suit with chevron patterns each time Edward saw him. "Do ya think it's reow? Millions visit it evewy year believing its reow."

"I've never understood the appeal of Christian or any other religious artifacts for that matter. Oh, for the love of Hades, could you please cancel the spell while we are here? I can hardly breathe," Alexander said as he stepped back into the hallway.

"Dat isn't ow it works. You know dat," and Mercurius also stepped back through to avoid the spell that had reduced the oxygen in the dungeon to debilitating levels for anyone exposed for very long.

"Oiy. You. Edward. Thomas wanted me to tell you that we are hot on the trail of your precious emerald. Clues led Nephrite up to an Indian reservation in Arizona."

"Native American Reservation," Alexander said, correcting Mercurius.

"Yeah, whate'er," Mercurius said, brushing Alexander off, "Nephrite does what she does best. She ripped da place apart. Turned out to be a school for littl ones. Most of da litto buggars got away through a portal with the ol' teacha, but not before some assistant and some kids got whacked. It's only a ma'er o time before we get it." He pulled the door shut, and he heard the lock turn. Edward pulled up the stone again and wrapped the tooth around the second top bar.

Edward waited and looked between the grate and the window every 5 minutes in anticipation of completing. It was late into the night when he went over and pulled the toilet paper back and saw that; indeed, the tooth had rusted out the bar almost completely. He pulled at the bars, and with less effort than he thought, both came away, leaving enough space for him to crawl through. He was about to crawl out when he got an idea.

Twenty minutes later, Edward had shimmied through the remaining bars, scaled up the window well, and out onto the castle grounds and disappeared into the trees.

~

THE FOLLOWING DAY Aura woke up in a soft down bed in her very own room on the third level of the treehouse. She had never had her own room before, and she felt a little scared being by herself even though she knew that Daniel was in the room next door. Aura went down the two flights of stairs, along the walkway, and into the kitchen area where Daniel was cooking breakfast. "Good morning Miss Aura," he said.

"Good morning," she replied. "Where is Kimberly?"

"Kimmie had to take off this morning. She will be gone for several days but don't worry. You will see her again," Daniel said with a smile. "How do you like your eggs?"

After breakfast, Aura was instructed to wear her shoes and be ready for a hike. He said they needed to see "The President" and gestured towards an old black and white picture hanging on the wall. It had eight people standing in front of an enormous Redwood tree. She wondered which of them was the President and how old they were now. Daniel had promised he would teach her how to activate and charge artifacts. She wondered if The President would be showing her or doing it for them. She had been taught about activating and charging, but this was the first time she would see it in person. She was excited.

They walked down the wood stairs to the tree opening and went through, and suddenly the treehouse was gone. At first, Aura wasn't worried that it would be much of a hike because Daniel only had flip-flips that seemed too small for his feet. But they walked and walked and walked. They had been gone for over an hour when Daniel finally stopped and said, "We are here." Aura looked around, and it was just more trees. "Is there another invisible treehouse here that the president lives in?"

"The President isn't a person; it is this tree right here." Aura looked towards where Edward was pointing; the same tree was in the black and white photo. "The President is believed to be the oldest living redwood tree. It is a giant sequoia estimated to be about 3,200 years old. To put that into perspective, This tree sprouted about the same time Moses helped the Israelites pass through the Red Sea on dry ground, and the Egyptians were swallowed by it. This tree is as old as many pyramids in Egypt and is older than the stone tablets that came down the mountain with Moses. It isn't the oldest tree in the world; that is here in California but further south. But this is the oldest Sequoiadendron giganteum, the giant sequoia."

"Aura, when you activate or charge an object, you want to be sure you match the object type with a similar energy source for the best results. Returning to the source or a similar geography can also increase the power of an artifact. So, for example, taking this hunk of iron back to where it was mined may be really good. However, another similar iron mine may be adequate. The alternate mine may even be better if there are other conditions that magnify the object." Aura remembered this similar lesson from her time with Makawee and told Daniel so.

"Good. So here is one of the objects we will charge today." Daniel pulled a mini tree stump from his wool parachute pants, but when Aura held it, it was clearly a stone. "That is petrified wood," he said. So petrified wood has its energy source from a living thing, so the alignment to the life-druid affinity works perfectly. We could return to the petrified forest where I got it and charge it there, but I think this will be even better. The President is not only one of the oldest trees in the world, but it also sits near a fault line and tectonic plate."

"But that is earth druid magic," Aura said.

"True, but all energy comes from the same source. Then it passes through objects such as a fault line, volcano, tree, or anything else. The energy has the same potency but now tends towards a particular affinity. That doesn't make it bad. In fact, sometimes it can be very good. It depends on what you are trying to do with your artifact. Think of it this way, imagine all energy coming from a universal source as the color white. Then as it passes through those affinity lenses, such as a lightning bolt or waterfall or something, it takes on a new hue of color—Blue for a liquid affinity, yellow for earth affinity, green for life, and so forth. Sometimes you may want an object to be as blue as possible with all liq filters regarding activation or charging. Other times you may want a combination of filters. Do you see this shark tooth here?" he lifted one of the many necklaces he was wearing with a giant shark tooth hanging from the end. "This was activated while riding a dolphin in the ocean. Both water and life. Blue and green."

"But you are not a liq," Aura said.

"Don't let other druids try to force you into one type of magic. We can discuss the colors red, orange, blue, red, and so forth, but colors are on a spectrum. Yes, your specific magic may be the strongest within one affinity, but that doesn't mean you don't have some connections and influence on others. You can be right-handed and still use your left for some things. Many druids can blend affinities for unique magic skills. I know full dé-thugach druids, meaning they are dual-gifted druids. Blacksmiths who forge polys are even more rare, being tri-gifted druids. There are few of those. They require cosmic, earth, and life magic to forge polygons. A true oracle is often a dé-thugach as well. Be open and flexible with how you look at magic so you don't box yourself into one type of thinking. Most teachers will focus on strict categories or lanes. Don't think that way. If you believe you only have one type of magic, guess how many you will have?" Daniel said rhetorically.

He approached The President and placed the petrified wood stone at the tree's base. "So, Aura, you have an object related to life magic. You have put it at one of the world's oldest and most potent life objects, which is also on a ley line, perhaps several in this region. What else might you do to enhance the activation of this object?"

"Would the time of day matter?" she asked.

"Very good. That is what I was thinking. At noon when we get the most sunlight. While sunlight is often associated with either frequency or cosmic affinities, light is required for all living things. Can you see how these things are not separate but rather blended? Let's activate this at noon, which will be here in a few minutes," Daniel said as he looked up at the clear blue sky. "That is the only time it would work anyway; otherwise, these trees cast too much shadow. I will activate this stone since I am the life druid. You could activate it, but it wouldn't be as powerful."

"And how exactly do you activate it?" Aura asked.

"There is a very simple incantation you speak while focusing on the object and energy from the surroundings. You take that all into your mind simultaneously and speak these words. 'Go dtabharfadh an Cruinne an cumas agus an chumhacht duit do lánacmhainneacht a bhaint amach,' which means 'May the universe endow you with the capacity and power to reach your full potential.' That is it. Those exact words don't matter as much as hitting that basic idea of a higher power than yourself infusing capacity and power so it can reach the measure of its creation," Daniel explained.

"What do you mean capacity and power?" Aura asked as she watched Daniel get into a meditation position in front of the tree.

"The capacity of a relic or artifact is the total amount of energy it CAN hold. The power of an object is how much energy it DOES hold. So if the most powerful object in the world had a score of 1000 (if we could measure these things objectively), then perhaps under these conditions, this petrified wood is gaining a capacity of 85 and also a power of 85. On this fictitious scale, the maximum capacity it can hold is 85. Today it would charge to 85, and we could recharge it to 85 in the future. But once activated to a particular capacity, an object is quite difficult to undo and then reactivate at a higher degree," Daniel tried to explain.

"So this won't be a very powerful object if it is only 85 out of 1000?" Aura asked.

"This will be powerful for our use. Just remember, some mighty relics and artifacts are out in our world. They are much more powerful than this but are also very rare and hard to acquire. Now hold the rest of your questions for a minute. Now is the time to activate this." Then Daniel did as he described and concentrated and muttered the phrase 'Go dtabharfadh an Cruinne an cumas agus an chumhacht duit do lánacmhainneacht a bhaint amach.'

Aura felt a wave of energy go through her. Not one she could see or would notice with any of her five senses, but rather one like a rejuvenating vitality throughout her entire body. As she looked around, the plants and shrubs began to expand, grow and blossom right before her eyes. Birds began to fly in circles around The President. The new growth, just starting to be seen on the trees, accelerated their expansion from what would take weeks to seconds. Wildflowers all over the area began to bloom spontaneously.

"Wow!" Aura said in amazement and wonder. "Are you seeing this?" she asked Daniel.

"Yes, and it never gets old. It looks like it extends for about 30' from The President this time. I once did this on spring equinox with a more unique relic, and it had a similar effect but extended much further," Daniel said.

"This is amazing," Aura continued to be astonished. Then coming back to her train of thought, she asked. "You mentioned other, more rare artifacts that could have much more power than something like this. Can you give me an example?"

"Sure," Daniel said, picking up the petrified wood and placing it back in his pocket like it was change from a dollar bill. "Imagine an artifact that almost everyone in the world knows about. Something ancient. Something tied to people's belief systems. We were talking about Moses from the bible a bit ago. What if someone found Moses' original staff (well, it was Aaron's staff, but you know what I mean). This staff brought about the ten plagues of Egypt, parted the Red Sea, brought forth water from a rock, and more. What if that object was found today? It is a one-of-a-kind artifact with unrivaled historical precedence and proven power. That is an example of an artifact that would be pretty high on the power meter, I would think."

"Was Moses' staff a druid artifact?" Aura asked as she followed Daniel back on the trail toward the treehouse.

"I gave that as a hypothetical so you could understand the concept. More important than that is why it would have so much power now. How many people know that story? How many people believe in that story, and for how many generations? Human thought is energy, and when that energy is focused around an object such as that staff, it empowers it in ways that ley lines, eclipses, and hurricanes can't begin to. This is why Kings and Queens have staves and scepters and crowns. Everyone in their kingdom believes that whoever is wearing the crown is King. That is why wars have been fought over crowns because a belief system surrounds that object that gives the wearer power. When used by a druid, that power isn't just political; it can control the forces of nature.

The rest of the walk back was spent in silence. Aura had a lot to think about. Her legs were getting pretty tired when she saw the tree with the hole in it. They didn't talk about druids, magic, artifacts, or anything like that for the rest of the night. They went back, made an early dinner, and enjoyed eating it on the deck high in the trees.

~

MERCURIUS' SPELL that removed much of the oxygen from the dungeon cell where Edward Blood was being kept had to be recast occasionally, but he was happy to do it. It allowed him to see Edward in his tortured state. He often thought about what Edward had put him through, so he took a lot of pleasure in visiting the dungeon. This morning he even had a little tune in his head he was humming as he walked down the long hallway to the big metal door at the very end. He put the key in, turned it with the familiar "clank," and pushed the door open. "Mornin' Edward," he said with all the sarcasm he could muster; only Edward wasn't there. Mercurius raced to the bars and immediately began feeling the effects of the lack of oxygen. He took out his semi-transparent apophyllite cluster and removed the spell restricting the oxygen. He then took in everything he saw all at once. Edward was gone. The bars on the window had been cut at the top and bottom. One of them was lying on the floor at his feet. Lastly, the picture had been taken from the wall, and now an empty brass frame was on the table facing the door. "Thomas!!!" he yelled as he ran out the door and back down the hallway.

~

AURA THOUGHT THERE WAS NOTHING like waking up atop the Redwoods as she woke up refreshed. She took a deep breath, which was always so difficult until recently. She climbed out of bed, got ready, and went to the kitchen, where Daniel drank honey lemon tea.

"Get something to eat because we will leave in a few minutes," Daniel said.

Thirty minutes later, they were standing in the main living room of the treehouse, and Daniel pulled out his octahedron, which had eight sides, each with a cut-out circle filled with a green energy glow. We need to go on a little trip this morning. He put the poly to his lips and blew on it softly while forming a picture in his mind. A green portal opened up before them. They walked through and came out the other side in a very different-looking geography. The redwoods had been replaced with pine trees, and the flat ground was now rocky and mountainous. Areas of the mountain were unusual colors of red, orange, yellow, and bluish-green. Just behind them was a building where men were walking out. Daniel took Aura's arm and pulled her close to the building so the men wouldn't see them. "We aren't exactly supposed to be here," Daniel said.

"Where are we?" Aura asked, thinking about how much easier it was to use Daniel's poly than Nane's.

"Richmond Mine, also known as Iron Mountain. It is about three and a half hours drive due east of my home. Welcome to an ecological disaster," Daniel said.

"What do you mean?" asked Aura.

"This mountain was mined for almost 100 years. Now, the water that runs through this area collects a lot of heavy metals and contaminates water downstream. A reclamation team here is trying to resolve the issue and manage the waste in the meantime. Three weeks ago, I met a guy on that team who was on vacation in the Redwoods with his family. See, once a life druid meets someone, they can use their poly to portal near where that person is. It also works for unique life organisms," he said.

"What do you mean 'unique life organisms'" Aura asked. "You won't have to worry about it because you aren't a life druid, but it means I can't use an ant or squirrel to portal to, but I can use a human or some trees or something a bit more substantial in their life force.

"But why are we here?" Aura said getting tired of asking the same question.

"Because we need to activate this hunk of iron, and because it came from here, I think we can get enough energy out of it even though we aren't earth druids." They waited for the men to get in a truck and drive up a dirt road. Once gone, the two walked up toward a ridge northeast of the building. "It sure is pretty up there with all those colors," Aura said. "All that beauty is the metals and chemicals exposed to light, water, and air. That is evidence of mining tailings that cause all the problems. See, this may not even work here. When so much ecological devastation has occurred, it dramatically diminishes the natural energy. But since we don't need much, I hope it will be okay."

"Okay, for what?" Aura asked.

"To heal you of your anemia. You are low in iron and other vitamins and minerals, which is likely due to problems with your small intestines being able to absorb them. So I'm hoping we can activate this hunk of iron and heal you," Daniel said. Aura smiled.

Daniel and Aura walked towards the ridge that had all the colors. When they had come to just below it, they stopped. "This should be fine." He handed the iron to Aura and said. Go ahead and activate it."

"Me?" she said, surprised.

"Yep. Neither of us are earth druids, so there will be no difference on who activates it." He responded.

"Where should I put it?" Aura asked.

"Wherever you think is best," Daniel said with a grin, waiting to see how she did.

The iron block was heavy in her hands. She found a place and set it down. "Why there?" Daniel asked.

"I don't know; it just feels better than over there," Aura said. She had picked a place further away from the tailings and colors. She set the iron on the ground and tried remembering the words. She had been trying to memorize them since Daniel had taught her. She concentrated on the iron and said, 'Go dtabharfadh an Cruinne an cumas agus an chumhacht duit do lánacmhainneacht a bhaint amach.' A small thump was felt under the ground, and some pebbles rolled down from a nearby steep rocky area.

"I think that may have done it," Daniel said, impressed that she remembered the incantation.

"How do you know," Aura asked, moving out of the way of the loose gravel sliding down.

"We try to use it," he said as he took the iron off the ground and sat before Aura. He held the iron between his hands, one above the other. Aura saw him concentrating when a small stream of greenish, grey energy left the iron and entered Aura. She did feel warm like the other day with her lungs. This time, she felt a burst of energy and vitality enter her.

"How do you feel?" Edward said after a moment.

"Really, REALLY GOOD!" she replied.

"Let's get back to the house then, shall we?" Daniel said as he got up and helped Aura off the rocky ground.

"How will we get back if no one is at your home? Who will you connect with to portal back?" Aura asked.

"You are beginning to understand all of this. That is good. Well, the tree I built the house in is a pretty unique life force, and I have found I can connect with that and portal there. You can't do that with most trees, but some redwoods are special," Daniel answered as he pulled out his octahedron, which now had only six remaining charged ovals. He put it up to his mouth and blew on it. A green portal opened again, and a moment later, they were in the treehouse, but as they walked through, they noticed that someone else was there.

~

AVANI HAD ENJOYED the last many months with Master Min. She was even getting used to Liang being around. She usually came up with the answers Master Min wanted sooner than Liang. Still, every once in a while, Liang would say something or respond in a way that was out of her depth and caused her to respect him deeply. He did seem to be naturally gifted, but so was she, which often set them as rivals, even if it was for Master Min's approval. Avani couldn't tell if Master Min had a favorite, but she liked to think it was her.

Master Min taught them about life druidism and how all life is connected. They learned about the "circle of life" in regular school. Still, Master Min taught it through the lens of energy and how energy isn't "used" but rather how energy transitions from one place to another or from one state to another. He used the analogy of electrical wires that power a home. "How does the electricity know where to go?" he asked. "Why doesn't electricity sit idle when you click the light switch? It is because energy goes to where it isn't. That is why and how light fills the immensity of space. Everyone thinks that space is void of light, but in reality, it is void of matter to reflect the light that is there. Trillions of stars send light in every direction, always trying to go from one state to another."

When eating a meal, he would talk about how the combination of a seed, water from rain, soil, and light from our star all combine to create the rice they were eating. The rice only stored energy that could be transitioned into the energy their bodies needed. It was going from one state to another state. And as a receptacle of power, they had the responsibility of spending their energy in ways that benefit the universe around them, creating harmony and balance.

Both kids thought he had an over-focus on balance and harmony. Master Min seemed to pay particular attention to the cost of anything you do. "Everything has a cost," he would say over and over. Liang seemed to get frustrated with Master Min's caution as well.

"We have magic powers. We can do whatever we want!" during lunch.

"No, you must always consider the cost. Always imagine the consequences of your actions. What have I told you about Newton's third law of motion? For every action, there is an equal but opposite reaction. In the world of energy, it is the same. Everything has a cost, and there are some things you simply should not do. There are forbidden paths you should not explore," Master Min said in a raised tone that was quite unlike him.

"What forbidden paths?" Liang asked.

Master Min looked frustrated, clearly having something specific on his mind. "Perhaps it is time," Master Min said with great consternation. For most of my life, I did not appreciate the cost of the magic that we do. I felt like balance would follow no matter what I did. Therefore I didn't need to take responsibility for my actions. I knew the need for balance, but I didn't feel it was my responsibility to maintain it. Almost 11 years ago now, before either of you was born, I and two former students of mine from years prior decided we wanted to try to replicate something that was talked about in ancient druidic lore. We wanted to create an artifact that could see into the future."

"Isn't that what cosmic druids do?" Avani asked.

"Yes, that is one of their gifts, but they can only see glimpses of future events, and usually, they are tied to a particular person or object at a certain point in time and a specific location. There can be multiple images that they can turn into what they believe are specific future events. Still, it is far from a perfect science. We wanted to create a device where we could look at any period of time, any place we wanted. The most dangerous magic is often performed when multiple druids cast a spell on the same object. It was myself, a frequency druid, and a cosmic druid that was working on this. We figured the combination of these three types of magic might work. We found a perfect quartz crystal. Therefore, it didn't have a single flaw and was perfectly clear. We found what we thought would be the ideal location at the perfect time and conditions, as I have taught you about when you activate an object. It was not far from here. I remember the day well; it was May 12, 2008, at almost 2:20 in the afternoon. I won't bore you with the details of the planetary alignment we thought would be just right. Or why we picked that place with a unique polarity balance for chaos and ordered ley lines.

The three of us focused on the object to activate it. We did not consider the amount of energy transfer that would occur. You both saw how Thomas Blood activated that stone in Indonesia and the aftereffects that can occur. Well, some people never learn.

An energy surge more immense than I have ever seen happened when we activated the quartz crystal. It is now known as the Great Sichuan Earthquake. A cataclysmic 8.0 on the Richter scale. We learned later that we had ruptured a fault line that extended over 150 miles. The ground displacement in areas was over 10 feet, either high or wide. The quake was felt in other countries it was so powerful. The earthquake caused more geohazards than ever recorded prior. Over 200,000 landslides occurred, and over 69,000 people died, almost all in this province. Liang, your sister, was one of the children lost in that earthquake. From that day on, I vowed never to teach again. I kept to myself and performed minimal magic only when it could help someone or something. When I met your mother for the first time and learned of her loss, it broke my heart because I had caused it. She was pregnant with you but had just learned that you would be born with a deformity. I felt like I had to help her and you, so I carved and activated the jet stone you now wear around your neck."

Avani and Liang looked stunned. "When I met her, and I learned of your potential, I realized I could no longer not teach, but I had an obligation to do a better job teaching, especially this principle of balance and harmony. Everything has a cost. Yes, the universe does rebalance itself. That earthquake was the first step in rebalancing after pulling so much energy. As a result, your sister is no longer here. Her death did enable your life. With your life comes the potential to do great things in this world. Both of you have great potential, and a burden and duty come with that. The more power you wield, the greater the responsibility you have to the universe around you. Do you both understand this?" Master Min looked at them both.

"It's like what Uncle Ben said to Peter Parker," Liang said. "Yes. It is good advice in comic books and real life. But understand this, if you are not a good steward of the power you have been given, I will not teach you," Master Min said firmly. "Do not make the same mistakes I have made. That is why I am here teaching you. That lesson is more important than any other I could ever give."

Chapter II

ANIEL AND AURA stepped through the green portal to find a man standing in the living room of the treehouse. He was very thin and frail. His clothes were tattered. It was Edward. When they walked through the portal, he took one look at Aura and fell to his knees. He put his hands to his mouth and began weeping. Aura was confused and took a step behind Daniel, who had a look of shock on his face. "Oh, my dear girl," Edward said.

Daniel turned to Aura and said, "Aura, this is your father. Edward, what happened, and where have you been?"

"Are you really my dad?" Aura asked very slowly.

"Yes, my darling. I am. I have been trying to get back to you for so long. Oh, you look so much like your mother. See, I have a picture of her right here." Edward pulled out the photo he had taken from the Brass frame. "Oh, the things you must have gone through. The things you must have suffered for all these years without a mother or father. Without knowing what happened. Without knowing you were so loved. I am so sorry, my dear. If you ever felt abandoned or alone. If you ever felt unwanted and not good enough. I want you to know that I wanted to be with you every moment of every day," he said with tears running down his cheeks.

With that, Aura walked up and gave him a deep and long hug. "What happened? Where were you?"

Edward recounted what happened since he left this same treehouse last time, how he chased Rosa but got there too late, and learned that she had a baby but was captured, imprisoned, and tortured for the past eight years. He told them how he felt when he learned she was alive, and Aura confirmed that it was likely at the moment she touched the fulgurite wand. Aura added what had happened to her on her birthday; how she got her mother's things from the stranger, what happened with the lights in the cave when she touched the wand, how the old woman gave her a desert rose, and how Makawee came and began teaching her magic and finally how she came to Daniel and how Daniel had cured her of her health problems. Edward and Daniel looked at each other as only longtime friends can where no words need to be said, and all things are understood.

"So you really do still have the fulgurite wand?" Edward asked.

"Yes," Aura said, ran up to her room, brought down the fulgurite wand, and handed it to Edward.

"Thank you. This is a priceless family artifact, one that you will likely inherit someday. Thank you for keeping it safe for me," Edward said sincerely.

"But how did you escape?" Aura asked.

Edward told about how he used his tooth to rust out the bars and escape. "That English bastard!" Daniel said. "I should have known it was him. I looked for you for years, but it was like you vanished off the face of the earth."

Edward continued the tale from his escape. "I was able to make it to some 'associates' in England who helped me get back to the U.S." Edward used air quotes on the word associates. Daniel seemed to know what that meant because he grimaced. "I owe them now," Edward continued. "They also gave me two stones I could use in the meantime. I went straight to the U.S. border office to find my poly. The last place I had it was when I was overthrown in the vehicle. So I went back to see if there was some evidence locker or somewhere I could get it. I went into the office and was taken into the back with the supervisory agent. I was about to explain the whole thing when I saw on his desk my tetrahedron being used as a paperweight holding down a stack of papers with photos of illegal immigrants being transported back to Mexico. Well, the memory of what they did to Rosa seized me, and to make a long story short, I took my poly and walked out. It turns out there was some video footage of the incident, so authorities may be looking for me," Edward glanced at Daniel. "From there, I found out what happened to you.

I went to your care center, where I learned you had recently been put in foster care with Makawee. Honestly, that was the first sigh of relief I had felt in 8 years. That feeling didn't last long. My poly wasn't charged, so I had to hitch a ride, but I made it up to the reservation and found it completely destroyed.

"What?!" cried Aura.

"I believe my cousin Thomas continues to look for my emerald and thinks you have it, so they followed your trail. Unfortunately for them, it dead-ended in Arizona. Makawee got away with almost all of the children. Unfortunately, Nane didn't make it. I got there just after the battle. Nane was barely hanging on at that point. I wish I had been a life druid for a minute to heal her. She told me that Brynn's parents needed to be told. She said that Makawee got away with the other students safely. She said it was Nephrite who mercilessly attacked them. She said she didn't say anything about Aura. Neither did anyone else. Nane told me she brought you up here just before they were attacked. Thankfully I had been charging my poly out the window of the truck that gave me a ride up to the reservation, that gave me a single charge which I used to get here."

Long into the night, Aura and Edward talked. Mostly they spoke of Rosa. Aura wanted to know everything she could about her mother. When Edward wasn't answering questions about Rosa or himself, he tried to get Aura to answer questions about herself. He wanted to know everything about her. "How in the world did you get the name Aura?" Edward asked.

"They told me my mom wrote it on my belly before she, well, you know," Aura didn't like talking about her mother's death.

"I see. I think I know why she did that. The day before I had to leave your mom, I told her that if I ever had a girl, I would want to name her Aura. She wrote that on you so I would know you were my child. What I wouldn't do to have her here. For us to be a regular family." Eventually, Aura fell asleep across the couch with her head on Edward's leg. Edward didn't move all night.

Aura woke up to Edward and Daniel talking. "Let it go," Daniel said. "I know you want revenge. You deserve revenge, but do you want him to capture you again?"

"I know where he will be, and he won't expect me. Thomas is up to something, and that maniac needs to be stopped. Whatever he is doing, it is reckless. He is the type of person that could wipe out the entire world and say 'oops,'" Edward rebutted.

"The 15th in Paris, they said?" Daniel asked, speaking in hushed tones to not wake up Aura.

"Yes, and then they said it was 2000 years old," Edward added.

"There are a ton of things in Paris that are 2000 years old. It could be any number of things. Did they say anything else?" Daniel wondered.

"Yeah," Edward said, suddenly remembering. "They also said it was a religious artifact, and millions of tourists visit it every year."

"Well, that narrows it down quite a bit more as the Christian religion started 2,000 years ago. It would have to be something associated with Jesus Christ," Daniel added.

"What are you guys talking about?" Aura asked, sitting up noticeably stiff.

"Your dad wants to stop his cousin from stealing an extremely rare artifact, but we don't even know what artifact it is or where it is, other than it is in Paris. Oh, and it is happening in two days. Daniel summarized.

"And you said it was something to do with Jesus?" Aura asked.

"Yes," answered Edward.

"Well, it's probably in Notre Dame," Aura said, stretching her arms high above her head. "All the artifacts from Chris's crucifixion are stored in Notre Dame in a rele, relia,..." Aura was trying to remember the word.

"Reliquary," said Edward excitedly.

"Yes, Reliquary. They moved them all from some other church to Notre Dame. They have a piece of wood they say is from the cross. They have some nails they say were used to crucify him. They have the crown of thorns. They have a bunch of stuff there," Aura said. "Some of them are even on display."

"Where did you learn all this?" Edward asked in amazement.

"At the center, I watched a LOT of TV. There was a show on the world's greatest treasures, and there was a segment on it," she said.

"I think she may have figured it out, but I still don't think you should go," Daniel said with grave concern.

"He needs to be stopped, and I can't let eight years of imprisonment and torture go without reprisal," Edward said. "Can you watch Aura while I am gone?"

"You will not leave me again. If you are going to go, I want to go with you," Aura insisted.

"Oh, so now you are going to put your daughter's life at risk, are you?" Daniel said, folding his arms and sitting back.

"I have to go, but maybe the two of you could go with me, but when it comes to Thomas, you let me deal with that alone. Can I take you and only be away from you for a few minutes?" Edward asked.

"As long as you stay safe. I would love to go to Paris." Aura said with a gleam in here eyes.

The most critical task to be done before leaving was to charge the polys. Edward's four-sided tetrahedron and Daniels 8 sided octahedron both needed four charges to be full. Tetrahedrons charge faster than any other poly. They can gain a charge within 12 hours under the right conditions, including strong wind or loud sounds. Daniel's octahedron, on the other hand, takes a whole day to gain one charge if it is placed touching a life force that is not his own. Usually, he would just put it in the tree, but he decided to ask Aura to wear it as a necklace under her shirt for the next two days, which she did. Over the following 48 hours, the four sides of Edward's poly were fully charged, while Edwards had 6 of 8 charges.

One of the two days was spent trying to make up for lost time. Edward and Aura played games, went on hikes, and enjoyed talking with each other. When they discovered they were both atmospheric druids, it seemed to bind them even closer. Edward took Aura on a little road trip. They walked into town. Edward had a friend that let them borrow a car for a few hours since they didn't want to use any of the charges on the polys. Edward drove down to his home and showed Aura where he grew up. The place was filthy, having had no one there over the past eight years. Aura was looking at the various pictures on the walls. She especially liked the one above the fireplace.

"I didn't know you had two younger sisters," Aura said.

"Yes. As you can imagine, I haven't seen them in a very long time. I'm not even sure where they are now. Last I heard, Mary was living in Utah, and Sarah was in Florida. When we return from Paris, we should visit them," Edward said. "My parents passed away years ago. You would have liked them. And oh, would they have liked you. My mother always wanted grandchildren."

Aura walked back to the kitchen. "Can I have this picture?" she said, pointing to a 5x7 photo hanging with just the three children. Edward looked like he was just out of high school, and the younger sisters were a few years behind him.

"Sure. Take whatever you like," he said.

Edward went to the fireplace's hearth and pulled up the stone again. He pulled out another bag that was tied at the top. Aura looked in and saw several other bags, including a row of gold coins, two rows of silver coins, and a stack of $100 bills. Edward took out two of the gold coins, gave them to Aura, and said, "Take these. You never know when you might need them." He grabbed some money and put it in his pocket of the clothes he had borrowed from Daniel. They were almost the same size, so sharing clothes wasn't an issue.

After returning to Daniel's, they ate dinner and went to bed early. They would need to travel before 7:00 am as that was 4:00 pm in Paris, which would be just an hour before Notre Dame closed. They all felt confident that Thomas would not steal anything when thousands of tourists are around with cameras. He was far too well known to do that. They were sure he would wait until after it was closed.

~

April 15, 2019

WHEN EVERYONE WAS READY the following morning, Daniel pulled out his octahedron, concentrated, and lightly blew. He once had a girlfriend who still lived in Paris. He used her life force to connect and open the portal, and the three of them walked through. The other end opened up onto a street with many apartments. "Let's not stick around here too long. That relationship didn't end as she would have liked," Daniel said.

They walked until they found a cab. Edward hailed it. "Notre Dame," he said. It took them about 40 minutes in traffic to get to the cathedral. Lucky for Aura, they nearly went right past the Eiffel Tower. The cab pulled up in front of "The Cathedral of Our Lady," and they got out. Edward paid the driver, who gave him back some change. A couple coming out of the sanctuary hopped right into the back of the cab, and he sped off.

The west facade of the cathedral is iconic from the parvis. The bottom has three arched portals. In the center is the portal of judgment, where the 800-year-old carvings show the accursed are chastised, and the blessed are welcomed into eternal life, according to Saint Matthew. On the left is the portal of the Virgin, illustrating Mary's assentation into paradise and her coronation as queen of heaven. The right portal, called the Sainte-Anne Portal, depicts scenes from the childhood of Christ. Above the three portals is the West Rose window, the smallest of the rose windows on Notre Dame. Flanking the Rose window, is the North and South Towers rising nearly 70 meters from the ground. Adorning the towers are the gargoyles used for downspouts, but additionally, between the towers are grotesques true to the fantastic universe of the Middle Ages that serve no function other than as decorations.

"Aura, do you see that window?" Edward said, pointing up to the West rose window. "Signs of Druidism go back as far as we have recorded history. See those circles in that window? The first circle represents the tribes of Israel. The upper half of the rose depicts the vices and virtues in pairs. The 12 signs of the zodiac cover the lower half of the window. Is religion being mixed with the zodiac? Those paired virtues and vices like Yin and Yang. Positive and negative. The two polarities. 12 is the main number in druidism because we have six affinities with two polarities of each. 12 types of magic. 12 Zodiacs and 12 Tribes of Israel. It isn't a coincidence.

Looking at Notre Dame from the front, it would appear small, being 44.5 meters wide. However, the length of the cathedral is 128 meters extending far back, which is only immensely appreciated once one enters the front doors, where you can see how this building can hold up to 9,000 people.

As Edward, Aura, and Daniel entered, they were directed upstairs to the upper room and then up and through the Chimera Gallery and the South Tower, where they could look over the parvis. The cathedral would be closing in 20 minutes. They needed to act quickly.

Returning to the ground floor, they walked through the large nave where the evening light passes the rose window coloring the symmetric French gothic pillars and arches. Aura looked back and saw the Grand Organ standing in glory under the Rose window. Chapels ran down both sides and around the choir, each with differing arrangements of altars, tombs, statues or paintings, and the occasional reliquaries of a patron saint. The chapels around the choir are called "radiating chapels," arranged like rays of light coming from the ambulatory.

"Daniel, Aura, look. He is going to try to steal the Crown of Thorns." Edward had realized why Thomas chose this week to steal the artifact. The Reliquary of the Crown of Thorns is only displayed during holy week up until Easter Sunday. April 15 was the first day the artifact had been on display in the last year. Edward had been trying to figure out how they would sneak into the sacristy and treasury, but there was the Crown of Thorns right in front of them. The reliquary was being displayed next to the crown of thorns itself. Preserved in a gilded, crystalline reliquary, the crown of thorns looks like a wreath comprised of brittle but elegantly woven marine rushers. It was displayed on a large red velvet cushion with a picture of the suffering messiah above it.

The crown of thorns placed upon Christ's head is believed to have been created from the Euphorbia milii bush, now commonly called the Crown of Thorns. After Christ's crucifixion, as recorded in the New Testament of the Bible, tradition states that his followers preserved several of the relics of their Lord's crucifixion. The chain of custody is not well documented prior to 1238 AD; however, after that time, the relics have gone through wars and revolutions. They passed through the hands of Charlemagne, Emperors, Popes, and Bishops and moved to Notre Dame in the early 1800s, where they have been preserved ever since.

"Aura, remember when we discussed the power of an object due to people's beliefs? One-third of the world's population is Christian—more than any other religion. Think about how many billions of people believe in Jesus Christ—the belief of millions for thousands of years. Think about how much energy an object like that has. That may be the most potent life-druid artifact in the world. I wonder what Thomas wants with it?" Daniel said. "We need to hide in one of the chapels where we can keep an eye on it until they close the cathedral down," said Daniel. "I'll cast a spell keeping us all hidden, and then after things quiet down, Aura and I will leave while you deal with Thomas."

A few minutes later, at 6:00, the clergy ushered the tourists and patrons out of the cathedral. Edward, Aura, and Daniel remained hidden in the chapel of Saint-Germain, where an altar was draped with a white cloth set against one wall with two candles. Aura wasn't sure how it was happening, but Daniel had out a purple amethyst stone and had cast a spell. At first, she thought it was similar to how the frequency druid at school did the optical illusion of the ball, but Daniel was not a frequency druid. After a minute of watching, she noticed that the patrons that were leaving, as well as the security and clergy, all walked past the chapel without even looking in. He was controlling what they would look at and see. Aura could tell this was quite taxing on Daniel, especially if more than one person passed at a time. Soon, only clergy were walking inside the cathedral.

Three clergymen were walking up to the Crown of Thorns display. They were preparing to move it back into the vault for the night when a hooded figure entered the front door and walked down the center of the nave. "Edward, look!" Daniel said in a hushed tone, pointing towards the hooded man. "It's too late. We can't get out now."

"Stay hidden here, and take care of Aura no matter what," Edward looked sternly at Daniel, who nodded. Daniel then took a green malachite stone from his pocket and concentrated. Aura and Daniel were now disguised as statues in the small chapel.

One clergyman turned, walking up to the hooded figure, and said, "I'm sorry. The cathedral is.." but the man stopped abruptly and grasped at his throat. The other two clergymen turned, grabbed their necks, and struggled for breath.

Edward handed Aura his bag of crystals and relics after taking out a small turquoise stone with brown and gold flakes. He then said, "Hold onto this for me, sweetheart. I love you!"

"Why don't you take your emera... I mean, the fulgurite wand?" Daniel asked.

"I don't want him to know I have it," Edward answered. Then he stepped out of the chapel of Saint Germain, threw his arms forward, and a pulse of static electricity surged from Edward's hands and hit the hooded figure full force causing him to fly back into one of the stone columns, his hood flew back revealing the face of Thomas Blood. The three clergymen gasped and sputtered for air as Thomas's hold on them was released.

Edward approached Thomas, who appeared knocked out on the ground. Just as Edward was upon him, he turned and hit Edward with a dark energy blast that launched Edward up to the 2nd floor, landing after hitting his head against the stone railing.

Seeing that Edward was in trouble, Daniel reached for a bloodstone which was an egg-shaped black stone with red blotches hanging from one of his necklaces. He placed it between his two hands, interlocked his fingers, and began muttering. Moments later, the sound of grinding stones from three chapels with tombs could be heard. The marble tops slid off as animated corpses started climbing out of the mausoleums. Thomas looked perplexed at how this was happening. One corpse had a gold crown and was wielding a sword and came at Thomas, who ducked and maneuvered away from the attack. Another corpse with a metal scepter swung, barely missing Thomas' head. The third tackled him to the ground, and an orange sunstone shaped like a pyramid flew out of Thomas' hands and slid across the floor near where the crown of thorns still lay on the red velvet pillow.

Daniel had to maintain focus, controlling the corpses like puppets. At the same time, he sprinted up the limestone staircase and over to Edward. While running, he felt for the seashell necklace around his neck. When he reached Edward, he placed it over his head, and a moment later, Edward came to.

223 | Dawn of the Druids

Thomas continued to struggle with the corpses while making his way to where his pyramid sunstone rested. Thomas picked up a golden candelabra from a platform nearby and swung, knocking two of the corpses back a few feet. He then swung at the one holding onto his leg, knocking the skull clean off the rest of the skeleton. Thomas then dove for his sunstone, and grasped it. Then, with it in hand, fire shot out and hit the corpses lighting the ragged clothing on fire. The clergymen looked up to see burning skeletons right next to them. They screamed and pushed back on their hands and knees into the middle of the transept, one of them knocking over the holy water font.

Edward then stood up from the balcony, and with another static pulse, he pushed the burning corpses into Thomas, who again got knocked backward onto the ground and into the holy water. The two burning cadavers approached the blood-streaked Thomas. One with a raised sword and the other with a scepter. Thomas extended his right hand towards the burning skeletal remains. He sent them hurling through the air at Edward on the balcony level. Edward used a gust of wind to redirect the fireball remains, which deflected them up through the ceiling of the transept and up into the roof and spire scaffolding. A large blaze immediately erupted. Daniel ran back to Aura. He grabbed her and raced to the far end of the nave. To the clergymen, it appeared that one marble statue picked up another statue and ran through the center of the pews.

Edward turned and cast a freezing spell on the holy water that Thomas was sitting in, which made his left hand and both feet stuck to the floor. He then cast another spell around Thomas that removed the atmosphere around his head. Not only did Thomas begin to asphyxiate, but without an atmosphere, no words could be spoken, as sound requires an atmosphere. Edward jumped from the 2nd balcony and, using a hovering spell, landed softly next to Thomas.

"8 Years you took from me. Your relentless pursuit of me cost me everything, including my future bride. You tortured me. We were friends! How could you do that?" Daniel screamed at Thomas. He then allowed Thomas to breathe by allowing the atmosphere back around Thomas' head.

A dizzy and disoriented Thomas said in an exasperated voice, "You were never willing," Thomas gasped, "to see the big picture, and then you got in my way. If you won't use the ancient stones to build power, you shouldn't have them."

"You are a monster, Thomas," Edward exclaimed.

A loud "crack!" was heard above. Edward looked up to see a sizeable burning support beam from the spire was about to fall onto the clergymen directly under the spire in the transept. Edward used the same shockwave again, but this time to move the clergy out of the way. They slid on the floor into the pews of the nave. Edward turned back towards Thomas, who used a dark energy pulse to push Edward directly under the falling burning beam. Looking on from the back of the nave, Aura screamed, "NO!" Then a large pile of burning rafters and wooden support structures fell. Daniel covered Aura's eyes.

Daniel then saw Thomas Blood free himself from the frozen ground, walk over to the display and take the crown of thorns. He then pulled his poly out of his pocket, and a moment later, Thomas Blood was gone.

Daniel lifted Aura and moved her to another chapel on the north side under the organ. "We have to go," his voice quivering and in shock as he looked over and saw Edward's legs protruding from beneath the blaze.

"We can't leave him!" Aura screamed, tears rolling down her face.

"He is gone. I'm so sorry, but I must get you out of here," Daniel said as he pulled out his poly and formed a portal in front of a white marble statue of Mary holding her crucified son. Daniel pulled Aura through as she fought to run to her father.

~

THOMAS BLOOD CAME THROUGHT THE PORTAL with the crown of thorns in one hand. He spat a large wad of blood on the ground. After the debacle activating the Imperial Hong Kong Pearl, he learned not to portal back to his office. So he chose just outside his home on the large round paved driveway in front of the castle. His cheek and eye throbbed, and his hooded robe had ash and burn marks. He felt something on his leg. He looked down to find a skeleton hand still wrapped around his ankle, which he jumped and kicked off.

He limped into the castle through the large wooden door painted dark blue where Syrpens greeted him. "What happened?" he asked, looking Thomas up and down.

"Don't worry about it," Thomas said. "Call Nephrite back. I ran into Edward. He won't bother us any longer."

"Did you get the Emerald?" Syrpens asked.

"I think he was telling us the truth the whole time. He doesn't have it. He didn't use it today, and I believe he would have used it if he still had it. So that path Nephrite is following will lead to a dead end. We have more important things to worry about now. Like getting this activated," Thomas said as he held up the Crown of Thorns. "And finding the other artifacts."

"I suppose we do," Syrpens agreed.

"Have Asha teach and prepare the children to go with me when we activate this here in a couple of months," Thomas ordered as he limped towards his office.

"I'll tell her right away," Syrpens said dutifully.

Continued in Book 2

Acknowledgments

The number of people that have influenced me in my life are countless, however, there is a very short list of people that without them, this book simply would never have been written or published.

Sahim for the "fan moment" that changed my life. My oldest friend who I can always discover more within Father Inire's Mirrors.

Belle for all the ideas and discussions about how to make the book better and always being excited about reading the next chapter. You have always been my most devoted fan.

About the Author

KEVIN PRINCE is a retired technology entrepreneur after being the founder and CEO of two cybersecurity companies. A true "child of the 80s" computer nerd with a background in computer networking, data analytics, encryption, cryptography and cybersecurity. Once retired his children encouraged him to write a book and the Druid of Destiny Series was born.

Kevin grew up in Utah and enjoys mountain biking, rock climbing, hiking and the various national parks that adorn his home state. He has 3 children and continues to live in Utah. He enjoys traveling, creating games, designing escape rooms, movies, writing and time with family and friends.

Kevin is also a Christian author, teacher, social media influencer, and speaker.

Contact Kevin on Social Media:

Instagram: https://www.instagram.com/druidofdestiny/

Twitter: https://twitter.com/KevinPrince1723

Facebook: https://www.facebook.com/DruidofDestiny

Website: DruidofDestiny.com

Book 2

in the

Druid of Destiny Series

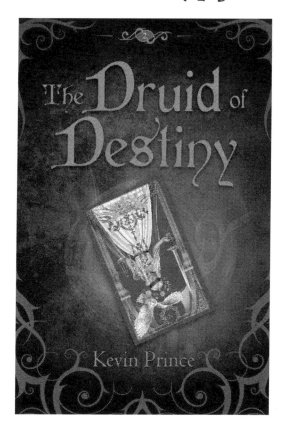

Book 2

THE FOLLOWING TWO WEEK in the treehouse were full of sorrow and grief. Aura couldn't believe her father was gone. He had already been gone longer than she knew him, but it felt like a hole was left in her heart the size of the Redwoods. She realized that when she didn't know who her father was, she didn't have a lot of feelings for him. But even with a short time, she had come to love him and hoped she would have the rest of her life with him. Being thrust back into a world without family was hard on her. Now she knew her parents were dead, and she would have to live the rest of her life without them. She felt so alone, even with Daniel trying to cheer her up. She could see that Daniel was struggling as well. He had lost his close friend. It didn't cheer him up even when Kimberly returned for a few days. Maybe being a druid wasn't that great after all.

One morning Daniel went to Aura after breakfast and said, "Aura, we have been falling behind on your training. That is mostly my fault. I haven't had the motivation to teach. You, understandably, don't have the motivation to learn. I feel if we stay together like this, your education will suffer. I need time before I can teach again, and you need a teacher. I want to take you to the man that taught me. Would you be willing to do that?"

"You mean I can't stay here with you anymore?" Aura asked with tears welling up in her eyes and feelings of abandonment surfacing.

"You are always welcome with me. ALWAYS," Daniel emphasized. "But you can't just stop your education. My old teacher is skilled; from what I understand, he began teaching again recently. I'd like you to train with him, and if you are uncomfortable or want to leave, you can always come back here. But you can't stay stuck; if you stay here, you will stay stuck. Will you at least consider it?"

Aura knew when an adult was doing something in her best interest and when they were doing something in their own best interest. She could tell that Daniel truly felt it would be best for her education to continue with this other teacher. "Does your teacher live around here?" she asked.

"Oh, I'm afraid not. He lives in China. He is a life druid like me, so your education will continue there. You will probably only be there a few months, and then you will be off to your next school. Even if I could teach you the rest of what you needed to know, you would need to move on in a few months. But again, you always have a home here whenever you need it. Also, with your dad, um, you are the sole heiress of that house in Meyers Flat. While you are gone, I will go down there and get that all cleaned up for you, so when you need a place to stay, it will be ready for you. I'll continue to ensure any taxes and things are handled. That officially gives you two homes anytime you need them," Daniel smiled, hoping Aura would.

"If you think it is best for me to go, I will, but only if you promise I can come back if I don't like it," Aura said firmly.

"I promise. I'll even stay for a few days with you in China to make sure you are okay before I leave," Daniel said.

The next day after dinner, Aura packed her belongings into her mother's grey duffel bag. She added the gold coins and bag of gemstones that her father had given her. She placed the fulgurite wand and the calcite in the cardboard tube. She kept the desert rose in her pocket. Daniel opened up a green portal, and they walked through it. They walked out into a forest with very different trees. The air felt different; Aura thought it was the humidity. Even the light was different, and it was so bizarre to watch the sun rise twice in a single day. Right in front of them was a very ornate traditional Chinese home. They walked onto the large patio, and Daniel knocked on the door.

"This will be a very long day for you, Aura. You just finished dinner, and everyone here is just finishing breakfast," Daniel said as he waited for someone to open the door. After a few moments, a young woman almost the same height as Aura answered the door by opening it with a small crack. She had long brown hair and jeans on. She wore a beaded bracelet on one wrist and a beautiful thick silver bracelet on the other. Both girls had similar skin tones and hair color, but that is where the similarities ended. They had very different noses, and Aura had amber eyes while the girl in the doorway had deep brown eyes.

"May I help you?" the young woman asked.

"Yes, is Master Min at home?" Daniel said, looking over the girl's head into the home.

"No. He is out collecting some herbs. You can come back later," she said.

"Oh, I am one of his former students. Are you one of his students now?" Before she could answer, an old man with a long white beard that split into two points at the bottom came walking up to the door. He had a bamboo basket full of fresh herbs. The door opened wide.

"Daniel, my boy. How are you?" Master Min greeted him. "And who is this you have with you?" he said, looking down at Aura.

"Master Min, this is my student Aura. Aura, this is Master Min, the life druid that taught me many years ago."

"It is very nice to meet you, Aura. What a lovely name. This here is Avani. She is one of my students. My other student is here" Master Min gestured at Liang, sitting on the center rug finishing his congee.

Master Min invited them both in. After pleasantries were exchanged, Daniel got right to the point. He told him about Edward, who Master Min had also taught. He described in detail what happened in Paris. The news came as somewhat of a shock to Master Min. Daniel explained the unusual past of Aura, her mother, and her learning that she was a druid. He talked about the eight years that Thomas imprisoned Edward. He spoke about Aura's training from Makawee and what happened to the home at the Indian reservation.

"I heard about what happened to the Notre Dame Cathedral. Everyone in the world did. They must have kept Edward's death, as well as the theft of the crown of thorns, a secret," Master Min said, now pulling on his beard.

"After Edward's passing, I don't feel I can properly teach Aura, and she needs to continue progressing. Master Min, she may be the druid of destiny," Daniel said with a clear solemnness.

Master Min turned to her and said, "How old are you, my dear?"

"Eight and a half," she responded.

"Really? When is your birthday?" he asked next.

"December 21," Aura answered, and both Liang and Avani looked astonished.

"That is a fascinating coincidence," Master Min said, still pulling on his beard, thinking. "Aura, you share the same birthday as Liang and Avani here. Isn't that remarkable?" That took aback Aura as the three children looked at each other. "That makes five, you know," Master Min said to Daniel. "Thomas Blood's two twins were also born on the same winter solstice during the same eclipse. I suspected that there were others. My guess is that there is one more."

"Aura, would you like to train here with me, Liang, and Avani?" Master Min asked, looking into Aura's amber eyes.

"I would like to continue to learn, and Daniel thinks it would be best. He promised I could go back if I didn't like... I mean, if it doesn't work out."

"Avani, would you help Aura take her things to your bedroom? It looks like you will have a roommate for a while," Master Min said.

Avani didn't like being close to people. Getting close meant they asked questions about you and your past, and she did NOT like that. But secretly, being around boys all the time was difficult, so this could be a good change. She gestured to Aura to follow her and led her up the stairs.

"Daniel, would you like to stay a few days while we get Aura settled?" Master Min asked.

"I think that would be best. I want to talk to you further about what you think Thomas Blood is up to," Daniel said, now changing the conversation away from the children. "An artifact that powerful in the hands of someone like that."

"Artifacts. Plural," Master Min said. "The crown of thorns is not the first artifact like this he has acquired."

~

Continue with Book 2

Made in the USA
Columbia, SC
23 September 2024

296b334a-8186-4118-b89c-47dd75959408R01